SHEELA-NA-GIG

Once they were inside the coach, Jane melted against the feel of Elaine's body and the surrounding leather upholstery, tasting the sweetness of the aristocrat's lips and tongue. Elaine's sharp little incisors bit and nibbled at Jane's lower lip until they drew a small bead of blood. Then Elaine pulled away.

'Thank you, Jane,' she whispered, 'for such a sweet kiss.'

'You are welcome, madam.'

'You are so lovely, dear Jane. Now let me see your breasts, my dove.'

Jane slowly unbuttoned her bodice, and wriggled her breasts free of the confines of her silken chemise and her corset. The sight of the other woman's rosebud lips enclosing Jane's pink nipples, of Elaine's teeth nibbling each teat into stiff expectation, made Jane weak with pleasure, and she arched her back to offer each tit more fully to this delectable treatment, and mewed as Elaine nibbled harder at her quarry.

SHEELA-NA-GIG

BRIDGET DOYLE

SAPPHIRE · SAPPHIRE

First published in 2000 by
Sapphire
Thames Wharf Studios,
Rainville Road,
London W6 9HA

ISBN 0 352 33545 9

Typeset by SetSystems Ltd, Saffron Walden, Essex
Printed and bound in Great Britain by Mackays of Chatham PLC

ONE

'Sister Jane, I understand that you can see spirits,' the beautiful woman said.

'Jane is a novice. Not yet a sister,' Mother Superior interrupted from where she sat behind her mahogany desk, looking over some correspondence. Mother Superior's pen was poised in her hand, but really she was listening to the interview with a frown of disapproval.

'Even better. Come forward, Jane, and let me see you.'

Jane was frozen momentarily to the spot. She roused herself with an effort and stepped closer to the beautiful woman, who stood in the bay window looking down on to the convent's ornamental garden. Jane kept her eyes lowered, and her hands interlocked in the wide sleeves of her habit.

'Look at me, child, or I will not be able to check that you are telling me the truth.'

'She must keep her eyes lowered at all times, Lady Melmouth, as a sign of modesty,' Mother Superior explained

'Not on this occasion, Mother Superior. Please tell her so.'

A pause. Then Mother Superior said, 'Jane, you may look at Lady Melmouth.'

It was a shock to Jane when she looked into the face of the visitor. Lady Melmouth was small and yet the tilt of her delicate chin commanded respect. She had glossy fair hair piled into an elaborate chignon. Clear, piercing blue eyes. Dainty nose, high cheekbones, cupid bow lips poised in a half smile. She wore pearl-drop earrings, a black velvet choker, a high-necked bodice and bustled skirt of black silk. She also wore kid gloves and carried a parasol of black silk and lace.

Jane felt awkward. She loomed above Lady Melmouth, her hessian habit and plain white head-dress disguising her slim figure and youthful features. Her hazel eyes were wide, and guileless, and bewildered.

'Can you really see spirits, child?'

Jane hesitated. 'Sometimes, madam,' she whispered.

Lady Melmouth nodded briefly and turned to Mother Superior.

'If you don't mind, I would like to speak to Jane alone for a few moments.'

'This is highly irregular, Lady Melmouth. To turn me out of my own office in order to speak to a lowly novice unchaperoned –'

'May I remind you that my brother makes substantial donations to this establishment each year?' Lady Melmouth interrupted sharply. 'I am sure he would be most upset to learn that I had not been made welcome.'

'Very well, Lady Melmouth. Ten minutes only. I shall check on preparations for evening mass.' Mother Superior bustled out, loudly clicking the door behind her.

Lady Melmouth smiled. 'I rather think I have made an enemy.'

Jane smiled back. 'It would not be difficult.'

'Does she give you a difficult time, Jane? Is she cruel?' Lady Melmouth asked softly. Jane looked down at the carpet and flushed a little.

'Only for my own . . . good, madam.'

Jane was surprised at the touch of soft kid gloves on her cheek, beneath her chin, as Lady Melmouth raised Jane's face and looked searchingly into her eyes.

'Do you enjoy such treatment then, Jane?'

'It brings me closer to my God, madam.'

'And you are clothed and fed and sheltered in return, are you not?'

'That also,' Jane admitted.

2

Jane's mouth felt very dry, and she felt a stab of disappointment when Lady Melmouth removed her hand.

'I could offer you better, Jane. I could offer you freedoms you may never have thought possible. A place of your own in the country, to live as you please, on an independent income. If you are willing to help me with one or two small matters. Do you understand me, Jane?'

Jane felt a tingle of desire run down her spine and its heat prickled her secret places. Was Lady Melmouth suggesting what Jane suspected she was? Surely not. Someone as beautiful and rich could pick up any girl who took her fancy at the opera or on a London Street. Stupid. Think straight. It was something to do with the spirits. That was why Lady Melmouth was here.

'If I leave with you now, Lady Melmouth,' Jane said slowly, in a low voice, 'I may never be allowed to return. Would you truly look after me for the rest of my life? I would ask very little.'

'Ah.' Lady Melmouth smiled at Jane's hesitant bargaining. 'The Mother Superior is indeed very jealous, isn't she? Never fear. I will not let you down. I shall take care of you, if you promise to help me faithfully. Are you willing to take the risk and leave these cloisters? Are you willing to trust me? That is the question, Jane.'

Jane knew that her fate was already sealed as she watched Lady Melmouth's elegant profile. The beautiful woman gazed serenely out of the window, waiting for Jane's answer.

'Yes,' Jane said simply.

'Good. That's settled. I'll arrange everything with Mother Superior. We shall be going on a long journey together. Of course I shall not be able to collect you until tomorrow.' There was a pause. 'Will you be . . . safe staying here tonight?'

Lady Melmouth held Jane's gaze for a few moments. Jane was shocked to see secret understanding, and a hint of cruelty, in her eyes.

'I believe so, madam.'

'Good. You can tell me how you fared tomorrow, on our journey.'

'Yes, madam.'

★

Mother Superior was very angry. When the evening meal was over, the last service of the day was sung, and the nuns had retired to their cells for contemplation, only then did she visit Jane's cell. She ordered Jane to kneel on the paved floor, and paced up and down in front of her.

'You have been a great disappointment to me, Jane. I have struggled to save your soul, and you are going out into the world with that strumpet of an aristocrat. Don't you realise what corruption awaits you?'

'If I had not agreed to leave with her, her brother may have ceased his endowments on our order.'

'That is as may be. If you had not been so forward about your visions, this would never have happened in the first place.'

'They are a gift from God, Mother Superior. You have said as much yourself.'

'Yes, I believe finally that they may be. But you must be careful not to abuse such a gift, do you understand me?'

'Yes, Mother Superior.'

Mother Superior paused before Jane. Her dark eyes flashed and her hands trembled.

'This may be the last chance I have to chastise you for the sake of your immortal soul, Jane, and I am determined to follow through my duty to the best of my powers.'

'Yes, Mother Superior.'

'Take off your shift.'

Jane closed her eyes and shrugged off the scratchy shift, wriggling out of it to kneel naked before Mother Superior. Her slender white body was graceful, long boned, her breasts small and firm with rose-pink nipples. Her head was cropped but auburn pubic hair curled between her legs.

Mother Superior took the cat-o'-nine-tails from where it hung upon the wall next to a small statue of the Virgin Mary. Usually novices would flagellate themselves during prayer. This time Mother Superior would mete out this punishment on Jane.

Jane saw a tremor pass through Mother Superior's body as she draped the tongues of leather across her shoulder blades. She wondered whether the nun was silently thanking God for the zeal and power to undertake this aspect of her duties.

Jane closed her eyes to better taste the pain of each stripe on her back. She loved the leap of lust in her breasts, her sex, every time she felt the blow and sharp pain of another weal. She muttered a Hail Mary under her breath to better control the passion searing through her body. She was so fortunate that Mother Superior took such special care over this chastisement.

'I am going to search you, now, Jane, one last time, for the Devil's mark. We have to be sure that your visions do truly come from God, understand me? If I reach a part of your body where you cannot feel, where there is no sensation, you must tell me. If a demon lurks inside you, we can discover its name and cast it out.'

'Yes, Mother Superior.'

Jane's breath became shallow and quick as Mother Superior took out of her pocket a small iron spatula, marked with the sign of the cross on its wooden handle.

'This was once used by a witch finder to discover the devils that possessed a young girl at this convent,' she reminded Jane. 'I pray it may not find anything this time. Prostrate yourself, child.'

Jane lay face down on the cold, hard floor. She pressed her breasts against the smooth, worn slabs and shivered with guilty pleasure as her nipples stiffened eagerly. She longed to touch herself between her legs but instead lay docile and flat, legs slightly apart. Mother Superior would soon see to that.

Mother Superior began her examination. She would always start at the neck and shoulders, work her way down Jane's back and spine, before she reached the smooth curves of Jane's bottom. First the older woman's hand would caress, then pinch, then apply the rough iron spatula with its tender little prickles, its tiny spikes of pain-pleasure. Jane would moan, and roll slightly, and confirm that she felt the pressure. Then Mother Superior would proceed down the backs of Jane's legs, to the tender soles of her feet.

'Turn over now, and lie on your back, child,' she would finally order.

Jane would obey. Already a slow delirium would have over-taken her limbs. She would feel anointed with warm juices between her legs, and her breasts now grew full and tender in their longing for greater cruelties, harsher treatment.

5

Mother Superior would take each globed tip of breast between her fingers and let the needle teeth of the spatula grind slowly over Jane's nipples. Jane would buck and moan at the delicious heat that seared though her body. Gradually her nipples would grow more and more sensitive to the tiny variations in pricks and smooth metal dragged across their tips.

Soon Mother Superior would need to straddle Jane and sit upon her pubis to hold her down. Then she would stuff a handkerchief in Jane's mouth to quiet her moans and kiss her lips, pressing harder and slower against her breasts. Mother Superior would pant slightly with this tender exertion, and she would grind her skirts against Jane's naked body.

'Now I must search your most intimate places, Jane. Spread your legs wide for me,' Mother Superior whispered. Jane nodded compliance eagerly. She felt she could not take much more tender punishment to her breasts.

As Mother Superior knelt over her, Jane splayed her legs.

Mother Superior crouched between Jane's raised knees, a predatory glitter in her dark eyes. Jane gasped as the older woman's cool fingers pried their honeyed way into her and probed her swollen sex.

'Do you feel this, Jane?' Mother Superior crooned.

Jane nodded, still gagged by the handkerchief. Then her back arched and she gave an involuntary squeal of pleasure as the older woman slowly scraped the spatula across Jane's aching sex, her stiff little clitoris. It was like a blossom of pure electric pleasure flowering over the rest of her body.

Slowly, deliberately, Mother Superior repeated the tantalising caress. Jane opened her legs wider, and raised her sex to meet Mother Superior's expert fingers, the wicked iron instrument she wielded with such subtle skill. Jane gave muffled moans as Mother Superior slowly inserted the wooden handle of the spatula into her quim to aid the tender invasion of her imperious fingers. Jane could not control the little spasms of ecstasy that jerked her body. She circled and bucked to increase the pressure she could feel against the fever spot inside her.

Just as she felt the passion reach a climax Mother Superior withdrew the pressure, leaving Jane panting and sobbing. Jane's hands strayed to her own breasts, to roll and pinch her own nipples in an attempt to ease the agonising hunger.

'Harlot,' Mother Superior hissed, slapping Jane's hands away. She knelt to suck on Jane's swollen teats, and nibble each one gently.

'I am going to make the final search now, my child, so make yourself ready,' she said at last.

Mother Superior slipped her hand further into Jane's eager sex, letting her thumb graze relentlessly against the girl's sensitive clit. Jane felt the fierce rush of orgasm culminate in a series of quick sharp jerks that flooded her sinews with unalloyed pleasure.

Just as she felt the delectable intensity begin to fade, she felt a sharp erotic intrusion into her arse-hole. Mother Superior had eased the wooden end of the spatula into her last secret place. The dual sensation of the older woman's fingers and the strange instrument was more than Jane could bear.

'Lie perfectly still, Jane,' Mother Superior whispered. 'I would not like to hurt you . . . too much.'

Jane obeyed. As always, Mother Superior applied just the right pressure to accentuate her expert rhythmic fucking. Jane felt a more suffuse, yet more intense orgasm flow through her as she looked up into Mother Superior's cruel face.

'I believe that you felt the test adequately throughout all of your body, Jane,' Mother Superior said at last, removing the spatula and her seductive fingers, now well oiled with Jane's come. She spread the juices across Jane's flat stomach and Jane shivered at the sensation. 'Which means you are not possessed by evil spirits – yet. Now, girl, cover your nakedness. Anyone would think you were proud of your body,' Mother Superior ordered severely. Jane obeyed, conscious of the other woman's possessive eyes watching.

Mother Superior sat on the iron bed, the only furniture in the cell.

'Kneel in front of me, Jane,' she ordered.

Jane knelt between Mother Superior's legs. Mother Superior hitched up her skirts, and spread her legs wider. She too was naked beneath her habit.

'Now make atonement one last time, Jane.'

'Yes, madam.'

Jane crawled under the older woman's skirts and lowered her face to the Mother Superior's sex. Her honeyed juices smelled of roast beef and vanilla, anointing tender folds already swollen and moist, already turned on by her assault of Jane. Jane slowly licked around the edges, enjoying the rough curls of pubic hair in contrast to the smooth, slick flesh. She flicked her tongue against the rosebud folds around the eager clitoris, gratified by Mother Superior's groans of appreciation. Then Mother Superior ground her sex against Jane's soft and tender mouth, and Jane obediently kissed deeply, and plunged her eager tongue into the older woman's quim, circling and waggling and avidly devouring as much as she could taste of the tender hidden fruit.

Mother Superior could not wait any longer. She came quickly and violently, biting her lip to hold back her cry of satisfaction.

Then she cupped Jane's face between her hands and kissed her long and slow.

'I'll miss you, Jane,' she said as she quivered with the last wave of orgasm. 'Go with God. Always remain on the side of God and He will reward you. As He rewarded me with our time spent together.'

'Thank you, Reverend Mother.'

'But remember: if you ever need to return here one day, you will need to make the act of obeisance before you will be welcomed back into the fold.'

Jane shivered. She had heard of only one other nun ever returning under such a penance, years ago. No one except Mother Superior knew the full details of that ritual, but Jane could guess at the range of cruel humiliations which would be involved.

'Yes, Reverend Mother,' she replied meekly – hoping she would never have to find out.

TWO

Megan was enjoying the unseasonable warmth of the autumn day. She had lain flat on a stretch of springy turf, surrounded by heather in purple bloom. Her eyelids were closed pink against the midday sun. Sometimes when she opened her eyes a buzzard wheeled across the blue arc of sky, faintly wisped by cloud, that vaulted above her.

She whistled Haf, the old collie she had volunteered to take with her to walk the boundaries of their property on her precious afternoon off. Luckily the dog had found plenty of innocent amusements – a rabbit hole, the scent of local dogs – to keep her occupied while her mistress dozed.

Megan realised that a rhythmic thudding sound had woken her out of her half slumber. She knelt upright, propped against a sunwarmed boulder, and looked down in the direction the sound came from.

It was Hazel Branagan, sinking some fence posts to replace those rotted down to uselessness, on the bounds of her neighbouring property.

Megan felt a frisson of curiosity. Hazel was a recluse, some would say an outcast, rarely seen in the village and rarely talked about. Mostly left well alone. Megan often wondered why.

Megan knew that Hazel had been born locally but had spent many years away, finally returning to purchase the land between

Megan's family's smallholding and the Melmouth Estate. Maybe the secrecy surrounding how Hazel had earned the small fortune which allowed her to live as she pleased was the reason she had been ostracised. Megan guessed as much from the meagre gossip she had gleaned from the older people in the village.

Megan continued to watch Hazel. The woman worked methodically, swinging a mallet against the top of the new seasoned fence post to sink it more securely into its footings.

Hazel was certainly fit. She needed to be to work her acres alone. She wore sturdy boots and woollen leggings and a cotton singlet, soaked through with sweat. Her bare arms were tanned and well muscled, now knotted with exertion. Her tanned face was striking: hooded eyes, straight nose and white teeth that flashed a grimace of effort every time the mallet struck home. Her hair was hay brown, bleached blonder where the sun had faded it this past summer. She wore her hair cropped short, which suited her strong features even if it was unusual. Megan wondered if it had been cut following an infestation of lice, but decided it was simply practical. Hazel Branagan did not have to please anyone with her looks.

Megan was surprised at how much she enjoyed watching the older woman work. Hazel's body was so lithe, without a spare ounce of flesh. She seemed to burst with health. When Hazel finished her task and put down the mallet and stretched, arching her back and uplifting her face to the warm sun, Megan still remained motionless, watching her.

Hazel could sense she was being watched as soon as she paused, stretched and wiped the sweat from her brow. At first she suspected it was one of the youths from the village again, and scowled, ready to set her hound on the trespassers if necessary. Max was still lying in the shade of a nearby boulder, panting, unperturbed, his big black paws spread akimbo to increase his contact with the cool ground. His contentment convinced Hazel that it was in fact a woman who watched – he would be up and growling if he perceived the slightest hint of threat. Hazel squinted against the sunlight and casually scanned the horizon. She caught a glimpse of the young girl watching her behind the large boulder on the other side of the stream. Hazel smiled to herself. No harm there then. Maybe even some amusement to be had.

She felt parched and tired but satisfied. She had replaced the last of the rotten fence posts surrounding her property before the onset of bad weather, so her livestock would be safely corralled for the winter. Hazel stretched once more. It felt like her body was singing from its exertion. The small of her back was sticky with sweat, and she could smell her own faint musk from crotch and armpits.

She walked down to the fast-flowing stream, cupped the crystal liquid in her hands to drink, then splash her face. The water was cold. It flowed from the lake higher up the mountain, and tasted sweet and slightly peaty. She filled up her hip flask for later use, then glanced quickly towards her voyeur. Usually she would strip off and wash before going home, a half mile's hike away. It minimised the fetching of pails of fresh water to the cottage. She shrugged. Why should she care about the sensibilities of the voyeur. It may even be a bit of a thrill. She had been celibate so long . . .

Too long.

With a sigh she untied her boots, kicked them off. Peeled off her leggings and singlet and climbed into the shallows, squatted to splash every area of her skin, sucking in breath at the water's coldness. She enjoyed the way the stream's current tugged at her blond pubic hairs, and tickled her pubis delicately. She felt a longing, stiff and hot and bitter sweet, in the tip of her clit and the base of her stomach. She dabbled her fingers against her sex, gently smoothing the delicate pink folds, before cleansing her arse crack of the sweat that had trickled there. Then she stood up. The cold water pressure had made her want to pass water. So she climbed up on the smooth granite boulder lying half way in the stream, squatted above the water and let the rush of golden urine arc down into the water, its warmth raising a little steam as it mingled with the babbling brook. Of course she was being an exhibitionist, offering a spectacle for her young voyeur. But it felt good, just squatting with the smooth stone beneath the soles of her feet, watching her pee scatter her own wavery reflection in the water.

★

Watching behind her boulder, Megan began to feel strange. She kept very still, clutching the moss growing on the boulder, observing Hazel's uninhibited behaviour. She felt guilty watching in secret, yet could not tear her eyes away. Hazel looked so beautiful naked. She had flat firm breasts, with brown aureole and nipples, tight firm buttocks, powerfully muscled legs. She reminded Megan of her younger brother, but Hazel's body was so much more pleasing and symmetrical. Hazel's narrow waist, firm shoulders and flat breasts, her high, narrow hips, added to her athletic appearance. Yet she was a woman, just like Megan. Megan gingerly cupped her own full breasts, her generous arse cheeks. So much softer in comparison with how Hazel's firm body looked, even though Megan worked hard on the farm, too.

Megan felt a mixture of envy and fascination. She wanted to touch the hard, clean line of Hazel's body. Her shy fondling of herself only inflamed her urges more.

When Hazel relieved herself, Megan felt a little start of shock and delight. The arc of liquid jetting from Hazel's coral-pink sex, visible through her blond triangle of pubic hair, glistened in the sunlight and made Megan's own heart leap with desire. Megan felt an insane urge to dangle her fingers in the jet of bright urine, then to softly stroke the glistening coral lips it issued from. She shivered with the thought of what delicious scents would be carried on the breeze from the woman below her, wished she had her collie's keen sense of smell. Hazel's vital physicality was such a powerful lure. Megan was glad she was hidden at a distance so that Hazel could not detect her quick, fevered breathing.

Watching the other woman had given her an urge to pass water, too. She bunched up her skirts and urinated where she squatted, temporarily drowning the little mosses beneath her with her own steamy jet. The sensation, shared at a distance with the woman below, eased the heat of her feelings a little.

Just then Haf noticed the woman and mastiff below and gave yaps of greeting before lolloping her way down the slope towards the stream. Hazel stood up and strode out until calf deep in water to greet the dog.

Megan groaned. She would have to call Haf back and reveal

herself. She let down her skirts and stood up, called the collie to her. Then waved awkwardly to greet Hazel.

To Megan's surprise, Hazel did not attempt to cover herself. She idly waved back, shielding her eyes with her other hand to peer up at Megan.

'Sorry,' Megan called, climbing down closer to collar the unrepentant Haf.

'Come down to the stream and have a drink,' Hazel said. 'You must be parched. You must have walked far.'

Which was true.

Megan stood for a while, looking down at the naked and beautiful woman. There was a ghost of a smile on Hazel's lips, in her hooded ice-blue eyes. The hint of a challenge.

Then Megan smiled back and climbed the rest of the way down. She crouched at the bank of the stream and scooped a handful of water to drink thinking of Hazel's piss-water, now far downstream, mingling with the clear crystal shallows.

Hazel, now fully dried by the sun, climbed on to the opposite bank and began to re-dress in a graceful, unhurried fashion.

'What's your name?' Hazel asked.

'Megan. Megan Lewis from Black Farm.'

'Ah, yes. You've grown. Eighteen, now, are you?'

'Nineteen.'

'And not yet wed.'

'No. Still helping out at home. We've just finished the hay making. It's been a good summer.' Megan offered this information as one farmer to another. Hazel nodded, finished buckling her trousers. She wore a man's belt of thick leather with a plain brass buckle. Megan watched Hazel's long tanned fingers, work callused, as they weaved the leather through the buckle. It made her mouth dry when she wondered how such hands would feel against her own soft skin. Megan looked down guiltily and scooped up a few more gulps of water.

Haf, now released from Megan's collar grip, and Max the mastiff were gingerly sniffing at each other, gently wagging tails. Hazel smiled at them indulgently, pushing a hand through her damp hair.

'Yes, it's been a good summer but I fear it will be a harsh

13

winter. I'm racing against time to secure everything.' She paused, looking sideways at the girl. Megan Lewis. Young and pretty, with milky skin warmed honey by the summer, and long chestnut hair that shone in a coiled plait. She wore a threadbare shift of gingham and a brown cotton shirt. Hazel could see the girl's full breasts and wide hips stretching the material suggestively. The girl had large grey eyes, timid yet intelligent. Curious and . . . aroused. The girl's dark lashes descended, shutting out the possibilities held in such a gaze, and the girl coloured prettily.

Hazel smiled and sighed to herself. Megan was a ripe berry, for certain. But Hazel had learned over the years that it was better by far to be slow and subtle in such matters. The outcome was always so much more satisfying. Besides, it would always be a risk with a local girl.

She knew the family. The Lewises were a large tribe, struggling to make a living for all of them from the meagre uplands. She wondered how long it would be before Megan was pressurised to marry someone, anyone relatively well off and remotely interested in her charms, so she could leave home and lessen the burden on her parents. Sooner rather than later, Hazel thought. Perhaps this winter.

Megan stood up again and smoothed her skirts.

'I must be off. I'm expected back for tea,' she said shyly.

As she turned to leave, Hazel reached out to stay her, slightly brushing the girl's bare arm. Even the experienced Hazel was surprised at the quiver of desire which she sensed running through the girl, and the strong leap of lust she felt deep inside of herself.

'If you like, I could put in a word for you at the Melmouth Estate. Get you some work there, for a year or two. If it is to be a hard winter, you getting a wage is bound to be of help.'

Megan's grey eyes searched Hazel's face and registered her meaning. The girl blushed, then nodded. She did not move any further away, even though they were standing close enough to feel each other's breath on their bare necks.

'Thank you. That's kind of you.'

Hazel had the grace to feel a little guilty. She wasn't being kind at all. The girl had taken her fancy. She nodded brusquely in return, and backed away, calling Max to her.

'See you again, soon, then. I'll send word.'

She turned and strode home across the purple heather, not waiting for more thanks or a farewell from the girl.

Fool, she thought, for giving in to her loneliness so easily at the first sign of temptation.

As if her life wasn't complicated enough.

After all, Lady Elaine Melmouth was expected home within the week.

THREE

J ane lay back on the satin sheets and giggled. Only a week since
she had left the convent, and she felt a different woman. Elaine
Melmouth had seen to that.

When Lady Melmouth had collected her in her liveried coach,
they had driven straight to London. The West End. Pall Mall to
be exact. Lady Melmouth had taken her to a private ladies' club.
This conservative establishment had an exclusive underground
section. In its Byzantine tiled basement was a massive heated
swimming pool as well as a range of smaller baths, Turkish baths,
saunas, and exotically dressed masseures and maids to attend to
every civilised need.

There were all manner of luxuries that could be ordered during
these ablutions. Russian cigarettes, venison pie and ice cream,
rose-tinted candy, the latest copy of the *Strand*, and a pot of
orange pekoe tea were the handful that they had sampled from
the menu together while they both soaked in huge enamel bath-
tubs after an initial sauna.

Lady Melmouth had gently questioned Jane about her background while they had chatted. Jane had told her she was an
orphan, raised at the convent before beginning to take holy orders
and becoming a novice, insisting that there was little more to tell
of her upbringing. Except that in the last year she had experienced
certain mystic flashes, which to her surprise had tended to be

accurate and treated seriously by those around her. Some interpreted the talent as a gift from God, others as evidence of possession or a diseased mind.

As she had lain in the scented water and confided this, Jane had craned her head to glimpse Elaine Melmouth's body as it reclined in a similar deep bathtub. Jane could only see Elaine's naked neck and shoulders and the very tips of her breasts above the milky water, but even so Jane had been mesmerised by the fine-boned classic looks, the porcelain skin. She wished she could see more of her benefactress. Meanwhile Jane's own steamy bath water loosened her limbs and soothed her muscles. She could feel the water lap against her rosebud clit, still sensitive after the night before. She could sense the little prickles from the spatula, reawakened by the water's warmth, across her nipples, and she throbbed inside at the memory of Mother Superior's caresses. She had closed her eyes and tried to picture Lady Melmouth dealing with her body in the same way that Mother Superior had. The images had sent shivers of pleasure down her spine.

But Lady Melmouth had not broached any intimacy with her in that respect, had not even questioned her about her final night with Mother Superior. Instead she had treated Jane with great affection but also with a certain imperious distance. Jane had easily submitted to Elaine's whims. She liked to. She was in awe of the older woman's beauty. Her ethereal grace seemed at odds with her inner strength, her assured aristocratic manner, and her flashes of wicked humour.

Elaine had taken Jane to Simpsons of Piccadilly and purchased a complete wardrobe for her. She was wearing some of those clothes now. A tightly laced corset over a chemise. A pair of silk drawers and stockings. Petticoats, a stiff bustle. An outfit of chocolate-coloured silk, which complimented the short shock of auburn hair she was now growing back after the convent's cropped austerity. The bodice was tight and many buttoned, the skirts generous, and they rustled whenever she moved. The constriction of the corset, and the cool softness of the silk, felt exquisite against her skin. She knew she should sit up, that she risked spoiling the lines of her dress by lying on the bed, but she was just enjoying the pressure of the lower part of the corset, which spanned her hips, then formed a downward 'v' which pressed against her pubic bone. She rocked her hips gently to increase the delicious constriction.

She wished she knew why Elaine had been so kind to her. But whenever she had plucked up the courage to ask, Elaine had firmly dismissed the subject. So Jane fantasised that Elaine had chosen her simply because she wanted a gentle and indulgent slave to worship her body and tend to her every sensual need – even if this had not proved the real case – yet.

Jane imagined stroking the nape of Elaine's slender neck, the subtle curve of her bare shoulders. She imagined massaging and easing every tension from them, the way the expert Turkish women had done to each of them at the club. She imagined being permitted to worship Elaine's breasts. She pictured them as milky globes with pale-pink nipples that darkened beneath Jane's loving attentions. She wondered what Elaine would order her to do next, and what she may wish to do with Jane's body in return.

Such thoughts left her warm and sticky and short of breath. Deliciously turned on. She may have totally misread the situation, and may only succeed to trapping herself in a fantasy cul-de-sac. Still, she could not help herself. It was torture but it was a wonderful thrill, too.

And it had to be dangerous to be so compliant with Elaine. To be willing to do everything she asked. Jane sensed whatever Elaine wanted would involve risk. Why else pay for chocolate-coloured silks and speak to a novice nun of her visions?

She sighed, sat up on the bed. Her own soft bed in her own private rooms, here at the Ritz. She could hear guests chattering in the corridor as they went down to high tea. Jane crossed to her dressing-table, brushed hair into some semblance of close cropped neatness, dabbed a little lavender water on her temples. She fingered the gold crucifix at her throat. That, too, Elaine had purchased for her.

She could not help but think she was being groomed to fill a part she had yet to discover.

Elaine had told her to meet her at the entrance lobby at 4 p.m. precisely, dressed in her best outfit. Elaine had even given Jane her pocket watch, delicate and ready wound, so she could honour the appointment punctually. Jane carefully secured her smart plumed hat, collected her suede gloves and purse before summoning courage to go downstairs. She took slow, measured breaths to still the nervous fluttering in her stomach.

Elaine was a little early too. She looked breathtaking to Jane. So perfectly elegant, so pale and ethereal, dressed in a crushed strawberry silk which glowed in the afternoon sunlight. She smiled at Jane as soon as she emerged from the elevator and swayed towards her. To Jane's surprise Elaine brushed Jane's cheek with a gloved finger. The action was swift and sensual, an act of possession here in the busy lobby with other brightly dressed women, on the arms of sober, smart gentlemen, bustling around them. Jane's eyes fluttered closed as she felt the closeness of the other woman – the scent of Elaine's citron perfume, the feel of her pert breasts lightly pressing against her own, of Elaine's steady breathing. She had to resist an urge to embrace Elaine, here in the entrance of the Ritz. She flushed, certain that even thinking such things was socially unacceptable. She concluded her susceptibility was due to her idle afternoon fantasies, and drew away from Elaine's siren touch to snap out of it.

'A small smudge on your cheek, my dear,' Elaine explained with a smile. 'There it is gone, and you look perfection.' She watched Jane's discomfiture with a smile of amusement. 'I'm afraid I must take you to meet some very tiresome acquaintances of mine while we are in London. Remember, you must follow my every instruction. Do not speak unless directly addressed, and then answer only the bare minimum. It amuses me to make you the Lady of Mystery. So, shall we go?'

The carriage carried them through the centre of the West End and drew up in front of a grand house in Harley Street. Jane blinked up at the vivid green railings, the cream porticoed entrance, before obediently following Elaine up the steps to the wide front door.

They were greeted by a butler who escorted them along a high hallway festooned with chandeliers, and introduced them to the company already gathered in the drawing room.

The room was decorated richly, with Persian rugs, objets d'art from all over the Empire, and acres of oil paintings – portraits of ancestors, landscapes of country estates – all crammed across the bright-crimson flock paper.

Elaine gently directed Jane to sit in a high-backed chair near the large balconied window. Elaine herself sat on a chesterfield sofa nearby.

Jane realised that the other people in the room were male and middle-aged and sitting stiffly in high-backed chairs set around a large marble fireplace. Each man nursed a brandy glass. Jane guessed they had just finished a long and leisurely luncheon, as they looked flushed and replete.

Jane was scared of men. She had only ever been in the company of priests before. She looked over to Elaine, who smiled reassuringly.

'So, Lady Melmouth, this is your prodigy?' the man with blond, greying side whiskers growled, scowling at both of them.

'This is Jane Claremont, gentlemen. Jane, may I introduce Lord Ashby, Dr Shetland, and Mr Barnes.'

The man who had just spoken was Lord Ashby. A younger man, with brown hair and a full beard, nodded to her as Dr Shetland. The other gentleman, more florid in appearance with red hair and whiskers, was Mr Barnes.

'You cannot hope to convince us that this slip of a girl is the answer to our problems, madam. I demand you end this ridiculous charade immediately.'

'You cannot demand, Lord Ashby, you can only ask. And I refuse. I still intend to take Miss Claremont to Morlanby. I have merely paused for the common courtesy of introducing her to you.'

Jane was surprised at the iron-hard tone to Elaine's voice. She seemed to have increased in stature, looking exquisitely cold and imperious. Jane could tell that these men were just a little intimidated by her manner and her social standing. Something Elaine seemed determined to exploit to the full.

'Please listen to reason, Lady Melmouth,' Dr Shetland entreated. 'Your brother's mental state is most precarious. He sees – or believes that he sees – all manner of phantasms. To take this slip of a girl to Morlanby in the hope of confirming or denying such hallucinations strikes me as both dangerous and frivolous.'

'Nevertheless, I am determined to do this – for the sake of my brother.' She looked from one man to the next. 'Do any of you dare to suggest that I do not have my own brother's best interests at heart?'

'We are not implying that –'

'Good, because I know him more intimately, care for his welfare more deeply, than any other living person. If he says he sees things, then I believe him. Sebastian never lies to me.'

'But, Lady Melmouth, as I have already explained to you, hallucinations appear very real, especially under the influence of opium –'

'You blacken my brother's name, sir, by listening to the gossip of his friends rather than to the testimony of his sister. He is over his youthful intemperance. He now lives in quiet seclusion at our estate.'

'But the effect of his earlier excesses may just be taking effect! I implore you to allow him to be committed to my care, so that I may attempt a complete cure before he deteriorates even further.'

Elaine looked very stern. Her lips were very pale.

'My brother is not insane, Doctor. Miss Claremont will help prove this to your satisfaction, I am certain.' She turned suddenly to Jane.

'You see visions, do you not?'

'Yes, madam,' Jane replied quietly.

'You have never partaken of opium, have you?'

'No, madam.'

'You see? There can be other causes, other explanations.'

'But this young girl is probably half crazed with religious mania – you cannot possibly hope to convince us with her ravings!' Lord Ashby spluttered.

'She is perfectly sane, sir. She has seen and predicted things vouchsafed by her own priest –'

'Who wishes to claim a miracle in his own backyard –'

'An honest man I have known for many years,' Elaine countered staunchly. 'Gentlemen. I propose to take the girl to Morlanby to discover what visions she encounters there, without telling her anything of the nature of my brother's . . . visitations. If her visions are similar to my brother's, then we would have

21

another way into the mystery, would we not? We could do so much more to help my brother's overwrought condition.'

'Lady Melmouth –'

'Oh, come, sirs, where is your spirit of scientific enquiry? Am I not offering you an opportunity to explore this matter further, and with greater objectivity? I am certainly not offering you a fake seer from the spiritualist circuit, a practised charlatan. Here we have a young, innocent girl, who knows nothing of the history of my family or our estate. What harm is there in taking this girl to Morlanby and seeing what she . . . encounters? I invite you all to Morlanby also, to monitor the experiment in any way you see fit. I believe the very act of embarking on such a serious and detached enquiry will ease my brother's current anxieties. If you all care about him so very much, will you not spare some of your own time and attention to try this scheme?'

Lord Ashby mumbled his outrage. Mr Barnes peered into the depths of his brandy and shook his head, too scandalised to speak. But Dr Shetland steepled his fingers and leaned forward in his chair. There was a genuine spark of interest in his grey eyes. Elaine had snared her first possible ally.

'I think it is indeed a project worth trying, Lady Melmouth. If you agree to our stipulations I think it would cause no further harm to your brother's present state. We must certainly tread very carefully. But who knows, this direct and independent confrontation of Lord Melmouth's visions may prove the first step to helping him distance himself from the troubling hallucinations, and begin his road to recovery. What do you say, gentlemen?'

The others looked angry, but seemed to sense defeat. They could not countermand their own appointed medical expert.

'Very well. We shall give the girl a two-week trial,' Lord Ashby said.

'Six weeks,' Elaine said.

'Four?' Dr Shetland offered.

Elaine considered, then inclined her head graciously.

'Very well. Please make your arrangements to join us at Morlanby on Saturday, gentlemen. Miss Claremont and I shall remain in London until you are ready to travel with us.'

Elaine shook hands with each of the gentlemen, who sprang to their feet as soon as she left her seat. Then they were escorted back down the hallway by the butler once more, and swept down to the waiting carriage before the men had any chance to rethink their agreement. Elaine gave instruction to the coachman to drive down to, and then make circuits of, Green Park until he was ordered to do otherwise. This accomplished, she drew velvet curtains across the carriage windows to grant the women privacy.

There was a long pause. When Jane attempted to ask about the strange interview, Elaine placed a gloved finger on the girl's lips until she fell silent. Then Elaine drew herself on to Jane's lap and began to kiss her tenderly. She kissed Jane's eyelids, her cheeks, and then her lips. She bruised her lips against Jane's full and fiercely, until she sought and found Jane's pliant tongue.

Jane melted against the feel of Elaine's body and the surrounding leather upholstery. She felt Elaine's heartbeat against her own breasts, and tasted the sweetness of the aristocrat's lips and tongue. Elaine's sharp little incisors bit and nibbled at Jane's lip until they drew a small bead of salt blood. Then Elaine pulled away.

'Thank you, Jane,' she whispered, 'for helping me back there.'

'You are welcome, madam.'

'Call me Elaine,' she whispered.

'Elaine,' Jane repeated softly.

'You are so lovely, dear Jane. Now let me see your breasts, my dove.'

The order was bold and direct, a challenge that echoed the appraising desire in Elaine's blue eyes. Jane felt a flutter of restrained lust. She slowly unbuttoned her bodice, and wriggled her breasts free of the confines of her silken chemise and her corset.

Elaine crooned softly, squirming a little in Jane's lap. Elaine gently cupped Jane's naked breasts in her gloved hands, squeezed the pert orbs, brushing against Jane's nipples softly with gloved thumbs.

'Exquisite. I shall suck each in turn, but only a little or I think you will grow greedy.'

The sight of Elaine's rosebud lips enclosing Jane's pink nipples, of Elaine's teeth nibbling each teat into stiff expectation, her tongue tracing each aureole, made Jane weak with pleasure. She loved the feel of the other woman's teeth and tongue, her insistent lips. Jane arched her back to offer each breast more fully to this delectable treatment, and mewed as Elaine nibbled harder at her quarry.

The creak of bit and harness, the sound of hooves on cobbles, reminded Jane that the coach driver could probably hear everything that went on inside the carriage, but she was past caring. No doubt Elaine's servants were used to being discreet. Hansom cabs were passing them on the street, ladies and gentlemen strolled in Green Park, all ignorant of what was happening here in this closed carriage.

Elaine shifted to sit astride Jane, hitched up her strawberry silk skirts, and unfastened her ruched bodice. She freed from her corset her own creamy breasts and presented them for Jane's enjoyment. Her breasts were small yet full with pink aureole. Her coral nipples were already swollen with desire.

'Now you may caress my breasts, Jane, but just a little, and very gently,' Elaine whispered, 'for I feel very sensitive and we must be quiet.'

Jane obeyed with tender ardour. She suckled until Elaine's soft sighs quickened into gasps of sharper passion. Jane eagerly lapped at the luminous firm flesh, suckled each teat and drew each forth tenderly between teeth and lips.

'That was wonderful, my sweet. I will let you have a little reward,' Elaine whispered at last. She rucked up Jane's skirts, stroked her thighs, stroked beneath Jane's silk drawers and along her tender sex, teasing the girl's swollen clitoris into erect and tantalising heat, letting her fingers stray into the petal folds of her vulva, probing deeper and stronger. Jane rocked her hips and buttocks to beg for deeper caresses, whimpered softly with frustration as she continued to suckle at Elaine's breasts.

Elaine twisted against Jane's body until Jane had no choice but to lie back on the padded leather seat, Elaine now lying on top of her and pressing against her. The feel of Elaine's breasts rolling over her own, with hard nipples pressing against soft flesh and her own erect teats, dragged her into a slow undulating ecstasy. Elaine kissed Jane tenderly, possessively. Tongue darted against tongue, pubis against pubis in an erotic dance of desire increased by every jolt of the carriage. Jane, possessed by the heady musk and feel and weight of the delicate woman who pinned her down, sought out Elaine's sex to tease with her own fingers. Slowly she stroked along the base of the clit, and across the very tip, until the slow sensual grinding motion of body against body increased in frenzy.

Elaine suddenly increased her pressure against Jane's clit and pubic bone, and kick-started another wave of intense orgasm. Jane moaned, unable to stop her body's tumult of release, the culmination of her feelings of attraction and sensuality in Elaine's company over the last few days. She embraced and kissed and licked Elaine's writhing form as the aristocrat started to quiver in orgasm. Somehow both women came together, trembling and pulsing and gently gnawing each other's shoulders to muffle their cries.

Jane felt such a syrupy, mellow come unlike anything she had ever experienced with Mother Superior. She came close to tears with the tenderness of it. It melted away all the tension of the strange interview with the three men, and somehow seemed a satisfying act after entering their strange, stiff, dining-room world.

For a while Elaine lay with her head against Jane's breasts. Then she roused herself and kissed Jane lingeringly on the lips.

'I needed that,' she said, 'thank you.' Then she called up to the coachman to drive them back to their hotel.

FOUR

On Saturday the two women were collected from the train station by another of Elaine's personal coachmen and the last leg of their journey to Morlanby was made by liveried carriage. Ashby, Barnes and Dr Shetland were due to arrive by the next London train in order to give Elaine a chance to prepare Sebastian and the servants and welcome the small party of local dignitaries who would also stay at Morlanby over the weekend.

The charming woodlands and streams gave way to bleaker moorland as they climbed upwards into Snowdonia. The heather still bloomed purple, but the ferns had begun to die back and their brittle russet almost glowed out of the wraiths of mist which slunk about the hollows. A few hardy upland sheep were the only visible things for miles at a stretch. Occasionally a crow or distant buzzard swooped from the grey cowl of mist to rest on a rocky outcrop.

Then they descended once more below the tree line into more fertile undulating farmland. The road looped alarmingly on the edge of a river valley, until they arrived at a portcullis and gatehouse. The coachman called to the gatekeeper in Welsh, and they were admitted to a winding avenue surrounded by woodland which led to Morlanby House. Jane admired the woodland, which contained oak and chestnut and silver birch and rowan, their leaves beginning to turn bronze at the edges.

Quite suddenly Elaine told the coachman to stop and Jane leaned out, expecting to see Morlanby House at last. But it was still some distance away, a prickle of chimneys and towers and mullioned windows glinting in the weak afternoon light.

Jane realised that Elaine had stopped to talk with two pedestrians on the other side of the coach. At first Jane thought Elaine meant to offer them a lift up to the house, but the aristocrat's face soon hardened into displeasure. Obviously she had recognised at least one of the visitors, and they were not welcome.

Jane looked at them curiously. A pretty peasant girl with shining chestnut hair and clear grey eyes accompanied by a tall fair man dressed in coarse work clothes.

'What are you doing here?' Elaine asked the man rapidly, her guttural hostility strange when formed by her musical voice.

'I've brought you a new maid. Lord Melmouth has agreed to hire Megan here in your absence,' the man replied in harsh contralto tones. Jane watched him more closely, and was intrigued to discover that the man was in fact a woman. A strong, good-looking woman with a man's bearing and icy, assessing blue eyes. As those hooded eyes rested on Jane, Jane began to blush. Jane looked down at her gloved hands, clasped in the lap of her silk dress, rather than hold that piercing blue gaze.

'I've no need for another maid,' Elaine said. 'Certainly not a protégée of yours.'

'Lord Melmouth thought differently,' the man-woman replied. Then she continued the conversation in loud, sing-song Welsh. Elaine flushed at the implied insult, but replied in equally strident Welsh.

Jane felt she soon became the object of discussion between Elaine and this fierce man-woman. The other girl, Megan, listened too, evidently with more understanding, for she stared at Jane curiously.

Elaine then questioned Megan harshly, startling her, and the girl spoke softly in reply. Abruptly Elaine came to her decision. She nodded in surly consent before she rapped on the carriage roof with her parasol to order the coachman to drive on, leaving the pedestrians standing to one side of the avenue, looking after them.

'What was that about?' Jane asked, curiosity winning out over timidity.

Elaine bit her lip, shook her smooth golden head slightly, as though ridding herself of a small annoyance. Her black plumed hat bobbed like the mane of a fretful pony, and her cool blue-green eyes flashed dangerously.

'Nothing important,' she replied coolly. 'I said I'd take the girl on trial. She can stay only if she pleases me in every way.' Elaine smiled wickedly. 'Did you like the girl Megan, Jane? She was pretty for a peasant, wasn't she?'

'Yes,' Jane replied. She wanted to say that her companion had also been attractive, but sensed that this would offend Elaine.

'You'll meet her later. She can be our lady's maid if she suits me,' Elaine continued, as though thinking out loud. Jane watched Elaine, noted her restlessness and the hint of malice behind her haughty composure. She wondered what the man-woman had ever done or said to cause such a reaction in the usually cool and composed Elaine.

When they finally pulled into the large drive in front of Morlanby, Jane was stunned at its grandeur. The house was more like a castle than a mansion. Three round towers were connected by ramparts to form an 'E' shape. The central tower had a large arch and huge front doors which opened into the main house.

The windows were small and mullioned, as befitted a fortress. Ivy covered the grey stone with a softening of green and wine-coloured leaves.

The castle was surrounded by manicured lawns and formal gardens . A single-storey chapel, built of granite, with a small bell tower and a shrine to St Brigid, was attached to the western turret.

'It's an odd family seat, is it not?' Elaine asked, smiling at Jane's frank admiration. 'Each generation of the Melmouth family has added something to it. The chapel, for example, was moved stone by stone from Ireland when the family first moved here, just before Edward conquered Wales. Strange how it was placed in that particular spot, and not within the protection of the court-yard, but we have always been eccentric. Goodness knows how we have remained in favour with monarchs all these years. I guess we are so out of the way they forgot about us. Now the family seat is ancient, and draughty, and obsolete. Still, I love it. From the upper storeys you can see the coastline stretching off in both directions, and sometimes on a clear day I fancy you can see Ireland itself, though it's more likely to be the peninsular.'

'It is beautiful,' Jane murmured, unsure what else to say.

'I'm glad you like it. But now we must hide you away before you are seen by Sebastian and the others. We must make sure you can prepare in solitude before the seance itself. There will be time afterwards to give you the full guided tour. Sebastian may even do that, he is so much better at remembering the facts and stories behind the place than I am.'

Elaine hurried Jane into the house as she talked, taking her up to her own private apartments in one of the turrets, away from the rest of the other guests.

Jane was relieved to be allowed to relax in the plush apartments Elaine had arranged for her at Morlanby rather than go down and greet all the other guests. The rich velvet curtains that draped Jane's rooms had now been drawn against the twilight, and the soft glow of firelight, aided only by the light of an oil-lamp on the bedside table, gave a rich glow to everything. Persian rugs and silken cushions were scattered on the floor. Portraits of naked rubenesque ladies were hung on the saffron-coloured walls.

The furniture of Jane's room was a mixture of austere Tudor and frivolous French. It comprised an oak chest, a mahogany dresser, a small Chippendale table and gilded chairs, a cheval mirror, and the elaborate four-poster bed itself which was carved in walnut and decorated with shameless cherubs.

Elaine had been most understanding when Jane had explained the rituals required to ensure that her mystical powers were at their height for the seance. Elaine had promised to ensure that the right approach to these preparations would be followed.

As a result Jane was on the floor tied to the bedposts, tethered to the foot of the bed. The ropes around her wrists were looped securely around the candy twists of the carved wood. Elaine herself had ensured the knots were strong. She had placed a gilt-framed pier glass in front of the naked Jane, then announced that she was going downstairs to greet and entertain her other house guests over a formal dinner.

Jane was so glad Elaine had understood so quickly what was required in preparation for the seance. She was certain that tender mortification of the flesh greatly increased her psychic powers, and Elaine had been only too happy to accept this theory.

Jane struggled a little against her bonds and sighed with contentment. She could feel the thick rope chafe slightly against her wrists and the hard wooden floorboards against her naked buttocks (a Persian rug had been rolled up to allow her such austere sensation). The fire burned merrily in the hearth, but she felt goose bumps at her exquisite predicament.

Jane was left to admire her own nakedness in the subtle silvered reflection of the cheval mirror. Jane had only just begun to accustom herself to mirrors – they had been banned as sinful objects at the convent. She had felt a little guilty assessing her appearance in the snares of their clear reflection, and now she gazed at her full naked body with dread and fascination. Her skin, covered with a thin film of sweat, glinted honey in the firelight. Her eyes were shining, her mouth soft and vulnerable. Her breasts stood full and rounded, like ripe apples, and her nipples were tender strawberry stalks. When Jane parted her legs, to sit cross-legged on the floor, she could see the coral slit of her swollen sex nestled in her soft auburn curls.

Jane felt so painfully aroused. The expectancy, the helplessness of her position, made her ache with pleasure. Elaine had promised that this bondage was only the beginning of what she had in mind. The thought made her squirm, and softly stroke her sex against the nub of her left heel.

Jane fought to keep control of her racing pulse when she imagined what Elaine might do to her later. She turned her thoughts to their arrival at Morlanby and considered the strange interview with the man-woman. She shivered when she remembered the lustful appraisal of the man-woman's piercing blue eyes.

Now she felt drowsy in the warmth of the fire and shifted slightly as she imagined what it would be like to be at the mercy of the tough blonde man-woman with the hooded eyes. How fierce and urgent her embrace would be. Jane rocked back and forth, moaning slightly, feeling her sex quicken under the pressure from her heel. Then she jumped guiltily as the door opened and Elaine walked into the room.

Elaine had dressed for dinner. She wore a low-cut, tightly fitting oyster silk with a high bustle, overlaid in elaborate embroidery and seed pearls stitched into the fabric. The effect was luminescent in the firelight, an erotic halo surrounding her slender curves. She wore full-length white gloves and a choker of natural pearls. Her hair was piled high, with blonde tendrils framing her face. She carried a small fan of ostrich feathers.

'You look beautiful,' Jane murmured, taken aback by such well-groomed radiance. Elaine smiled.

'Thank you. I wanted to impress our guests to the utmost. I explained that you wished to rest and fast in preparation for the seance tomorrow. I did not explain the other details of your preparation.' She came closer. 'What were you doing just now? Caressing yourself?'

Jane nodded, blushing in spite of herself.

Elaine stood by the mirror now, looking down at Jane where she sat fettered. 'Come, Jane, tell me what you were thinking of as you caressed yourself? I shall be able to tell if you are lying.'

Jane hesitated, uncertain whether to tell the truth.

'I was thinking of the woman in man's clothes that we met on the road today,' she admitted reluctantly.

Elaine frowned. 'Really? We shall have to see if we can offer more powerful distractions.'

There was a knock at the door.

'Enter,' Elaine called. 'Ah, Megan – yes, please put the tray on the table there, and come stoke up the fire.'

It was the girl with the chestnut hair, neater now and dressed in the plain black dress and white apron of an upstairs servant. She bent her supple body over the coal scuttle to replenish the fire, then turned to notice Jane with a start.

'Perhaps you could tell Miss Claremont a little more about Miss Branagan, Megan. She seems curious about her. How did Hazel Branagan take you under her wing?'

'She is a neighbour, madam, and has been very kind, but I know little of her. I'm grateful that you accepted me for the post,'

Megan replied in English with a sing-song country burr. Her grey eyes, bright as a Persian kitten's, slid over Jane's nakedness with guilty satisfaction.

Jane wondered if Megan admired the fragility of long pale limbs and heart-shaped face, just as Jane had admired herself for the past two hours in the cheval glass mirror. Vanity was one of the worst sins to surrender to in the convent. It was even considered a sin to glance at one's reflection in a pail of water, worthy of a penance of twenty Hail Marys and extra flagellation in the evenings. Jane guessed, with an erotic shiver, what dreadful punishments Reverend Mother would have meted out for the past two hours of glorifying in the beauty of her own flesh. What extra penance she would have ordered Jane to suffer for enjoying the way that Elaine and Megan were now looking down at her nakedness.

'Miss Claremont is in preparation for the seance to be held tomorrow night,' Elaine explained in a clear, matter-of-fact tone. 'Does it shock you, Megan? Do you think such things are the work of the Devil?'

Megan looked down at the Persian rug beneath her feet, shifting from one foot to another.

'No, madam. Although my family are chapel, we believe in spirits too. It's sensible to lay any unhappy ghosts to rest.'

'So you have heard of the haunting of Morlanby?'

'Not much, only the odd rumour in the village,' Megan hastily denied.

'Well, whatever you have heard, do not speak of it in front of Jane. She must have no prior knowledge to jar with her own perceptions tomorrow night.'

'Yes, madam.'

'Now pour a saucer of tea.'

'Yes, madam.'

'Does Jane's nakedness bother you?' Elaine persisted. 'I'll cover her with a sheet if it does. It is just a method of purification in our religious order, one she became used to at the convent.' Elaine smiled down at Jane wickedly.

'Convent?'

'Yes. She is a member of a rare sect, just like Sebastian and me. Do you think that Popery is next to Devilry, Megan?'

'No, madam. We all worship the same God.'

'How surprisingly open-minded of you. Miss Branagan must have broadened your horizons. She is very well travelled, you know.'

'So I believe, madam,' Megan replied. She seemed shy and bewildered at the direct interest the Lady of the House was taking in her opinions.

Elaine took the saucer of tea from Megan, and sat on a gilt chair which she positioned close to Jane.

'I know you are fasting, dearest, but after our long journey a little weak tea will do you good. The food this evening was indifferent and the conversation very boring, so you did not miss much remaining up here this evening. Now, you must be parched.'

Elaine bent over Jane and let the naked girl take a sip of tea from the saucer. Jane could see Elaine's creamy breasts, barely contained by the silken décolletage, could smell the patchouli perfume which she wore this evening. Elaine's eyes were tender and possessive. Jane neglected to sip, in awe of the rustling beauty ministering to her, and a little hot liquid splashed on to her naked breasts, making her *moue* then glow with silent pleasure at the sensation. Elaine smiled in slow understanding.

'Ah, take care how you scald yourself.' Elaine took out a lace handkerchief and dabbed at Jane's breasts, letting the material graze over the stiff nipples.

All the while Megan remained by the table, unable to leave until dismissed. Her eyes widened slightly as she watched the furtive caress.

'Megan, put this saucer back on the tea tray for now. Miss Claremont has supped enough. But pass me the sugar tongs.'

'Yes, madam.' Megan hastened to obey. The sugar tongs were heavy silver, embossed with the Melmouth coat of arms. Elaine handled the ostentatious instrument thoughtfully.

'Lovely, are they not? I always suspected they may have a more practical use.' With a smile Elaine leaned forward and stroked Jane's breasts with the cold precious metal. Jane felt her skin burn at the touch of cold smoothness, then felt an exquisite jolt of pleasure as Elaine pinched each sensitive nipple in turn between the tongs, holding and pulling and turning each imprisoned bud so that it twisted slightly.

'More, oh please, more,' Jane crooned, arching back against the decadent clamps as Elaine applied greater pressure. Jane was vaguely aware that Megan was still there, that she was watching these goings-on with shock and fascination on her young face. Jane suspected that Megan enjoyed witnessing Elaine play with her. She certainly enjoyed being Elaine's tender prey. She loved the look of sharp satisfaction on her noble tormentor's face. She wondered how much of this erotic punishment was due to her admission of finding the wild woman Hazel Branagan attractive. Jane reminded herself dimly to find out more about Hazel Branagan's history. But then she lost track of such thoughts as she surrendered totally to the heat and pressure that flowed from her nipples all over her body. She twisted and writhed against Elaine's grip on each of her nipples in turn so that the delicious torture could be increased even further.

Suddenly Elaine stopped and handed the tongs over to Megan.

'Please take these back to the tray.'

'Yes, madam.' Megan handled the tongs carefully, laying them on the white linen napkin beside the sugar basin.

'Now pick up a sugar cube with them and lay it upon Jane's tongue.'

'But I cannot –' Jane protested.

'I said lay it on your tongue, my dear. Of course, I shall not let the whole cube dissolve in your mouth. That would be worthy of at least a month in purgatory after all. This taste of sugar will not break your fast, so indulge me. Do as I say, Megan.'

Megan approached, a single white sugar cube pincered between the tongs that had so cruelly tortured Jane's nipples a few moments before. Megan's smooth brown hands trembled slightly, holding the sugar with delicate pressure so that it would not crumble.

'Jane, put out your tongue,' Elaine ordered curtly. Jane obeyed, and Megan delicately balanced the sugar cube against the flat of Jane's tongue. The sticky sweetness dissolved there for a few seconds, then Megan removed the cube.

'What should I do with the sugar now, madam?' Megan asked Elaine, as Jane ran her tongue around her mouth, across her lips, feeling light-headed with its cloying sweetness.

'Oh, I'm not sure. I know, drop the remainder of the cube into Jane's belly-button,' Elaine ordered carelessly, watching the proceedings from her gilt chair as if it were a throne.

Megan obeyed, as Jane lay as flat as she could while still tethered in order to balance the cube on her abdomen. It slid to nestle in her belly button like a bright jewel against her honeyed skin. Pure and white and profane.

'Is that all, madam?' Megan looked back at Elaine, clearly worried about what her next order would be. Elaine's beautiful face remained impassive for a few beats, as though she was considering the question carefully. Then she smiled indulgently.

'Yes, thank you, Megan. You may take the tea things and go. We shall not need you again tonight. Please bring breakfast trays and a kettle of warm water for washing at ten a.m. for both of us.'

'Yes, madam. Thank you. Good night.'

As the door clicked behind Megan, Elaine broke into musical laughter.

'That may have been distressing to the poor girl,' Jane protested. 'It is her first day in service and she is very innocent.'

'So? I shall not adapt my behaviour to fit her peasant morals,' Elaine replied sharply. 'Besides, if she was recommended by Hazel Branagan she must already have the leanings within her. I am merely providing her with opportunities to uncover them, a chance she may never otherwise obtain. Much as I have offered you certain sensual opportunities, my dearest Jane.'

Elaine knelt beside Jane, bent over her belly and lapped at the sticky sweetness now melting there. 'Should I lick lower, my sweet Jane? Or should I call Megan back to provide that service?'

Elaine did not wait for a reply. Her tongue darted against Jane's mound, assailed Jane's clitoris with quick darting jabs that made Jane cry out with sharp passion. After hours of waiting, the assault made Jane swoon with need.

'Quiet, my sweet,' Elaine warned, pulling away, leaving Jane to quiver with arousal. 'Sebastian is the only person who shares

35

the tower with us, but he is a light sleeper.' Jane nodded, biting her lip.

'Let me put a little ointment over the scald on your breast,' Elaine offered. She went across to the dresser and returned with a small jar. 'It is perfumed with neroli and is very nourishing to the skin. There –' her fingers smoothed the tincture across the pink mark on Jane's breast '– is that not soothing?'

Jane nodded, speechless at the delicious sensation of Elaine's long, tapered hands smoothing the contours of her breasts in wide circular strokes. Then Elaine stroked and massaged her belly, then her upper thighs, smoothing down her calves before caressing her bare feet, smoothing even the soles. Great waves of relaxation flowed over Jane, and her body stretched and blossomed beneath her lady's smooth and supple fingers. All the while Jane ached to have Elaine caress her sex once more. Her thighs spread open wantonly, exposing her pink slash between the auburn curls of pubic hair, as she tried to entice Elaine back to her throbbing clitoris. Elaine caught and held Jane's gaze in the mirror, even as she continued to massage Jane's slender inner thighs.

'Do you not find yourself beautiful to look at, Jane?'

Jane nodded dumbly, shamefully.

'Were you permitted to admire yourself like this in the convent?'

'No. We even had to bathe in our shifts, so we would not catch sight of our own nakedness.'

'One day soon I'll shave you here –' Elaine tugged teasingly at Jane's pubic hairs '– so you can admire yourself even more easily. But I am too impatient tonight. Perhaps I'll arrange for Megan to perform that duty.'

Jane's excitement grew at the casual announcement of future delicious humiliations which may involve the pretty servant. Elaine smiled knowingly. Then she rose and fetched a candlestick and matches from the bedside table. She dismantled the candle carefully from the holder. It was a new, thick, beeswax candle.

'I have an idea for a little sport. Are you game?' Elaine whispered, as her fingers finally trailed against Jane's moist and willing sex once more, dipping slowly between Jane's nether lips. Jane gave a little cry of delight, savouring this tender pressure against her open, swollen sex. Then she nodded, helpless to resist anything that Elaine might suggest.

'Good.'

Swiftly, carefully, Elaine slid the fat candle into Jane's hungry pussy. Jane shivered and raised her hips to accept the smooth pillar of beeswax easily. Elaine propped a silken cushion beneath Jane's buttocks so Jane could better cradle the candle inside her. Then she struck a match and carefully lit the wick where it lay between Jane's legs. Jane could see the reflection of the lit wick flickering between the milky 'V' of her thighs in the mirror.

'There, is that not a beautiful sight? Now, I am going to straddle your lovely mouth, and you must bring me to passion quickly and fervently, before the flame reaches your beautiful pubis and singes your cunt. Do you understand?'

Jane nodded eagerly as Elaine's skirts surrounded her in fragrant darkness and Elaine's naked sex danced above her eager lips.

Jane flicked her tongue out to taste the perfumed sweetness of Elaine's pink slash, which mingled with the remains of the sugar cube. The juices slid down her throat and Jane thought that Elaine tasted of fresh apricots. Jane's tongue was firm and hot with need and pried apart the honeyed folds lasciviously, while Elaine rocked against the frantic caress of Jane's lips and tongue.

'Oh yes . . . faster . . . I have thought of nothing else all day . . . more, my little nun. I command you to bring me to passion now!' Elaine murmured above her, urging Jane on to more fervent worship. Jane grazed the firm bud of Elaine's clitoris with her front teeth and felt Elaine buck with the sweet pressure. Jane felt sharp need between her own swollen vulva, felt the flicker of candle flame heat between her parted thighs, and the danger of it made her burrow her tongue further into Elaine's sweet tunnel, circling as far as she could into the slick flesh as Elaine quivered and shook against Jane's mouth and gave a final small cry of orgasm.

Slowly Elaine slid away from Jane's face. Jane could feel the juices and musk of her aristocratic mistress on her chin, on her tongue, and swallowed the sensuous evidence of her lady's enjoyment. Then she looked down at the burning candle. She could feel the heat of the flame higher up her thighs, and she winced as a little wax dripped against her raised buttocks. The wick had burned down enough to almost threaten her pubic hairs.

Elaine knelt between Jane's parted legs and blew the candle out. The gutted flame sent a thin spiral of smoke upwards.

'There, you see? No harm done. Congratulations,' Elaine whispered, her eyes glinting with mischief. Then Elaine took hold of the rapidly cooling candle and gently rocked it further inside Jane, while her index finger circled Jane's tender nub. 'Does that feel good?'

Jane could only nod mutely as she felt the swell of an orgasm rise within her, like a great wave she must ride to the bittersweet break. She writhed, her hips rocking against Elaine's fucking motions with the waxen dildo. She moaned as Elaine nibbled at her breasts and nipples, the nape of her neck. She felt the shockwave spread from her clitoris, from deep inside her vagina, from her tender tortured nipples, filling her mind with a pure white light of mystical ecstasy. The force of it finally left her languid and spent.

Elaine's silken-sheathed body lay against Jane's naked flesh, embracing the girl until she grew quiet. Only then did Elaine undo Jane's bound wrists and kiss her.

'Now rest for a few hours, Jane,' Elaine whispered, removing the candle and smoothing Jane's cropped hair. 'We have an important day ahead of us.'

Jane stood up and stretched the stiffness from her limbs. She sensuously rubbed her taut thighs, her chafed wrists, feeling aglow and totally alive. Yet she knew that Elaine was right, and she must get some rest. She looked down at the silken sheets and counterpane on the elaborate carved bed.

'It looks too luxurious,' she said doubtfully, stroking the satin coverlet with wonder. Elaine laughed.

'Well, a queen once slept in it, what else do you expect? Go ahead and sin. Sleep on a soft mattress in a gilded bed for tonight. I shall have fun punishing you for your shameless enjoyment tomorrow. Here –' Elaine took out a garment from the dresser drawer '– wear this if it will make you feel more holy.'

It was the hair-shirt which Reverend Mother had packed especially for Jane, along with a plain rosary of ebony.

Elaine pecked Jane on the cheek. 'I'm too tired to continue with the mortification of your flesh tonight, but I promise to redouble my efforts tomorrow. If you need me for anything, I am just next door. Good night.'

'Goodnight, Lady Elaine.'

When Elaine had gone, Jane stood admiring her own naked body in the mirror for some time. Then, with a shiver of anticipation, she shrugged on the hair-shirt. Its prickles scratched at her soft skin and she shimmied against them, glad of the familiar subtle torture. Then she knelt at the foot of the bed to say a rosary before she entrusted her body to the sensual snares of sleep and a soft bed.

She knew that tomorrow she would be ready for whatever was expected of her. God, memories of Reverend Mother, and of course Lady Elaine, would see to that.

FIVE

The next morning Jane was roused by Megan drawing back the curtains and letting the sunlight dazzle her eyelids into fluttering open.

'Good morning, Miss Claremont,' Megan said. 'Lady Elaine said to wash and dress you ready for a morning walk with her, and to offer you this as a small breakfast to sustain you.'

Jane sat up, conscious of the rasp of hair-shirt as she rubbed her eyes and yawned. She noticed the fire had been remade while she slept, and felt guilty. She wandered into the bathroom to use the water-closet, then stood by the window while Megan poured a copper kettle full of hot water into a porcelain basin for her.

She gazed out of the window and admired the view. The parkland below looked lush and green, spreading down to the river in one direction and the sea in another. Late roses still bloomed in the formal terraces, between clipped yew and box hedges.

Megan dipped a soft flannel into the steamy water and rubbed a little sandalwood soap on to it. Jane approached awkwardly now she realised Megan meant to wash her rather than leave her to her own ablutions She had never had a maid before. She silently let Megan take off the hair-shirt. Then Megan gently and methodically began to flannel her down.

The clean, warm water was refreshing, and soothed some of

the fever in her skin from the night before, although it fired anew at the sensation of having this young girl tend to her so intimately. She felt lulled by Megan's capable hands, their backs tanned brown by a summer of farmwork. It was pleasant to submit to the maid's calm unhurried care.

Megan dressed her in fresh silk underclothes, laced her into a corset (but not too tightly, to permit a country walk) and dressed her in a skirt and bodice of dark-green lawn, which was accompanied by a wide hat with a chiffon veil. Jane found that she held her breath as Megan fastened each of the little buttons of the bodice. Jane hoped that Megan's competent fingers would brush against her bare skin, but they did not. She felt a little ashamed, as though she was exploiting the maid, but it seemed as though Megan was enjoying her duties. Jane wondered why she was so silent and then remembered that as a servant she could not speak unless she had a message, or was spoken to.

'Thank you, Megan,' Jane said awkwardly when Megan finished her tasks. She thought the girl blushed a little.

'You are welcome, Miss Claremont. Lady Elaine said that once you have breakfasted you are to knock on her door and she will take you down.'

Jane was relieved. 'What time is it, Megan?'

'Half past ten.'

'Thank you, Megan.' Jane searched for the right words to let her leave, 'That will be all,' she said at last.

Megan smiled cheekily, bobbed a curtsey and left.

Half past ten. At the convent Jane would have been up five hours already. She would have breakfasted on thin watery gruel, not this ambrosia made with full cream which Elaine deemed suitable for Jane even during her fast of preparation. Jane permitted herself six spoonfuls only of the porridge, as it was a shame to let the food go completely to waste, and treated herself to a bone china cupful of Earl Grey tea. Then she knocked on Elaine's adjoining door.

Elaine was wearing a black riding habit and tricorn hat that suited her slim petite figure. She smiled at Jane, took her hand, and hurried her down the wide staircase, through the main hall. They rushed out on to the terrace and down the gravel drive before anyone else could see them. Jane looked back at the castle, its fortress-like bulk grey and lovely in the sunlight. She was still in awe of her surroundings and the swift change in her circumstances.

'Come, Jane. There will be plenty of time to tour the house later. I thought we'd get some fresh air, while the weather is fine. Do you ride?'

'No.'

'Then you must walk beside me while I do, for I have missed my favourite mare for too long not to exercise her today. I'll introduce you to Willow.'

The mare was beautiful, a calm and affectionate horse that snuffled Jane's hands curiously while Elaine crooned nonsense and patted its glistening flanks, well muscled with health. The horse pranced the cobbled courtyard, held in check by the stable boy, ready bridled and saddled. Elaine mounted with ease before taking the reins from the stable boy.

'We'll be back around one o'clock.'

'Yes, madam,' the boy said.

Jane followed the horsewoman. Elaine kept to a walking pace for a while, then cantered around the park and back to Jane. Her eyes were shining, she was laughing and her cheeks were rosy with exercise.

'She is a fine mare, isn't she? Perhaps I'll have time to teach you how to sit and walk her, at least. But not today. Let's go down by the river, and make a circuit back through the woods.'

Jane looked about her in wonder. The autumn day was fine and warm. Squirrels darted and bounced between the park oaks and chestnuts, collecting acorns, while finches and sleek crows and the occasional wheeling buzzard could be seen on the wing. Jane found herself smiling, admiring the fast-flowing river that soon wound itself beside them before swerving away down to the sea.

'The estate is very large, and there are many fine coastal and moorland walks, but today I want you to see Maiden Falls. It's just through this stretch of woods – the oldest on the estate. These beeches are centuries old,' Elaine informed Jane, as she pointed with her riding crop in the direction she wanted them to go.

They walked the wide bridle path that led off the main avenue, and it seemed to Jane that they had entered a huge natural cathedral. The beech trunks were wide and covered with mosses. Their branches vaulted high above them, russet leaves murmuring in the breeze and filtering the sunlight into subtle glints that dappled the path. Leaf litter was piled like doubloons against the exposed tree roots, roots as thick as a man's arm.

Soon they heard the thunder of water, and the path widened to show the tumbling lacy white waterfall which cascaded from rocky outcrops into a deep wide pool below, which was formed by a smooth bowl of eroded granite. A series of rounded stepping stones were placed at the point where the pool thinned back into river. Beyond, the other mossy bank rose through rowan trees to moorland, the heather blooming purple against the clear blue sky.

'This point marks a boundary of the estate,' Elaine explained, pausing her mount and looking down at Jane's enraptured face. 'It's lovely, isn't it?'

'Oh yes,' Jane murmured.

'Some say it is a sacred place. It has been venerated for generations. Every Midsummer's Day the women of the village come here to throw sweetmeats, trinkets and flowers into the pool, to give thanks for fertility and to offer prayers for a good harvest.'

Jane knelt against the largest granite boulder that bordered the pool, and traced the elaborate spirals that had been carved into the hard grey rock. The marks were so old that the edges were smooth and lichens filled the deeper grooves.

'The ancients carved those. The reason for them was forgotten long before my family ever owned this land,' Elaine said, as she dismounted and tethered Willow, who snickered and pawed before bending her neck to crop at the smooth grass of the clearing. 'They say the carved rock holds great power, if you believe such nonsense. Which is one reason why I thought it might be appropriate for the continuation of our own little rituals in preparation for the seance. Take off your bodice.'

The command took Jane by surprise, but one look at Elaine's haughty features showed she would not be refused. Jane fumbled with her buttons, and let the garment fall beside the boulder. She shivered a little as the breeze caught at her bare nape and shoulders and her cleavage above the whalebone corset.

'Now hitch up your skirts, and turn to lean against the boulder.'

Jane obeyed, facing the smooth carved granite and propping her hips and knees against its bulk. She gave a sigh of satisfaction as she felt Elaine pull down her cami-knickers to massage her bare arse with leather-gloved hands.

'Did you enjoy last night, Jane?'

'Yes, very much.'

'Tell me, how many spoonfuls of porridge did you take for breakfast?'

'Six,' Jane whispered, and gave a start as she felt Elaine's insolent fingers probe her arse and sex provocatively. She spread her feet wider to allow Elaine easier access, even as she feared how exposed they must be, and wondered whether anyone would discover them. Elaine laughed.

'I knew you would not be able to refuse good food when offered it, little nun, and now I have an excuse to punish you just a little. Three blows against each arse-cheek, I think, for each sinful mouthful of porridge which has broken your fast.' She let the tip of her riding switch stroke Jane's bottom. Jane gave a shiver, and felt her nipples harden in expectation.

The riding switch was almost as vicious as the cat-o'-nine-tails Reverend Mother had used at the convent. Jane bit her lips to stifle her cries as each blow landed on her bare flesh, alternating across each buttock. The crop whistled through the air, and each slap against flesh left a tender mark that stung in the cold breeze.

'That will do for now,' Elaine said, 'I do not wish to draw blood. Turn around.'

Jane obeyed, leaning back against the boulder, still keeping her skirts aloft.

Elaine pressed against her and kissed her hungrily, nipping her underlip savagely. Jane gloried at the feel of the soft wool which encased Elaine's breasts, as they crushed her own. The cold smoothness of granite behind her soothed her stinging bottom.

Elaine's gloved fingers pressed with expert possession against Jane's clitoris, while her palm pressed down upon her corseted pubis until Jane felt a spasm of pure lust shoot through her abdomen.

'Don't move,' Elaine ordered as Jane began to squirm and ride Elaine's leather-gloved fingers. With a groan of tortured desire Jane stilled herself, letting Elaine have her will. She looked up at the sunlight glinting through branches so that she would not have to watch the dark passion in her lover's eyes, the sullen pout of pleasure.

'You little hussy, how wet you are,' Elaine murmured. 'How wide you open yourself. Do you want to be filled, my sweet nun?'

'Yes,' Jane whispered, and whimpered as the prying leather fingers withdrew, and her sex was left starving for caresses, molten hot in the cool breeze. Then Jane sighed with bliss as she felt the leather handle of Elaine's riding switch slide into her willing sex. She embraced its girth easily. She sighed as Elaine gave the teasing little prods with the crop against Jane's fever spot. The thrusts grew deeper, more insistent and unleashed shivers of passion, gasps of joy. Just as she thought she would reach the peak of orgasm, Elaine paused to let Jane pant once more in tortuous expectation.

'Now you must use the riding crop inside me,' Elaine whispered, handing Jane the instrument. Elaine hitched up her own skirts and placed one booted foot high against the boulder, to grant Jane easier access. She parted her silken knickers to entice Jane to obey, even though Jane still quivered with unsatisfied passion.

The martyred Jane sank to her knees in the soft grass and kissed Elaine's sex with a frenzy provoked by her own near-orgasm. Elaine grabbed locks of Jane's short hair to direct her ministrations, and Jane flicked her tongue obediently at the very tip of the delicious coral clitoris before easing the handle of the riding switch, still covered with her own juices, in between Elaine's swollen pink folds to fuck her tenderly. As she worked she imagined her own fanny was thus filled and serviced, and felt her own juices flow unhindered down her thighs.

Elaine's eventual cries of orgasm mingled with the rumble of the waterfall.

'Good.' Elaine bent to kiss Jane, tasting her own juices on

Jane's tongue. 'I suppose the ancients would say that we have reconsecrated this place, don't you think? Now dress quickly, before we are discovered by one of our guests taking a stroll. I'll take you to the chapel where you can pray for your sins in preparation for this evening.' Elaine smiled cruelly. 'Tell me, are you terribly unconsummated? Do you long to experience the peak of your passion?'

Jane nodded.

'All the better for your psychic powers, my dear. You told me so yourself. Be sure to not touch yourself down there while you are at prayer.'

Jane nodded meekly, secretly wallowing in her tortured sensitivity. As Jane picked up her bodice to dress, still heady with near-orgasm, she thought she caught a glimpse of someone watching on the other side of the falls.

'Who was that?' Jane asked, as Elaine remounted her mare, carefully rearranging her skirts. The mare snickered, as though echoing Jane's question.

Elaine arched an eyebrow and followed Jane's gaze. 'I do not see anyone. Perhaps it was Sebastian. They sometimes let him take a solitary walk in the mornings, if he has slept well enough.'

'Then why did he not call out and greet us?'

'I've asked him not to speak to you until the seance. And besides we were rather busy. Now come.'

Jane obeyed, blushing with the implication that someone may have been watching them all along.

The chapel was grey and unprepossessing granite on the outside, but its interior, in Jane's opinion, reached perfection.

The walls were whitewashed and adorned with medieval depictions of the stages of the cross. The scourging, the crowning with thorns, the crucifixion itself were all portrayed in faded but gory detail. There were mahogany pews and oak panels and a high vaulted ceiling of decorated plasterwork. There, painted in gold leaf and lapis lazuli, were the four cardinal symbols of the lion, the bull, the angel and the griffin, surrounding the Melmouth coat of arms.

The altar was protected by an elaborate screen of carved walnut, but Jane could see the carved and painted rendition of Christ on the cross that, even from this distance, looked chillingly realistic. To one side was a Lady Chapel which contained a beautiful marble figure of the Madonna. This smaller shrine was decorated with flowers and honoured with votive candles.

There was a single confessional booth at the chapel's entrance, and a porphyry pedestal to hold the holy water. Little alcoves held plaster images of the saints linked with the Melmouths, Anthony and Mark and Brigid and Jude. Jane walked about it all with awe. Not even the convent's chapel was as rich and ornate as this.

She breathed in the frankincense and rose petals and felt at peace, as she finally knelt in the Lady Chapel to tell her rosary. Her breath began to mist in the unheated chapel, and her body to numb, until there was only her and the image of the Madonna in the whole world.

But after a while, Jane became aware of whispered voices in the entrance behind her. At first the language was Welsh, even though Jane understood it was banned on the estate, and Jane guessed it was servants who had sneaked here for a gossip. Then the language changed to English, perhaps as someone more senior passed by, and Jane recognised one of the voices as Megan's.

'How are you settling in?' the other voice questioned. Jane recognised with a start the contralto voice belonged to Hazel Branagan. 'Do you think you have done the right thing?'

'Yes, I think so. Everything is so clean and plentiful and lush here! It's a different world from the farm.'

'And what about the Mistress, Lady Melmouth. Do her eccentricities disturb you?'

'If I am to be truthful, I would have to say that they excite me,' Megan whispered. It sounded almost like a confession, and that she wanted to be absolved.

'What about their religious persuasion? Does this exotic high churchery offend your senses?' Hazel persisted, not commenting upon Megan's admission.

'Again, it is exciting. But I do not understand it.'

'It is a particular sect. Very strange. I am not even sure it is still recognised by the Pope or the Church of England, although I myself was confirmed in this faith when I was a girl.'

'When you first lived here?' Megan prompted eagerly.

'I'm not here to talk of that, Megan.' Hazel sounded severe. 'This is just a quick visit to check you are content to remain. Remember, I'll fetch you home whenever you wish, if things become too difficult. Or . . . you know, you can always come and stay with me if ever they won't have you at home.'

The offer hung on the air and caught at Jane's chest so that her breath was suspended, waiting for Megan's reply. She felt strangely jealous of the maid and wished she had received such an invitation.

'Thank you. You are kind. But I think I shall remain here for now,' Megan said quietly. 'This place, that strange nun . . . it all intrigues me.'

'The nun enjoys the martyring of her flesh, does she? Then she is a true initiate to the faith.' Hazel's voice was lighter, as though she smiled. 'She looks a pretty little fanatic. Did she truly look fine naked?'

Megan giggled. 'Ah, beautiful. I should not have told you.'

'I am interested, and I'll not spread gossip.'

'The nun is in the chapel now. Lady Elaine told me to fetch her, but I cannot see her.'

'She'll be in a corner of the Lady Chapel. It is the coldest and most holy place.'

Jane shivered to be known so well by a stranger.

'I'll go now,' Hazel continued. 'I'll visit you in another week or so, and I'll give word to your family that you are well.'

'Thank you.'

Then there was silence and Jane returned to her prayers.

When a light hand touched Jane's shoulder she almost felt it would be an apparition made flesh. But of course it was Megan.

'Lady Melmouth told me to fetch you, so you can rest for a while in your room before the seance,' Megan whispered, glancing around the chapel as though it was indeed a devil's grotto.

'Thank you.' Jane rose slowly, rubbing her stiff knees. She felt a frisson of excitement as she felt the soreness of her buttocks, due to Elaine's earlier chastisement, when she moved.

'Do you disapprove of the chapel, Megan?' she could not resist asking as the maid escorted her quickly back out into the daylight, down the steps of the formal gardens and the wide terrace leading back to the main house.

'It seems a little strange, after the plain village chapel,' Megan admitted.

'It is a unique church, of a unique faith. Perhaps it will die out with the Melmouths.'

'What is so special about it?'

'Perhaps Lady Melmouth would be the best person to explain,' Jane said mysteriously.

'Do you think they would want me to convert if I remained in service?' Megan asked doubtfully. It was obviously weighing on her mind.

'That would depend on whether you were suited to embrace such a passionate and unique faith, I am sure.'

'You are very devoted,' Megan observed, stealing a sideways glance at Jane.

'I was lucky, and found my calling early in life,' Jane replied serenely. She paused to look up at the castle's austere bulk, blocking out the low afternoon sun. 'I hope my preparations will give me the power to do some good here this evening.'

Megan took her elbow gently, leading her on.

'I'm sure you will,' she whispered in encouragement.

'YOU!' a voice rang out in anger.

The two girls turned to find Lady Elaine, hissing in disapproval at Hazel Branagan as the man-woman crossed the formal gardens. Elaine paused in the main drive, leaning on her parasol, glaring at Hazel, waiting for her to catch up. The tall wild-woman walked towards her, faced her down. Both women seemed oblivious of Megan and Jane, standing in the porchway.

'You have a nerve, coming here a second time. I suggest you leave before any of my guests catch sight of you. What was your errand this time? Do you have another whore to foist upon me?'

Megan stiffened at the reference.

'No. After all, you seem perfectly capable of picking your own. You have a taste for girl-nuns these days? How refreshing for you,' Hazel replied. Jane flushed, recalling how her hooded blue eyes had appraised her yesterday, and dismissed her as so much trash.

'You are going to jeopardise everything as usual, Hazel Branagan. Don't you realise that Ashby is here? I forbid you to step foot on my estate ever again.'

'Your estate? Has Sebastian handed over the keys to his castle already? Are you about to escort him to the sanatorium and have him sign a power of attorney? And then what? Are you finally going to marry Ashby just in order to get what you want? Your ambition is getting the better of you.'

Elaine's parasol sliced through the air and across Hazel Branagan's cheek, leaving a thin red cut. Hazel smiled, but the smile did not reach her cold blue eyes.

'Take care, Lady Melmouth. You may damage your pretty little fashion accessory. And I may retaliate next time you try such a move.'

'Never mention my brother in such a way again,' Elaine said slowly. Her face was impassive, but her eyes flashed icily. 'Leave us now,' she commanded. 'Never come back.'

Hazel gave a mock bow.

'As you wish. Next time your sheep stray on to my land I'll slaughter them rather than let your estate manager know. Take care never to cross my land again on your rides or rambles. You'll get the very same welcome from me.'

Hazel turned and strode rapidly down the drive, letting her tanned hands sweep across the clipped yew hedge that banked the path. The restrained gesture suggested she was on the edge of real violence.

'I'll not be threatened on my own land by a peasant, do you hear me, you ungrateful bitch!' Elaine yelled after her.

'You're a bitch on heat yourself, Elaine bach,' Hazel called, not bothering to look back. 'Don't think I cannot tell the signs. Have fun at your seance.'

Jane and Megan hurried inside, anxious Elaine would not realise they had witnessed her loss of composure. Elaine stood in the driveway for some time, watching Hazel walk rapidly down the avenue.

Later Elaine crept into Jane's bedchamber to find the young woman composed, kneeling and telling her rosary beads silently.

She was dressed in a high-necked plain gown of dove-grey, and her short auburn hair glinted in the candlelight.

'Are you ready? I can ask Father Dominic to say a short mass for us in the chapel before you go down, if you like.'

'No, I would prefer to take communion tomorrow morning if that is acceptable.'

'Why is that?'

'To atone for any sin involved. Reverend Mother used to say seances, even if they help the afflicted, smack of necromancy.'

'Mystic visions are a fact of our sect. She should reconcile herself.'

Jane stood up, and smoothed her skirts.

'Do I look presentable for your guests?' she asked.

'You look beautiful.' Elaine approached and embraced the young woman. She rested her hands on the girl's hips, brushing her breast tips against Jane's.

'Please don't, not now,' Jane whispered breathlessly. The entreaty sparked a leap of lust in Elaine. She could feel Jane trembling, and she knew the girl was still terribly aroused after this morning.

Elaine slowly unbuttoned the top of Jane's gown and reached for her naked breasts. Slowly she rolled and pinched the girl's stiff nipples. Elaine watched emotions flit across the young novice's open face: shame, guilt, desire, lascivious need. She unhooked Jane's skirts and stroked the warm mound of her sex through silken cami-knickers.

Elaine wanted to chastise this tender young girl again. Jane's nubile and yielding body, the girl's tortured, shameful obedience, was an opiate which Elaine craved. Elaine's family had always indulged such urges, and she needed to fulfil them even more at times of danger, when everything hung in the balance.

Elaine remembered the way she had played with Jane last night, the way she had chastised her at Maiden Falls this morning, and Elaine itched to do even worse. She remembered the little beads of raised pink welts, the delicate blue bruises left by the riding switch on Jane's bare arse. Elaine pinched and stroked the bruises through Jane's cami-knickers. Elaine smiled in satisfaction as Jane drew breath sharply, then sighed in response to the cruel caress.

Elaine's fingers sought and stroked Jane's moist sex, occasionally grinding her thumb across the folds at the base of her clitoris so that Jane grew weak and pliant in her arms. Jane began to kiss and suckle Elaine's lips, Elaine's neck. Then Jane dipped to lick and nibble Elaine's breasts in gratitude.

Elaine ploughed her fingers still further into Jane's sex, enjoying the yielding undulations of her against the pressure, the small quivers and pulsation of delicate muscles against her fingers as she frigged quicker and harder – but not quite hard enough to let the trembling girl come. Elaine guided Jane's hand, so that Jane's fingers fondled Elaine's hungry quim to the same rhythm, compliant and eager. Elaine smiled, letting herself give in to orgasm, knowing she would keep such release from Jane to ensure she was receptive during the seance. If Jane did well this evening, Elaine would reward her in the morning. Elaine would enjoy doing that almost as much as she enjoyed tantalising Jane into this constant sensual state.

As Elaine came, she tried hard not to think about Hazel Branagan. Tried not to think of Hazel's strong face, her brooding blue eyes, the cruel sensual mouth. She tried not remember the touch of Hazel's hard, knowing hands that had once brought Elaine to the precipice of a passion she had never experienced before or since. To remember would only bring ruin.

Instead, she kissed Jane's forehead tenderly and said, 'Now we must go down and begin the seance.'

SIX

They were waiting for her.

Jane hesitated in the vast hallway, and Megan gave her a knowing look – half sympathetic, half anxious – before hurrying past with another guest's cape to hang carefully on the coat hooks formed from stag's antlers. Jane glanced at Elaine.

'My brother's idea, to invite a few local dignitaries. I suspect he wanted protection from Ashby, Shetland and Barnes for the evening. Don't worry, they are mostly harmless, and I shall be with you,' Elaine encouraged.

Jane took a lungful of air and slowly exhaled.

'Good luck, Miss Claremont.' Megan curtseyed and made her way back below stairs, her boots striking the stone flags with brisk regularity. Jane's breath, like incense, wraithed after her.

Jane wanted to stop while she still could. But what were her options? If she offended the Melmouths, she could never return here, or to the convent. She could die on the moors of exposure, or in a workhouse of malnutrition. Neither choice was appealing.

Besides, she had enjoyed such a luxurious existence these past two days. She loved the convent for the peace, for its ordered cleanliness, and of course she had loved Reverend Mother in her way. But she also loved satin sheets and silk dresses, and the attentions of the beautiful woman who stood beside her.

Elaine took her elbow, propelled her forward, imploring,

'Please go in, do this for me, please.' A faint whisper, like the rise and fall of a sighing breeze, rattled the huge front doors as they passed by. Jane wondered, as she looked at the cool and collected blonde beside her, whether she was in the thrall of an angel or devil. But she knew she had already made her choice. She would do what she could to convince the sceptics that the demons which plagued Sebastian were more than merely his sick imaginings. Any troubled conscience which resulted would be hers to unburden at her next confession.

Jane drew herself up to her greatest height, and the two women entered the drawing room.

The room was large and bright with candles and, it seemed to Jane, milling with people. The guests had just dined and so were all dressed richly – the women in jewel silks, the men in white ties. They chattered in animated groups, clustered around the huge fireplace, where logs crackled and glowed between elaborate iron fire-dogs. A large oak table was laden with silverware and crystal that sparkled against crisp linen. Decanters of port and platters of cheeses and vases of hothouse flowers vied for attention. Two lurchers bounded from the hearth side to greet Elaine, and snuffle Jane in friendly welcome.

Jane felt her cheeks flush as everyone turned to look at her curiously in the brief silence which followed their entrance. She noticed Lord Ashby, with Dr Shetland and Mr Barnes, talking to each other in a group, smoking cigars and leaning against the large marble mantel. They were with a lithe young man, who was pale and thin but had a kind, mobile face.

'Elaine, there you are at last!' the young man called, before picking his way through the crowd to greet them as the general conversations resumed. Up close Jane could see that he was younger than Elaine, with the same thick flaxen hair, and classic Grecian features, but with large tawny eyes which glinted restlessly in the candlelight. There were shadows under his eyes. He was holding a glass of claret and smoking a cheroot.

'Jane, this is my brother. Sebastian, this is Jane Claremont.

To Jane's surprise Sebastian took her hand and shook it warmly.

'You are most welcome here,' he said.

'Thank you, sir. I am honoured to be here.'

Although Sebastian's manner was slightly distracted, she was cheered to see that he was intelligent and in high spirits. She had half expected a mental and physical wreck, after the way Lord Ashby and Dr Shetland had talked of him. She noticed a special smile exchanged between brother and sister.

'I see you have been charming our guests in my absence,' Elaine said.

'Of course. Only the best from our cellars on Halloween, you know that.'

Jane was shocked at the reminder of the date. Halloween. No wonder this had been set as the date of the seance. She had lost track of the days during her sensual affair with Elaine.

'Everyone is keen to begin the experiment, if Miss Claremont is quite ready.'

Jane could not help but smile back at the boyish grin which offered conspiratorial support, even though the pit of her stomach was clenched with nerves, and her shoulders were chilled and stiff with the effort of appearing calm.

She had not expected she would be performing to such a large audience. She suspected they would want entertainment, rather than the scientific enquiry Elaine and Sebastian had stressed.

Sebastian waited until Jane nodded that she was ready before he spoke out loud to the gathering.

'If everyone would like to take their seats, I'll arrange for the lights to be dimmed and we'll begin.' There was a ripple of applause as people moved to obey. 'This is Miss Jane Claremont, ladies and gentlemen, a gifted psychic and a novice in our holy order who knows nothing of our family history. She has agreed to open herself to the vibrations of this place and tell us what she can gather about my . . . my affliction.'

There was a muted round of chatter, and Jane had to restrain herself from bowing to the audience. She wanted, above all, to retain a little dignity.

'Ah yes, the little filly from the convent – did she get here via the music hall?' Lord Ashby called out with disdain.

'You have already met with us in London, Lord Ashby, and you know full well of Miss Claremont's pedigree. Shame on you,' Elaine replied above the ripples of laughter.

As she spoke she directed Jane to the raised dais at a distance from a semicircle of seats where the guests were positioning themselves. The raised dais was framed by velvet curtains. A stage, Jane thought with alarm, even as Elaine lowered her into the heavy wooden chair placed on the stage.

'Just a moment, Lady Melmouth. Dr Shetland has proposed certain checks upon the young . . . lady to ensure that she does not indulge in any parlour tricks.'

Elaine's jaw clenched in annoyance. She let her hand rest gently on Jane's shoulder. Jane swallowed hard, and her diaphragm fluttered nervously.

'Restraints?' Elaine asked.

'Yes, Lady Melmouth, just to ensure the proceedings can be considered scientific,' Dr Shetland explained eagerly.

'Without your agreement to them we could not possibly permit this charade to continue,' Lord Ashby added provocatively.

Elaine and Sebastian looked at one another.

'Please, Elaine,' Sebastian murmured, as he exhaled a plume of smoke from his cheroot with studied carelessness. He turned to Jane. 'Miss Claremont, will you agree?'

Jane nodded slowly.

'Very well, but I really think you could have informed us of your plans sooner,' Elaine said, with an edge to her voice.

'I have everything ready here. If you could assist me in the preparations, Lady Melmouth, for the sake of decorum?'

Jane faced the expectant audience as Elaine loosened her dress, and stripped her to her underskirts and chemise, under Dr Shetland's instructions.

'Could you, er, examine Miss Claremont most carefully while we look on? We need to check there is nothing hidden on her person which she may attempt to "materialise" during the seance.'

'Very well.'

The men in the audience plucked at their beards with dry, trembling fingers, and the women fluttered their fans, troubled yet titillated by this unexpected preamble.

Elaine gently and methodically smoothed the palms of her hands over Jane's thinly clad body, warming to her task. Jane felt Elaine cup her breasts, graze slowly across her nipples. Jane flushed at the memory of what they had done together just ten minutes before. Passion had hardly begun to be subdued, and again her body was being stroked into arousal – this time while others watched avidly. All these strangers, her elders and betters, stared at her with fascination while her mistress searched her as directed. She hoped the audience could not guess what pleasure she derived from being used in this way.

Jane started with shock as Elaine's hand slipped under her petticoats and fingers dabbled her painfully swollen and moist sex. Elaine's clear blue eyes were bright and mocking, a half-smile on her lips, as she continued to taunt Jane's cunt with knowing digits, searching deep into her crack and kneading her arse cheeks as she knelt for better access. Jane stood with her legs spread, keeping very still, feeling the torture of arousal and desperately trying to keep her face impassive. She wanted to squirm against Elaine's impertinent fingers but knew she could not register the slightest hint of her pleasure.

So many eyes watching her as though she were a common whore or circus performer, suspecting, but not daring to admit that they knew exactly what was going on beneath Jane's crisp white petticoats. Jane trembled with fever as Elaine slicked an index finger, wet from Jane's juices, into Jane's tight little arsehole, and wiggled provocatively. A bead of sweat slid between Jane's breasts, and she bit her lip to prevent herself from crying out at such bliss.

'It seems there is nothing hidden on Miss Claremont's body,' Elaine said at last in a clear, calm voice, as she finally withdrew her prying fingers and stood up, moving away from Jane's semi-clad body which throbbed with suppressed lust.

'You are quite certain there are no rolls of ribbon or cotton which Miss Claremont may later produce as evidence of ecto-plasmic spirits? I believe it is a common trick at spiritual meetings in London,' Dr Shetland persisted. There was a catch to his voice despite his detached manner.

'I am sure, Dr Shetland. Would you care to check yourself?'

Jane stiffened at such a challenge and looked down in fear.

Dr Shetland coughed slightly.

'No, that would not be seemly. Now, could you assist me in

securing these leather restraints on Miss Claremont? You won't mind them, will you, Miss Claremont? They are pretty comfortable, and they will ensure you do not move about in the dim lights necessary for the seance.'

Jane looked at Elaine, and nodded silently to give her permission.

Jane sat on the heavy wooden chair, still dressed only in her undergarments. The wide leather restraints were fastened about her wrists and ankles by Elaine, then padlocked to the legs and arms of the heavy wooden chair by Dr Shetland. As a final indignity, lengths of silken cord were wrapped loosely around her waist and chest by Elaine, the ends of which were handed to members of the audience by Dr Shetland, who told them to hold on firmly throughout the seance no matter what happened.

'Are you satisfied that Miss Claremont is now sufficiently restrained?' Elaine asked at last. Lord Ashby nodded, as did Mr Barnes, and Dr Shetland took a seat with them in the front row.

'Now we must extinguish some candles, to provide muted light, and we must remain quiet, to permit Miss Claremont to concentrate.'

Elaine and Sebastian sat in the front row once the candlelight had been reduced, and their guests became silent in expectation. The room was now suffused with the more golden glow of the firelight. A sudden gust of wind sent a draught down the chimney, making the log fire flare and the few lit candles flicker. The audience tittered nervously.

'Please place one of those tall candlesticks in front of me on the platform,' Jane requested in a clear, steady voice. 'Thank you,' she added as Sebastian hastened to obey.

She let herself watch the single flame of the candle and breathed deeply, evenly, to calm herself. She tried to ignore the others who watched her. All except for Sebastian and Elaine. Jane reasoned that they really believed something was present, or they would never have undertaken this seance, would never have thrown her to these wolves. They were the eye of this storm.

She had to believe in them. She had to do what was required of her. There would need to be more than an array of parlour tricks to convince Dr Shetland and the others that Sebastian could sense something real. She prayed for the help of her guardian angel.

Jane took a final, measured breath and lay herself open to the castle, the surrounding land, to Sebastian and whatever was haunting his sleepless nights, in an effort to guess their source.

The force almost winded her. Something huge and dark and ancient. A power that was angry with Sebastian, and with his three gentlemen friends.

Jane thought she saw a figure, a shadowy woman standing by the fire. A hallucination brought on by fasting and prayer, or a real apparition?

Jane shook her head. She felt weak and strange. She could feel a presence clawing at her chest, wanting to get through. Not the powerful force, something weaker but just as angry and more vocal. Maybe she could handle this lesser presence more easily than the ancient force. As Jane denied the powerful force and beckoned the lesser presence, the casements rattled as anger flew about the room. The candle flame grew to three times its original size and flickered rapidly.

'There is a curse on your land,' Jane said finally in as slow and measured a fashion as she could muster. An understatement, if ever there was one.

'Nonsense, very melodramatic and second-rate,' Lord Ashby declared loudly, and some laughed.

'Yes, there is a curse,' Sebastian agreed clearly, and his tone quietened the laughter. 'But how to remove it? That is what I need to know, Miss Claremont. Could you find the answer from the spirit of this land, this castle?'

Jane looked at him. She wanted to refuse, explain the spirit was too powerful to articulate in this after-dinner atmosphere. But there was such a look of entreaty, of restrained terror, in Sebastian's handsome face. A look echoed by his sister's concerned face. Elaine was asking Jane to help. Jane must do what she could.

'Please,' Sebastian persisted, 'what can you tell me?'

The others were getting restless. They had not planned on their urbane but highly strung host taking this quite so seriously. The bearded sceptics twitched as more candles gutted about the room, and the velvet curtains billowed. Some of the ladies gave little cries of fright. Jane summoned all her courage.

'I shall try,' she said simply.

Jane let a sliver of the lesser power in the room speak through her.

'Sebastian, do you still bear those marks I gave you?' the rasping voice asked, and laughed viciously. 'I thought to give you spunk and you let me down again. Trying to seek a way out of your duty, your fate –'

There were more words, damming up with the effort to get through, and behind them Jane sensed an impatient presence which made her temples throb with the effort of keeping it back.

It was enough for Lord Ashby to stand up, muttering curses, and for Sebastian to become deathly pale.

Others stood up also. All concentration and attention on the seance was gone, as people tried to ignore this turn of events. With an effort Jane cast out the gravel-voiced spirit, sublimed it into the candle flame and away into the ether. The older, darker spirit went of its own accord.

Jane was as shaken as her audience had been. She had not bargained upon actually contacting any entities and she had touched upon real manifestations. One elemental in its power, and she knew that it intended to return. Soon.

Elaine stood, also looking very pale.

'It seems we will not have many playful spirits tonight. Perhaps Halloween is not the best time to try this diversion after all. Will anyone join me in the green room for a nightcap, perhaps a game of charades? I am sure the spirits will not follow us there.'

'Only the brandy, perhaps,' someone joked.

There was a ripple of relieved laughter and people filed past Jane where she remained tethered to the chair, her ribbons loosely strewn about her. They glanced at her with distaste and disapproval, and a little awe. They discussed how she could have trained her voice to speak so low when 'possessed', as though she were a mechanical specimen that could not hear their comments. Jane fixed her gaze upon the candle flame in front of her, to hide her embarrassment, until most had gone.

Eventually Megan slipped into the room, murmured something to Dr Shetland, and between them they freed Jane.

'Lady Melmouth said you should rest now, retire as soon as you are able, and she will speak with you about this tomorrow,' Megan whispered respectfully as she helped Jane to dress once more. Jane nodded. She was shivering, chilled to the bone although it was not cold in the room.

Megan guided her closer to the fire so that she could warm herself, then was called away to relight more candles. Jane chafed her hands, staring into the log-flames, too exhausted to climb the tower stairs to her bedroom immediately.

'The voice . . . how did you do that?' It was Sebastian, offering her a brandy which Jane took gratefully.

'Was it someone you recognised?' she asked, taking a few sips.

'Yes.'

'Don't be ridiculous, Sebastian. Let us go through and join Elaine.' It was Lord Ashby, scowling, trying to lead Sebastian away.

'It is not ridiculous.' Sebastian turned to Jane. 'It was the voice of my – of Elaine's and mine –' He paused and closed his eyes before he resumed with an effort. 'It was the voice of our dead father.'

Jane blinked in astonishment.

'You should not convince yourself of such insanity, especially in your present overwrought state,' Lord Ashby said firmly, 'or you'll not sleep again tonight. I'll expect you in the green room in five minutes or I'll return to physically drag you there.' Lord Ashby's nostrils flared angrily, and he departed without acknowledging Jane's presence.

Sebastian turned to Jane.

'I apologise for Lord Ashby. He always acts like a prig when he is frightened and is too cowardly to admit it.' Sebastian smiled suddenly, and his kindness made her smile too.

'I understand, Lord Melmouth.'

'Please, call me Sebastian always. Thank you for confirming some of my infernal nightmares tonight. Even if my friends are not convinced, it reassures me there is a truth in what I say.' He refilled Jane's brandy glass from a decanter and she again sipped the fiery liquid. It made her light-headed on an empty stomach, but it soothed the knots in her shoulders and neck and temples. 'You're still trembling a little,' he observed. 'Did our spirits frighten you so much?'

'It was just the effort, after fasting and preparing for the seance. And nerves, in front of so many people,' Jane replied quickly, unwilling to admit how powerful the force she had detected had been. Sebastian nodded as though he understood, regardless.

'You saw the woman, didn't you?' he asked abruptly.

Jane nodded.

'I'll show you where I first saw her, when I show you round Morlanby.' Sebastian shivered, then smiled uncertainly. 'Elaine had told me that you were a rare soul, and I am so glad she found you when she did. They would have bundled me off to Bedlam by now if it had not been for you.' Jane looked down shyly at such praise, unable to meet the earnest tawny eyes. 'Please stay and help us find the secret of this curse, and how to lay it to rest. Are you a rare enough soul for that?'

The room tilted and swayed, as though reality had taken on a whole new significance. Such an invitation was tempting. Even so Jane felt nauseous at the very thought of tracking down the source of the power she had sensed. It had not threatened harm to her, but it may yet harm Sebastian. She wished she could reassure the handsome youth. She wanted to tell him that she had invented everything, learned ventriloquism and performed parlour tricks with Elaine's connivance just to delay any plans to declare Sebastian mad. But Sebastian would not have believed her. He knew Elaine better than Jane did, and knew she would not indulge in such obvious theatrics. Jane smiled at the irony of it. She had dreaded the seance because she was afraid she would sense nothing and that her acting skills would fail her. She had worried at failing to fulfil the promise she had given Elaine to help Sebastian. But now Jane was as convinced as Sebastian that were was something which plagued him. And she was half afraid to stay.

Yet Jane knew she would stay. She had to. She was in Elaine's erotic thrall. She was charmed by Sebastian, and now she was also intrigued by the power of his demons. She wanted to free the young man from whatever darkness overshadowed him.

'Yes, I will stay, and try to discover more, if Elaine agrees,' she said quietly.

'Thank you, Jane,' Sebastian replied. 'I'll help you in any way I can.'

Jane was touched by the look of relief on his handsome features. 'If you can help us lay these unquiet spirits,' he continued, 'you'll earn my eternal gratitude and my sister's deepest affections. You'll always have a home here, especially if you have helped restore this place to peace and happiness.'

'That would mean much to me,' she replied politely, and realised with surprise she told the truth. She would want to live out her days in this beautiful landscape. She almost felt as though it was a home which had awaited her all her life. With an effort she roused herself from such sentimental thoughts and turned to Sebastian with sudden resolve.

'I promise I shall do my very best to help you, no matter how anyone else might object,' she said firmly.

SEVEN

Hazel woke with a start. She thought someone had been banging at the door. Elaine? Then she realised she must have been dreaming. Why would Elaine visit her little 'hovel', she asked herself bitterly, sitting up in her narrow wooden bed and rubbing her eyes.

She could detect a sliver of light through the thick shutters, could hear the sighing of a high wind wrapping itself around the cottage before it swooped from moorland to sea. Soon the direction would change and the inland breeze would bring rain. The tang on the air told her that. Hazel had a sense for such things. She stood and stretched and hitched the front door open to look out at the morning.

There was a covering of hoarfrost on the small lawn, upon the leaves of the rhododendron and fuchsia that hedged her small concession to a garden. Hazel huddled further into her Aran sweater and prodded Max's supine bulk until the dog growled and ambled outside to relieve himself. Then he trotted about sniffing, checking nothing had breached the garden boundaries overnight (give or take a few voles and hedgehogs). Hazel smiled as the self-important Max snuffled brittle grasses, and executed a slow, stiff jaunt across the lawn. She had never known a dog so slow to rouse itself on cold mornings, even if he was the best guard dog she had ever possessed.

She looked up at the sky – a steely blue, with thickening mackerel cloud. It was cold. Colder than it should be for this time of year. She had to break a thin film of ice over the water butt to fill her kettle. She hooked the big cast-iron kettle over the embers in the hearth and collected a few logs from the stack in the lean-to next to the cottage to kindle the fire back into life. Max ambled back in to take up his station in front of the hearth and she closed the door behind him.

With a little warm water in a tin bowl she quickly scrubbed her face and armpits, loins and feet with a flannel, then dressed in her long-johns and vest, corduroy trousers and shirt. Max wagged his tail appreciatively as Hazel opened the shutters and began to cook porridge on the small range. He knew he would have some of it, cooled down, for breakfast.

The fire and breakfast woke Hazel up and warmed her through before she ventured out. She laced up her boots; shouldered herself into her thick serge jacket. She rammed her cap low on to her short cropped hair and wrapped a scarf around her neck. Then she banked up the fire and shut up the cottage before striking out on the upland track with Max trotting at her heels.

She kept up a swift pace until her breath was warm enough to mist the cold air, and she had begun to sweat a little. Then she let up on herself, pausing to look at the view. It was so beautiful. She still felt a kick in her chest when she saw the sweep of moor, the white slash of waterfall flowing through it. A bristle of russet and dark-green woods surrounded Morlanby's dove-grey castlements. Then, more distant still, a sliver of beach and the shining horizon of Irish sea.

She remembered her time in America and Canada, how the landscape had lacked this infinite variety. Hundreds of miles of mountain, forest, lake and snow field – even the wilderness of the Klondike – however majestic, had not touched her like her homeland. She shivered as she remembered the bitterness of winters she had spent in the Northern territories. Ten minutes away from the cabin and you could be dead. Perhaps the spectre of that bone-white cold, the constant threat of hypothermia and frostbite, lived on in her muscle fibres. Perhaps that was why she sensed the coming winter would be worse than usual for this temperate country.

She leaned her back against the slender trunk of a young mountain ash, reached out and stroked a cluster of its remaining bright red berries. They had been abundant this year. Sign of a bad winter. Nature's way of storing sustenance for the months ahead. Also a sign of bloodshed, the old lore said. When she remembered, she grimaced. She wanted to forget all she had learned from the old woman, Deidre, who once lived in her cottage. As a girl Hazel had sheltered at Deidre's cottage when she was caught out in the rain on long rambles, and had listened to the old woman's tales as she sat by the fire. Stories Hazel remembered, and would often relate to Elaine when she returned to Morlanby. Such memories had prompted her to buy the property when old Deidre had died. But right now thinking of Elaine, of anything connected to her, filled Hazel with restlessness.

She remembered more fully the dream she had experienced just before she had woken up that morning. Elaine banging on the door, rattling it on its hinges, begging to be let in. Hazel supposed it was the high wind that had made her dream of such a thing. But the wind had not prompted what had happened next in her dream. Elaine had been drenched, her blonde hair plastered to high cheekbones, skirts clinging against her hip curves. Hazel had dreamed of undressing Elaine tenderly, peeling away the wet clothes to uncover the ivory skin, the full breasts, the long legs which lay beneath. Hazel blinked, took a breath at the memory of how vivid the dream had been. She had smoothed the palms of her hands over that sumptuous flesh, the body she had once known as well as her own, all the while murmuring consolations and kissing away the tears on Elaine's cheeks. Elaine's arms had slipped about Hazel's neck, and Hazel had clasped Elaine close, letting the fire warm them as they had kissed and stroked and sucked each other hungrily. Elaine had whispered Hazel's name over and over, telling her how much she was loved and needed, declaring that they must never be parted again.

Hazel remembered the dream with a moistening of her sex and a swelling in her breasts. She remembered how it had felt to stroke Elaine's hard nipples, the tender flesh of her inner thighs.

How she had brought her own hard-muscled thigh between Elaine's long legs, and felt Elaine's soft mound press against it eagerly, and Elaine had begged to be taken, possessed by Hazel once more. Hazel closed her eyes and rubbed herself as she remembered the dream, felt the old lust rise in her loins once more.

Elaine.

But it was madness. Hazel had woken to find herself alone, just as she was alone now on this mountainside. She had been wound in a tangle of sheets and blankets, with the door rattling in the wind as though an angry spirit wanted entrance, and Max growling throatily in response, even as he slept. Hazel clenched her fists, and shook her head to free herself from the cloying languid mood her dream had left behind. She had enough to think about without wasting time, torturing herself with impossible fantasies. Hadn't Elaine ordered her angrily off Morlanby property, demanded she never returned, just the day before? Her old lover was gone, and was real only in dreams.

As Max grew restless at the pause in their journey, bounding to the brow of the hill then returning to sit at her feet, she pulled the muffler closer around her neck and continued along the sheep track, over the lower hump of the mountain and down towards the Lewis farm. A thin trail of smoke drifted from the chimney of the low-slung random stone house, and Hazel could see figures moving in the courtyard. There was a good chance that Megan's father was still working close by. Hazel struck up a punishing pace, picking her way across rough mounds of heather, eager to have her errand over with.

Hazel was pleased to find Huw Lewis busy in the stables, seeing to his horse's tack before going down to the nearest town. Hazel had forgotten it was market day. She chatted to him rapidly, offering her spare bantam in exchange for one of his cockerels, to which he easily agreed. She smiled, pleased. Her hens would lay and breed better for it. Then she mentioned she had seen Megan the previous day at Morlanby, and that the girl planned to stay for the time being, in spite of the rumours of what had been happening there, that the young lord was teetering on the brink of violent religious insanity. Megan had seemed content and settled in her duties and wished to remain for a month at least.

Huw's two eldest sons, Ewan and Jon, were in the courtyard readying the cart, laden with butter and cheeses for market. They were burly youths, with dark hair and eyes the same colour as Megan's hidden under beetling brows. When they overheard Hazel's report Ewan said, 'Would have been better if someone had not given Megan fancy ideas, then she would have stayed safely at home.'

Hazel ignored the jibe.

'She'll come back a strumpet, after all those goings-on at Morlanby, and we'll never be able to marry her to a decent man,' Jon added, raking a contemptuous stare across Hazel's appearance. Hazel suppressed a smile. As if she was meant to be humiliated at the stupid young buck's low opinion of her marriageability. As if Megan could only wish for marriage.

'Even if there are poperies and devilries afoot in Morlanby, Megan should be safe enough for now,' his father replied. 'Better for her to have good food and a soft bed along with hard work this winter, for we could only have given her the hard work. Now shut up, and help me hitch the mare.'

Huw had bridled his carthorse and led her out, nodding briefly in thanks as he passed Hazel who stood by the stable entrance. Hazel nodded back, surprised at such candour and gratitude from the usually dour old man. His sons disapproved, for they scowled even worse.

'Would you like anything from market?' Huw called back towards Hazel as he turned the cart in the courtyard.

'No, but thank you. I'll be over next week with the bantam. And I'll tell you what news I've got from Megan. I know you are too busy to visit her.'

Huw nodded and put up his hand as his sons opened the courtyard gate to give him access to the road. Mrs Lewis stood in the kitchen doorway, wiping her hands on her apron, watching her husband depart. She waved towards Hazel too.

'Will you come in for a cup of tea before you walk back?' she called across.

'No thank you, Mrs Lewis. I've too much work to get back to. Next week, maybe.'

Mrs Lewis nodded and returned to her kitchen. Hazel turned ready to walk home and found the young men still hanging on the courtyard gate, watching her.

'Isn't natural for a woman to be out of wedlock. Even an ugly woman ought to find herself a husband, don't you think, Ewan?' Jon said as Hazel and her mastiff walked past them.

'That's right, Jon. Woman is Adam's rib and useless if she isn't bearing his children. The Bible says so,' Ewan replied. Then he turned to Hazel. 'What about you, Miss Branagan? Are you courting yet?'

Hazel did not bother to reply.

'You must be very lonely, all alone on your hillside. Perhaps you would like one of us to pay you a visit next Sunday? Or maybe both of us next Saturday night? We're often in the mood for a bit of . . . company after a night down at the Black Bull,' Jon continued, while Ewan guffawed.

Hazel smiled at them thinly. Her gimlet eye was enough to silence them. 'I would not recommend it. Neither myself nor Max are very sociable,' she said quietly. Then she walked on past them both, choosing to leave things at that on this occasion. They were both young still. They would find other interests soon enough.

Hazel hoped. Bullying men of any age she could do without. She had met enough of them on her travels. She sighed at having to face it again so close to home. Men who resented her, sensed that she had no need for them, but could not leave her alone. She guessed it was some vague dissatisfaction, some sexual swaggering, some jealousy of her independence. Perhaps it was just outrage at her manly clothes and proud bearing that prompted it. But she had never bowed down before it, given in gracefully, and she was not about to start. She made a mental note to load her shotgun, just in case they came calling one drunken night like they had threatened. Next time they baited her she would not be so tolerant, even if they were Megan's brothers.

She smiled when her whitewashed cottage, nestled between rowans and firs, an island in a sea of pasture and hawthorn, came into view. Some of her sheep, little tails flicking, were grazing ferociously, scissoring and tearing at the sweet grasses before chewing the cud as though they were elderly monks mumbling prayers to themselves. They gave baas of annoyance as Hazel and Max skirted them and she laughed. She was glad to be home again, alone and free, even if she was plagued by the ghost of Elaine in her solitary bed.

Just as Hazel reached the haven of her home once more, in Morlanby Megan was preparing a bath for Lady Melmouth. She was discovering that this was an elaborate procedure, one which Elaine was very exacting about.

Elaine was still in a negligée of creamy lace, idling over a breakfast of fresh bread rolls, butter and jams, with a pot of Darjeeling tea. She had directed Megan to stoke the fire high, set out the copper half bath, and fill it with several kettles of hot water mixed with just the right amount of cooler water to make the bath steam fiercely. Then Elaine handed Megan small glass vials filled with precious oils – the heady sweetness of ylang-ylang, frankincense and lemon grass – so that a few drops of each could be added. Then a sachet of dried lavender was to be steeped in the waters, and a handful of fresh rose petals were fetched from the hothouse to scatter on the surface of the already perfumed waters. Megan then collected a pile of thick towels to lay over the arm of the chair and warm by the fire. She placed a towel on the carpet next to the bath, to catch any drips.

'I think that everything is ready now, madam,' Megan said at last.

'Do you have the oatmeal soap? The natural sponge? The lemon-juice and thyme mixture for my hair?'

Megan checked the small lacquered table and ticked off the items.

'Yes.'

'Are my fresh clothes laid out ready on the bed? You have set out my dark-red gown?'

'Yes, madam.'

Elaine looked up at last. Megan was surprised to notice that the aristocrat's porcelain features were drawn, and there were shadows below the clear blue eyes. Elaine pushed a slim hand through the mane of blonde tresses she had loosely tied back with a lace ribbon, and Megan noticed how it trembled.

'Did you sleep well last night, Megan?' Elaine asked.

'Not very well, to be truthful, madam. I suppose it's because I'm not used to the house yet, but every sound of the wind at the window or gusting down the chimney seemed to wake me with a start.'

Elaine nodded gravely, as though this confirmed her suspicions.

'I did not sleep very well either. Which is why I want this bath to be perfect, to soothe the tension out of me, do you understand?'

'Yes, madam,' Megan replied in a tone that betrayed she did not fully understand. Elaine smiled at her consternation.

'Good.'

Finally Elaine crossed to stand next to the bath and shrugged off her negligée. Megan tried hard not to stare at the lady's naked beauty. Her breasts were like rounded, polished marble, her belly smooth with a tiny pot, her hips and bottom were curved and caught the light like the surface of a peach. Megan looked down only to admire the firm rounded calves, the high arched feet. As she looked at the delicate toes she wondered what it would be like to suck each one in turn. The thought made her look up again and rest admiringly on the inverted triangle of blonde curls which covered Elaine's love mound. For some reason Megan remembered the Song of Solomon from the Bible. Elaine's body was so perfect and ripe, like the fruits of an exotic harvest. Megan felt her breath catch, standing so close to the naked woman, even as these wild thoughts ran through her head.

It took a few moments of awkward silence before Elaine inclined her head serenely, rousing Megan from her thoughts.

'Well, Megan, hurry up and test the temperature with your elbow. I don't want to be scalded.'

Megan bent to obey. The heady fragrance of the steam filled her nostrils. The water was very warm and inviting.

'Seems just about right, madam.'

'Good. Then take my hand and help steady me while I step in.'

Megan took the slim hand with her own and held it like an awkward courtier. Elaine settled into the bath, sitting back and sighing at the soothing warmth.

'Take the small saucepan and scoop water over me, Megan.'

'Your hair as well, madam?'

'Yes, yes. I want to be cleansed completely after such a restless night.'

Megan dipped the small copper saucepan into the scented water, then slowly poured its contents down Elaine's spine, over her breasts, over her head while carefully shielding Elaine's eyes. With each scoop Megan's hand grazed against Elaine's firm calves, and Megan grew hot at the glancing contact. She wished she did not have to watch how the pale skin, delicate as Dresden, glistened as rivulets of water trickled downwards over Elaine's fine-boned shoulders, her long, tapered neck, those pert breasts. The morning sunlight added to the effect, adding ethereal quality to the aristo-crat's nakedness. The long blonde hair, when dampened, turned to the colour of old gold and clung in long tresses across her breasts, her shoulder blades, like an exotic seaweed.

There were pink roses in Elaine's cheeks now, and her aureoles and nipples matched the colour exactly. Megan wanted to reach out and stroke her lady's cheeks, her lips, her nipples with an index finger, just to check the perfect flesh was real. The urge made her warm and sticky and she sensed Elaine's grey-blue eyes watching her curiously.

'Now you must soap me down, Megan. Look, I'll stand up to make this easier for you. I know you are not used to the duties of a lady's maid, but must you act so dreamily? The water will cool before we are finished, and I'll make you draw another bath to complete my ablutions to my satisfaction, if you are not careful.'

'Please forgive me, madam, I am quick to learn,' Megan stammered, although she sensed the light tone of mockery in Elaine's voice beneath the annoyance. When she risked looking into Elaine's eyes, she was shocked by the knowing challenge there.

'Then soap me down, and perform the task well if you want to stay in service at Morlanby.'

Megan carefully soaped up the natural sponge with the bar of oatmeal soap. It took an effort not to tremble as she smoothed the sponge across Elaine's shoulders, down the delicate spine, following the curve of the tight buttocks and continuing down the long, shapely legs. Then Megan soaped the sponge again, and its froth of bubbles smelt fresh and exotic.

'Hurry, Megan,' Elaine said in warning as Megan showed hesitation.

'Yes, madam.'

Megan rubbed the sponge carefully along Elaine's collar bone, over her full breasts. Megan felt her breath catch and her abdomen quiver, as her hands glided the sponge across those rosebud nipples, and felt the weight of those breasts. She desperately wanted to squeeze them and put her lips to them, suckle at the soaped-up beauties. It would mean instant dismissal, but maybe that single sensation would be worth it.

Megan had not felt so tempted by another woman's flesh since she had seen Hazel Branagan naked. She wondered at the overwhelming desires she felt even though Elaine's body, curvaceous and petite, was so different from Hazel's lean lines. And Jane Claremont, the young nun, she remembered guiltily, her beauty was different again. But Megan had also felt a soft desire for her. Megan flushed guiltily.

'Carry on, Megan. I think my breasts are clean enough, thank you.'

Megan jumped, and her hands held the sponge aloft as though she had just been burned by Elaine's flesh. She resoaped hastily, trying not to glance at Elaine's glistening calves. Then she hazarded a quick glance up at Elaine.

Elaine was watching her under drooping golden lashes.

'Soap my belly next, Megan. Then pay particular attention to my thighs and privates.'

'Yes, madam.'

Megan carefully soaped the beautiful belly of her mistress, admiring the curve of her hips and her dip of navel. She soaped Elaine's calves, and knees, letting the sponge drip warm water behind the knees, which made Elaine sigh and shiver at the ghostly erotic caress. Then Megan soaped Elaine's thighs, stroking the tender flesh of the inner thighs reverently. Finally, she approached her mistress's privates, and let the soft natural sponge glide against the pink slash of slick flesh swelling from dripping gold curls of pubic hair.

Elaine let out a low moan, and shuffled her feet further apart in the copper bath so that Megan could soap and stroke her fanny more easily. Megan hardly noticed, so intent was she on her sensuous task. Megan felt as though a band of iron gripped her chest, and a slow fire burned between her own thighs, and her breath came hot and quick as she stroked the silken folds of Elaine's labia, keeping up a subtle rhythm. Megan thought of how she had washed Jane the day before, and had managed somehow to maintain her distance from the joy of intimacy with the young woman's body. Now the memory of Jane's beauty, how firm and warm she had felt beneath the flannel, returned vividly to add to Megan's quickened lust. She waited for Elaine's curt order to stop soaping those beautiful privates but Elaine only breathed soft and shallow in the quiet room as Megan continued to caress her sex with the sponge. Megan gently squeezed the sponge, letting warm water drip over the swollen pink hood which hid Elaine's clitoris. Slowly, shyly, the nub grew hard and offered itself for more caresses. Then Megan stroked Elaine's sex-lips once more, until they too unfurled. She let the sponge graze softly against the sensitive clitoral tip for a fleeting second, before she continued the long, full-length strokes downwards along Elaine's sex. letting the sponge slip between her arse-crack provocatively.

After long moments of such treatment Elaine gave little gasps of appreciation, and her fingers fastened around Megan's scalp, digging into her hair possessively.

Megan paused, breathing shallowly with effort. They were frozen for a while in this position. The fire crackled, and Elaine dripped, and Megan felt small beads of sweat on her upper lip which she slowly licked away.

'Should I stop, then, madam?' Megan asked at last, her voice a quiet rasp. Even as she spoke she watched Elaine's coral-pink clitoral tip, how it throbbed with arousal, and longed to place the tip of her tongue against it, to cool its hot ache. She longed to let the fingers stroke her own sex, which had swollen into fevered longing.

She tore her gaze away and looked up into Elaine's face when her mistress did not answer immediately. As Megan crouched beside the bath, and looked up the column of skin that was Elaine's softly rounded belly, through the valley made by her breasts, to the beautiful face, Megan's heart and stomach flipped over. There was no mistaking the parted lips, the half-closed eyes, misted over with desire.

'Leave off the sponge for now. Continue with your tongue,' Elaine whispered.

Megan felt stunned. She wondered whether her ears had deceived her, and she had hallucinated the latest order because it was what she wanted to do most in the world at that moment. She needed to lap the sweet, swollen sex of her mistress, she was compelled to.

Carefully, with great reverence, she let the tip of her tongue touch the very tip of Elaine's pink, enticing clitoris. Elaine let out a sigh of appreciation. Elaine parted the flesh surrounding the hard bud with her index and ring fingers, letting her middle finger glide across the very tip in a firm massage whenever Megan paused in applying delicate licks. Megan felt dizzy at the sight of her mistress pleasuring herself with such languid abandon. Megan watched as Elaine circled the base of the shiny pink nub before stroking its very tip and hastened to copy the circular pressure with her own tongue. As Megan continued dabbing and probing with her hot, tender tongue, Elaine's fingers sought out her own sex-lips, dipping a second finger and a third slowly into her rose-pink sex, plowing the delectable furrow in front of Megan's fascinated face. Soon Megan could lap at beads of juices flowing like honey from the centre of Elaine's cunt.

The taste of honey-musk mingled with oatmeal and rose petal was bringing Megan to a peak of arousal. Only Elaine's jerk at a handful of hair caused her to look up at her mistress once more, and realise there was another order for her to carry out.

'Strip, Megan, and step into the bath with me.'

'Oh no, madam, I couldn't!'

'You must. Right now.'

Megan looked into Elaine's eyes, smudged dark with impatient passion, and knew there was no chance to refuse. Megan quickly stripped off her clothes and stepped into the copper bath. The warm, scented water pooled round her calves, and the fire kept her skin warm, but she shivered.

Elaine scooped up the little copper saucepan and poured water over Megan's naked body, smiling at her.

'This will keep you warm,' she whispered, even as she sponged the maid's body. 'The contrast of your tanned hands and neck against the pale flesh of your torso is most erotic, you know,' Elaine observed as she let the sponge slide between Megan's thighs and glide against Megan's sex. Megan closed her eyes, and her hips bucked slightly against the slick pressure, soothing her fevered sex and clit only to arouse them still more. She opened her eyes in surprise as Elaine abruptly ceased the caress, and threw the sponge back into the water.

'Now rub your body up against mine, Megan. Let your body soap mine. It's softer than the sponge's caress, I'll wager.'

'If you wish, madam.'

'I do most certainly wish.'

Megan felt awkward as her arms circled Elaine's narrow waist. Megan's elbows pressed slightly against Elaine's hip curves and her palms rested against the apple of her arse cheeks. Standing this close, Megan's nipples slid across Elaine's upper breasts. Elaine's breasts jutted into Megan's, lifting them slightly. Elaine's smooth lower belly glided across Megan's mound, and Elaine's triangle of curls jutted against the curve of the very top of Megan's thigh. Elaine slowly shimmied against her. Elaine's swollen clit glided against Megan's soapy thigh, circled and pressed urgently. Megan felt her own hard little clit grow hot and eager against Elaine's belly, and groaned at the torture of it.

'Come, Megan, sway against me too – yes – just as if we were dancing slowly,' Elaine crooned, even as she pressed her nipples further into Megan's soft breasts, and licked the delicate nape of the maid's neck. Megan trembled, unable to contain herself. She let her fingers find and massage her own hot cunt even as Elaine began to frig herself once more, grinding against Megan for extra pressure, one arm circling Megan's waist, stroking a tender hip-bone delicately.

Megan felt she would soon crumple at the bliss of being in this embrace, but had to let her arm fall from Elaine's waist to steady herself. Elaine immediately took hold of Megan's arm and guided the maid's palm towards her. Slowly, insistently, Elaine rubbed Megan's palm up against her sex. Megan let her fingers circle and explore Elaine's sex, honoured to be allowed to touch her mistress in this way, even if she was uncertain what to do. Megan tried to think about what she most enjoyed when she caressed herself, even though she felt nervous. Megan let her fingers probe deeper into the tender flesh and slip into Elaine's wet sex to circle eagerly against the quickening cunt walls.

Elaine came violently and quickly, and the sight of her soft face in passion was enough for Megan to climax too. Megan pulsed and quivered against the fingers of her other hand, which still dabbled against her own slick quim in eager satisfaction.

For a few moments, Megan embraced Elaine, and felt the other woman quivering slightly until her passion was fully spent.

'Very good, Megan. You learn quickly,' Elaine said at last.

'Thank you, madam.'

'Did you come?'

'I believe so.'

'Good. If you're not certain, I'm sure Hazel Branagan will tutor you in how to finish yourself next time you two meet.'

'Madam?' Megan asked, still stunned and slow after making love to comprehend Elaine's meaning.

'Oh, nothing. Please rinse me off, and then rinse yourself off too, while I watch.'

Megan dipped the saucepan once more and let the warm water flow down Elaine's planes and curves. Megan felt a hot stirring in her clit and knew with dismay a renewal of lust. But she knew that Elaine's mood had changed. Megan did not dare reach out and touch that perfect flesh again. Instead Megan poured water over her own body, rinsing it of suds, wishing the water would cool her ardour rather than inflame it. Some chance of that while Elaine watched her with a slow, cool smile.

'Now step out of the bath, dry yourself and get dressed, Megan. This you must do before you help me out of the bath, so be quick.'

'Yes, madam.'

Megan stepped out on to the towel laid over the carpet, reached for a fire-warmed towel and swaddled herself. All the while she was conscious of Elaine watching her. Megan rubbed dry her solid hourglass figure, her ample hips and full breasts, with resigned briskness.

'You clean up quite well, Megan. Hazel still has good taste. You remind me of the figures my brother brought back from India. Full and round, images of a fertility goddess.'

'Thank you, madam,' Megan said doubtfully as she dressed herself in guilty haste. Elaine laughed at the maid's sudden shyness.

'Towels are cloth, which also comes from India; do you know that, Megan? We shall educate you in such things while you are at Morlanby. Now hurry and bring that fresh towel to me.'

Elaine stepped out of the bath as Megan surrounded her with the large towel, and rubbed her dry with careful vigour, as though applying herself to a task which would help to rub away the memory of what had just happened.

'That's enough, child, or you will rub me raw. I'll stand by the fire to dry a little longer. Fetch the lotion on my dresser – yes, that one. Now smooth it across my body. It helps keep my skin soft and supple. Do you find my skin pleasing, Megan?'

'Yes, madam.'

'Then treat it gently. Yes, that's right.' Megan's palms burned to feel Elaine's soft breasts and arse and thighs beneath them once more, even as she obediently applied the lotion. Megan tried to be as methodical as possible, to resist licking and nibbling the fresh creaminess of Elaine's skin.

'Tell me, Megan, will you remember all the procedures of my bathing ritual in future?'

'I believe that it's already branded into my memory, madam,' Megan muttered with some feeling. Elaine smiled, and inclined her head in approval as Megan laced up Elaine's stays tightly and helped her step into her petticoats.

'Good, then you will be able to see to Miss Claremont's bath tomorrow with the same thoroughness. Perhaps you will both find something novel in the experience too.'

Megan stiffened at the suggestion even as her heart quickened at the idea.

'Is that an order, madam?' she hazarded.

'Yes, I believe it is, Megan,' Elaine replied silkily. 'And I have one other order to give you. Will you obey it? Or would you rather I asked it of you as a very great favour?'

Megan flushed slightly as she fastened Elaine's cream blouse. Elaine was mocking her. As if she could refuse Elaine anything, the great Lady Melmouth herself. As if she wanted to refuse her anything after what they had just done together.

'I am happy to be of use to you, madam. What else would you like me to do?'

Megan half suspected she would be ordered to bathe and seduce yet another female guest, but the flippant command did not come. Megan looked up and was surprised at how quickly Elaine's expression had changed. Now Elaine appeared almost sombre, and took one of Megan's hands in between her own.

'Promise you will keep watch over Jane around the other guests when I am not there. I do not wish her to be upset by those arrogant boors any more than is strictly necessary. And whenever you can, please attend to Sebastian also. Let me know of any concerns you have if either Jane or Sebastian look even slightly upset. Do you understand me, Megan?'

'Yes, madam. This I will do gladly.'

Megan felt the pressure of Elaine's hands around hers relax at this promise.

'Thank you, Megan. I am glad I can count on you. Lord knows, I need all the help I can get for the next few days. Now you may go. You may return to clear up the bath things after I have left on my walk.'

'Very well, madam.'

As Megan reached the door Elaine called out her name.

'Yes, madam? Is there anything else?' Megan asked.

'Thank you for the bath. I enjoyed it very much.'

'As did I, madam,' Megan blurted out, before hurrying out of the boudoir and shutting the door behind her.

On the way back downstairs, Megan paused and leaned against the cool stone walls of the turret. She brought her wrists to her nose and sniffed. She could smell the scent of ylang-ylang lotion on the palms of her hands, and the subtler tang of Elaine's musk.

It took quite a while before her heartbeat returned to normal and she felt brave enough to face the other servants without betraying her guilty carnal pleasures on her pretty, mobile features.

EIGHT

Elaine felt languid and relaxed as she descended the main staircase, ready to bid goodbye to her overnight guests. She was surprised at the subdued mood in the drawing room and guessed that others had spent a restless night also. Sebastian and his three gentlemen friends had left early for a shoot on the moors. Dr Shetland had considered such exercise and fresh air would help Sebastian to settle after the excitement of the seance – and keep him safely away from Jane, of course, Elaine had gathered wryly. She had debated whether she should insist on joining the shooting party, but decided against it. She needed to rest and recharge her batteries. Battling against the constant interference of Dr Shetland, the outspoken malice of Lord Ashby and the silent disapproval of Mr Barnes was all taking its toll on her. The vultures circling around Morlanby, hoping for their piece of meat every time Sebastian faltered, were getting bolder. She would have to remove their influence for good, and soon.

Still, the morning bath with Megan had been a reviving therapy, she remembered fondly. Whenever her livelihood hung in the balance, she needed the consolation of another woman's flesh. But even here she must be careful, with the ever-watchful Ashby, the earnest Dr Shetland, and even that clod Barnes staying at Morlanby. They would have their spies, would be eager to blame her lusts on madness, and lock her up along with poor Sebastian.

Elaine noticed that Jane was sitting quietly in the window seat of the drawing room, working on a piece of embroidery, occasionally looking out across the park. Elaine gave her special smile of encouragement even as she was approached by the local magistrate, Dunwood, and his wife, who were ready to take their leave.

'I've never had such a restless night,' Mrs Dunwood complained, eager to list the shortcomings of Elaine's hospitality.

'I am sorry to hear that,' Elaine uttered smoothly. 'Perhaps when you visit us again at Christmas you will find the castle more comfortable.'

Mrs Dunwood looked disappointed at the hint that she would have to wait six weeks before being invited back. She glanced disdainfully over at Jane, to vent her ill-humour.

'I would arrange to have the house blessed if I were you, Lady Melmouth. Such goings-on! Who knows what the girl has unleashed.'

'Exactly what did you see and hear last night?' Elaine asked, trying hard to sound genuinely interested in her guest's bad dreams, no doubt brought on by a hysterical tendency.

'Well, on the way up to the room last night, I could have sworn I saw a young woman with dark hair standing by the landing window, but when I approached she simply disappeared.'

'Really?' Elaine responded politely, inviting more details. Perhaps it had been Megan, anxious to avoid being buttonholed by a demanding guest, who had then slipped her way through a servant's door when Mrs Dunwood noticed her.

'And later, when I was actually in our room, while I was getting ready for bed and Mr Dunwood was still downstairs, I distinctly felt a kiss on my cheek.'

'A kiss?' Elaine suppressed a smile.

'Yes, a fleeting peck, but of course no one was there.'

'A mischievous spirit, then. Not harmful,' Elaine offered as consolation.

'But later on I had the most dreadful dream. I awoke in a cold sweat and had to order some hot milk and honey before I felt calm enough to go back to sleep.'

'What was the dream about?' Elaine asked, her curiosity sharpened.

'I am not sure, I cannot remember much about it now. Except the woman with dark hair I had seen in the corridor was there again, and seemed very angry, almost in a passion about something. When I awoke the fire was guttering, letting putrid black flames billow into the room.'

'Ah, no doubt that was the cause of your unrestful dreams. My apologies. I'll arrange for that chimney to be swept. Jackdaws so often nest in the chimneytops and block their flow.'

'Try bird netting,' Mrs Dunwood suggested practically. Elaine nodded and smiled, not bothering to explain that the candytwist chimneytops were unsuitable for such additions.

'Here's our carriage pulling up, dear,' Mr Dunwood pointed out, looking down at the drive. Elaine accompanied the couple through the hallway and down the steps. After Mr Dunwood had handed his wife into the carriage, he turned to Elaine to say goodbye.

'On my way up to the room last night, I thought I saw a mastiff wandering the corridors,' Dunwood offered abruptly. 'When I tried to seize its collar to lead it back downstairs, the beast simply faded away. I told Ashby this over breakfast and he said it must have been too much brandy in the early hours, but I am not so sure.'

'Thank you for telling me,' Elaine said kindly, liking the man's integrity. 'Perhaps you could write down these events, and send me the account? It would help us in the research we are undertaking here.'

'Certainly, Lady Melmouth. I had doubted the veracity of spiritualism but after last night . . . well, it's good to have an open mind, isn't it? My best wishes to your brother. I hope he is soon fully restored to health. Good day.'

Elaine smiled to herself as she waved after the departing carriage. A magistrate, no less, reporting that strange hallucinations had taken place at Morlanby. That would certainly make it more difficult to convince Sebastian that he was merely imagining things, that his hallucinations were a sign of creeping insanity. When she bade goodbye to her other local guests, she heard very similar reports from their lips, and also asked them to make a short note of them in a letter to her.

Round one to Lady Melmouth and her little psychic nun Jane.

Her hostess duties acquitted, Elaine booted up for a walk with the dogs, trying not to think of the nightmares that had plagued her own sleep. Nightmares about Hazel, cold and silent, refusing her help, refusing her understanding, refusing her. Elaine shuddered, thrusting the memory out of her mind. She wished that Hazel Branagan had never returned. She needed her wits about her. Everything else must wait until after Sebastian and Morlanby were safe.

Still, she wondered if Hazel had enjoyed watching her with Jane at the Maiden Falls the previous day. She knew it had been Hazel who watched them from the opposite bank. She wondered what tales Megan would report to Hazel after this morning's bathing ritual, also.

Jane was still sitting in the drawing room when Elaine went in to collect her dogs from the fireside. Jane's elfin face looked healthy, but was very pale. Her expression was pensive, and she jumped slightly at the sound of Elaine's voice.

'Come help me walk the dogs, Jane. The fresh air will do you good.'

'Thank you.'

They wore cloaks against the chill air, and struck out down the long avenue, the dogs gambolling ahead in high-spirited games.

'Look, they are trying to catch their own tails,' Elaine said, laughing. 'A sign of change in the weather, a high wind I think the locals say.' She tried not remember Hazel's young face when she had first imparted that piece of folklore to Elaine, as they walked in the park on such a day as this. She glanced back at her fortress, Morlanby, the one constant friend she could rely on. The windows reflected slivers of brightness from the wan sunlight, and the place looked serene after its unquiet night, still harbouring its secrets.

Jane smiled at the dogs' antics and threw a few sticks for them.

'How are you feeling this morning?' Elaine asked.

'Fine, but a little tired.'

'That's understandable.' She watched the nun's pretty face

fondly, and hooked arms with her as they continued the prom-enade. The watery sunlight struggled free of cloud once more to glow upon the chestnut trees, their finery of golden leaves drifting down one at a time in the gentle breeze. 'That was quite a show you put on last night.'

Jane turned to face Elaine and looked at her searchingly.

'Did you sleep well last night?'

'Not very,' Elaine admitted. 'Perhaps it's the strain of entertaining. I'm used to having Morlanby just for myself and Sebastian.' Elaine paused. Jane continued to gaze at her expectantly. Elaine noticed a more determined set to the girl's chin. Elaine's existing respect for Jane's skill as a medium, and her strength of character, increased.

'Very well, if you must know, I had bad dreams like everyone else. I was somewhat impressed with last night's seance. I'll admit that the voice you produced at the seance did startle me a little. It was very like my dead father's voice.'

'Your father – yes, Sebastian mentioned that too.' Jane frowned. 'So he used to bully Sebastian, did he?'

'He bullied anyone he got a chance to, my charming father. But yes, Sebastian was particularly singled out. He was disappointed that Sebastian was more poet than soldier. Thought he could quite literally whip him into shape and tried out the theory once or twice.' Elaine laughed bitterly.

Jane nodded thoughtfully. 'Sebastian is still afraid of him, even now.'

Elaine bit her lip. 'I'm not sure this has much to do with your business here.'

'If you want me to truly help Sebastian –'

'Yes, of course I do,' Elaine replied quickly, 'and I am grateful for what you have done so far. It queers things for Ashby, having such a public display of things going bump in the night. I don't know how you did it, but it seems to have worked a treat. Of course Ashby will try to belittle your performance. He'll try to prove you were in cahoots with Sebastian, but I'll challenge every move he makes.'

They had reached a Grecian-style summerhouse. Elaine paused to train the clematis that clung to the sunniest wall, wrapping the last new growth further round its trellis to withstand winter winds. Then a sudden hailstorm sent them, laughing, into the shelter of the summerhouse. They peered up at the single dark-grey cloud responsible, watched the too-white beads of ice bounce off the lawn and giggled as the dogs took shelter with them, the hail's glancing blows annoying even their tough hides.

Chestnut leaves, curled and fine as tissue, had been blown on to the shelter's wooden bench and Elaine scooped them away before she and Jane sat down. Elaine felt a need to huddle closer to Jane, to put an arm about the girl's shoulder and kiss her gently. Their tongues arched and circled each other seductively. Elaine still felt languid after her bath with Megan and could have kissed for hours, but Jane soon pulled away.

'So do you truly believe in the realm of the spirit after last night, Elaine?'

Elaine shrugged and continued kissing.

'Is it important?' she purred.

'Well, it is one of the reasons that you brought me here.'

'You are determined today. Can't we just kiss and cuddle?'

'I'd like to know what you believe. It would help me.'

Elaine sighed. She wanted to say no, she did not believe and be done with it, but that was not strictly truthful. So she thought for a while in silence.

'I believe there are things beyond our ken, things which can affect us, and seek to communicate with us if given half the chance. But unlike my brother, I prefer to believe that such forces are benign, and act only in our best interests. There, are you satisfied? What do you believe yourself, little nun?'

Jane looked grave.

'In this instance, I believe that you are correct. The power here is benign to you, but it is currently angry at Sebastian. I want to discover why that is, so we may help Sebastian.'

'Do you believe it means Sebastian harm, then?' Elaine asked, intrigued in spite of herself. It was clear Jane believed in her talents, and in the veracity of the haunting. Elaine was not about to contradict her while she could help Sebastian.

'I believe that Sebastian must face it and choose by his best instincts or it will bring him harm,' Jane confirmed slowly.

'There are more things in heaven and earth, indeed,' Elaine murmured. 'But promise me you will help him to do this, promise you will do everything you can to protect him.'

Jane looked down, scuffing at the dead leaves.

'Of course I promise to do everything in my power,' she replied.

The hailstorm had ended and the dogs, impatient at their tarrying, snuffled their skirts, tails wagging. Elaine laughed and stroked each one in turn, watching as Jane relaxed enough to stroke the dogs too. Elaine's hand brushed against Jane's on a shaggy mane.

'Enough serious talk, let's finish our walk.'

Elaine was satisfied at the ghost of lust that crossed Jane's clear eyes. Elaine realised that she was turning into a cunt tease these days. Nothing else seemed to soothe her restless anxiety.

Evening mass was attended by a few servants and villagers – Elaine was pleased to see that Sebastian had returned and that his companions, hating popery, had not accompanied him to the service.

At last a chance to talk with him.

After the service Father Dominic accompanied Sebastian back to the house, and they caught up with Elaine and Jane. Elaine linked arms with Sebastian affectionately.

'So, Seb, how do you feel now?' she murmured.

'All the better for last night. I must admit it felt good to realise everyone slept as badly as I did after it.' Sebastian grinned wickedly.

Elaine glanced across at the priest.

'Did you experience any bumps in the night, Father?'

'I slept well enough but there were some disturbances in the chapel.'

'What sort of disturbances?'

'Candles overturned, vases toppled, that kind of thing. Could just have been the high wind causing unusual draughts.'

'But you are going to bless the chapel just to be sure.'

'Yes, and I shall bless your apartments also.'

The two young men exchanged a gaze of rare understanding.

'I am so glad you decided to come here, even if you had not quite completed your seminary training in Mayo,' Elaine said kindly. 'As an old college friend you have helped Sebastian so much these past weeks. Certainly more than Father O'Leary ever did.'

Father O'Leary had always been her father's ally. Nothing like the gentle spiritual man walking beside her. She was glad the old coot had been forced to retire and she had happily sent him packing back to Ireland.

'I had to come here when I heard that Sebastian was upset. Even God can wait for Sebastian.' Dominic smiled shyly, his dark eyes soft as he looked across at Sebastian. Sebastian smiled back and turned to Jane.

'You must let me take you on a tour,' Sebastian said. 'It may help you pinpoint the source of the force you uncovered last night.'

'I am not sure that's a good idea right now, Seb,' Elaine interjected, flashing a warning at Jane. Sebastian was overwrought, needed longer to recover from the impact of the seance.

'Thank you. I'll gladly accept your offer later,' Jane said in defiance of Elaine. 'But first I would like a chance to walk the estate alone, see what I can detect by my own powers. Then I will wish to know the history of certain landmarks, certain rooms. You will be able to help me in this way?'

'Certainly. It will be a relief to be doing something constructive – going out to meet the visions rather than waiting for them to visit me every night.'

Elaine did not say anything to object. She was surprised to realise that she trusted Jane to look after Sebastian in his quest almost as much as she trusted Father Dominic to care for him. The realisation gave her hope.

NINE

Hazel stood on the coastal path, watching Megan, who waited for her on the beach. They had agreed to meet a good mile beyond Morlanby's boundary, and Megan was now sitting with her back against an outcrop of rock, enjoying the sunshine, bundled up in a grey woollen cloak. The day was bright and clear. Perhaps the last such that they would have for some time. The distant sea was turquoise, flecked with choppy waves beyond the shelter of the bay. In the distance a fishing vessel tacked against the breeze.

'Penny for them!' Hazel called, giving Megan advance notice of her approach. Megan looked up and waved.

'I'm thinking of nothing, to be honest, except how rare the day is.'

Hazel leaned against the rocky outcrop, which looked like the spine of a leviathan as it arched from the cliff and stretched out towards the sea. She shaded her eyes with the palm of her hand and gazed out at the horizon.

'They'll have a good catch today,' she commented as she watched the fishing vessel, gulls wheeling in its wake. Then she took a breath to ask what was really on her mind. 'So, how went the seance?'

'Well. Rather better than expected, perhaps. The servants say there was definitely a spirit, a *pwca*, about all night. In the morning

89

all the horses were sweating as though they had been ridden all night, even though they were safe in the stables, and the gentlemen had to go on a walking shoot and leave their mounts to recover. As for the humans, I'll wager not one had a quiet night.'

'It could have been the weather. It was a rough night.' Hazel gave a wry smile. 'Was Lady Melmouth content with the results?'

'I believe so.' Megan glanced away guiltily. Hazel wondered if it was out of loyalty to Elaine or something deeper.

'And the nun? How does she fare?'

'She remains, to find out how to lay the spirits, with the help of Lord Melmouth of course.'

'Exciting times indeed,' Hazel said calmly. Megan looked up at her, grey eyes troubled with darker depths.

'Why did Lady Melmouth ban you from the estate?' she asked bluntly.

Hazel shrugged. She did not feel like explaining to the girl anything more than what was strictly necessary.

'Bad blood. Family history.'

'The housekeeper said that you lived at Morlanby until you went away, that you were brought up there by the old lord as one of his own. Is that true?'

'Yes,' Hazel said baldly. She crossed her arms and continued to look down at Megan, daring her to continue with this line of questioning. At the back of her mind Hazel noticed the flush in Megan's cheeks, the glitter in her eye, the rosiness of her lips, parted to taste the sea breeze as though it were a peach. Hazel thought of Megan's other lips, hidden by her skirts, and longed to caress and kiss them. Hazel took a long breath in order to control herself.

Megan glanced back to the horizon, giving in, thinking of another approach. Hazel watched her transparency with amusement.

'Wouldn't you like to sit on the beach? The sand is quite warm and very firm,' Megan said, patting the compact sand with her palms to prove her point. Hazel hesitated, wondering if she could put her self-control under such a strain. Then she gave in abruptly and sat beside the pretty maid. She noticed how Megan's breasts began to rise and fall more quickly, and how her hand crept closer to Hazel's own, lying palm upwards on the sand.

'So do you know anything of the bathing rituals that are carried out at Morlanby?' Megan asked shyly, glancing at her sideways.

Hazel looked down at her sharply. She felt her collar prickle uncomfortably.

'Why, what do you know of them already?' she asked roughly.

Megan blinked.

'Only that they are very pleasurable. I never knew such luxurious ways existed.'

Hazel grabbed at Megan's wrist, unable to bear the innuendo and simmering desire between them any longer.

'Has Lady Melmouth been educating you in her sluttish practices, is that it?' Hazel asked angrily. 'Has she told you to taunt me in this way?'

'No, no, truly,' Megan protested.

'Is this what you want?' Hazel forced her body up against the girl, pressing her back on to the sands, hiking up her skirts at the same time. She felt the girl quiver and squirm beneath her, felt the heat of sheer lust between them like an infinity loop.

'Do you want me to fuck your skirts, little Megan? Have you been turned on by an aristocratic slut who can't keep her legs closed so soon? Perhaps your brothers were right about you,' Hazel hissed, as she dragged Megan's knees far apart and, keeping the girl's wrists pinned in one of her own, gazed down at the wanton pouting sex lips naked to the sea breeze. God, but Megan looked beautiful. Hazel felt a pain in her clitoris, as though it was gripped by a cruel vice, just looking at Megan's juicy quim. Truly she had been without a woman far too long. Distracted, she let Megan struggle free.

'I don't care what you think of me,' Megan sobbed. 'I want you to make love to me.' Megan let her own fingers stroke her sex, inviting Hazel to watch the display. 'Look, am I not beautiful enough for you? Here.' She loosened her blouse, letting her breasts spring free. Hazel found their fullness, their hard brown nipples, intoxicating. 'Look how much I am aching for you,' Megan whispered. Megan parted her sex lips still further so that Hazel could feast her eyes upon the little red tongue of clitoris swelling from beneath its coral hood, the shining juices on the engorged labia. 'Please love me, I can't stand this much longer. No matter what I do to myself in bed at night, the ache is always so much fiercer the next day. I grow so wet at the thought of you. Please, Hazel.'

Hazel could barely resist. The pain of longing was unbearable. Gently, idly, she let her rough fingers skim the tender flesh of Megan's cunt. Megan almost screamed at the ecstasy of her touch, pressing against Hazel's fingers. Then Hazel lay on top of her once more, mouth grinding against mouth, licking the salt and sand from Megan's cheeks before devouring those breasts, letting her teeth graze across the solid little nipples while her hand pressed into Megan's yielding sex.

But at the back of her mind was a tiny buzzing doubt. The girl should not be so eager so soon. This had to be Elaine's manipulation. Megan had easily been seduced into this heightened arousal by Elaine for a purpose. How could Hazel slake her lust until she knew it was truly a two-way thing and not a three-way thing which involved Lady Melmouth?

Perhaps she would be no better than the miners she had seen in Klondike saloons, rutting their lust into any drugged flesh, if she took Megan now. Perhaps she would be as depraved as Elaine herself if she continued to take advantage of Megan's arousal.

'No,' she cried out between gritted teeth and, with supreme effort, dragged herself away from the supine girl, who was whispering the foolish nothings of those lost in desire.

Megan exclaimed an oath at the visceral pain of such abandonment.

'Oh Hazel, what is wrong? Please, hold me again. I love the way you kiss, the way you suckle my breasts. Oh, don't leave me like this!' Megan's fingers played once more with her sex as she spoke. Hazel watched with red-hot lust as the girl's rhythm increased, rubbing her clitoris until she brought herself to a quick, hard climax, sobbing with relief as she did so. 'See? But it's never enough, I'm always triggered again, and only you can truly bring me off, bring me peace . . . please.'

Hazel stood up, backing away, not sure whether to believe the girl. Should she fall for this latest line of seduction?

'Cover yourself, girl,' she ordered at last, 'before someone comes along. Why are you in such a state? Perhaps Morlanby truly is corrupting you.'

'You're so cruel,' Megan hissed, 'to ignore the effect you have on me.'

'Maybe I am,' Hazel agreed harshly, 'but later on, when you learn the nature of my love, you may thank me for showing such . . . restraint,' Hazel sneered, wiping her hands, moist with Megan's juices, against her corduroys. 'Meanwhile I suggest a quick swim in the sea to cool your ardour.'

'Do you find me so ugly?' Megan asked, the catch in her voice betraying disappointment as she sat up and rebuttoned her blouse with trembling fingers. Hazel looked at the horizon in an effort to keep her self-control.

'No, Megan,' she said more gently, 'I just prefer not to couple like an animal on the beach the first chance I get. I've been celibate for years. I think I can wait a little longer for the right moment.'

Megan stood up, taking Hazel's hand shyly.

'How am I going to stand the wait?' she sighed coquettishly, putting Hazel's hand to her cheek. Hazel cursed herself for a fool. Why deny herself, and the girl, a bit of fun? For a personal morality meaningless to a society that already condemned her appetites? At least she could be sure of not getting the girl with child, she thought wryly, if she went ahead.

She knew her apprehension was because of Elaine. Elaine had been jealous of Hazel's interest in Megan. Elaine had half-seduced the girl, sent her forth like a poisoned chalice. How could Hazel make love with Megan, knowing she was only finishing off what Elaine had started?

Hazel's anger at her ex-lover bubbled over.

'Leave me alone now!' she yelled, pushing Megan from her. 'I have explained all I can. Now go home, or I won't be responsible for my actions!'

'But when can I see you again?' Megan begged. Hazel could see the girl was too frightened to refuse but desperate to try for another rendezvous.

'I'll meet you here next Thursday noon, if my temper has cooled by then and you act a little more demurely. Now go!'

'I'll be here Thursday,' Megan called, even as she ran across the beach towards the coastal path. 'You can love me or not, I don't care, as long as you kiss me.' She yelled in a flirtatious romantic gesture, 'Goodbye for now,' and waved, then was lost in the undergrowth of gorse that lined the coastal path.

TEN

Jane had managed to slip away from the house without being noticed by anyone that day. Which suited her, because she was on a quest for spirits.

The day was bright and clear, and the mosses on tree bark, the plumage on chattering jackdaws, glowed in supernatural brilliance. Jane walked briskly down to Maiden Falls, and let her palms glide across the carved stone that had witnessed her chastisement and humiliation with Elaine's riding crop. Now that she could be alone and quiet in the place, she sensed a strong elemental presence. She tested the theory with two slender willow twigs she plucked from the river banks. She held them delicately crossed the way dowsers tested for springs. They went haywire in her hands – and not just because of the tumbling waters. Ley lines crossed the site of the stone.

Jane began to follow one of the lines of power. She lost its trace a few times, had to go back to the stone and begin again, but eventually it led her up towards the chapel. Which was just as she thought. Then she went back to Maiden Falls, and began to follow another of the many ley lines. This one that she now pursued was heading down towards the beach.

She had paid such close attention to the dowsing rods that she did not notice Megan until the girl almost bowled her over.

'Megan, what is wrong?' Jane asked in surprise, as she noticed how agitated Megan seemed. Megan only stared at her blankly, as she tried to pull her clothes into a neater state. Then Megan began running again, back in the direction of Morlanby.

Jane felt it best to respect Megan's privacy and let her go. She guessed that she would have wanted the same if positions were reversed.

So she continued down to the beach.

Jane was about to leave the shelter of the trees when she felt an arm encircle her waist, a hand clamp around her mouth. She let go of the divining rods and struggled. But she could not escape the vice-like grip of her assailant, whose hot breath rasped at her neck. Jane decided to go limp and let herself be bundled into the grass-covered mound beside the coastal path, until she had a chance to see her assailant. The full sunlight after shade dazzled her, even as her attacker pinned her to the floor, straddling her on all fours.

Then she recognised that it was Hazel, and a shiver ran down her spine. Jane, still unsatisfied after the sexual teasing Elaine had subjected her to, was now lying beneath the wild woman she had fantasised guiltily about since she had first arrived in Morlanby.

'What are you doing?' Jane asked, trying to look authoritative and to sound annoyed. But secretly her heart was thudding at the thrill of it. Hazel Branagan, the handsome enigma, her tall frame dressed in corduroy trousers and a crisp white man's shirt. Hazel's piercing blue eyes gazing down at Jane with diamond-like precision, raking over Jane's supine body, assessing her soul. That hooded dangerous look Jane had first admired, the knowing smile and flash of even white teeth, entranced her. Jane felt as though Hazel had guessed the secret fantasies and predilections that had seethed through her imagination since she had first set eyes on Hazel Branagan. She could sense the dangerous sexuality of the wild woman and longed to be the object of her lust.

Nevertheless, Jane made a play of struggling to get up, only to be dragged to the ground once more with ease. This time her skirts were hitched up, and she had lost the top two buttons to her bodice.

Hazel's long fingers lazily undid the rest of the buttons, and then idly traced a pattern on the soft skin just above Jane's corseted breasts. Jane's breath grew shallow at the gentle and insistent caress.

'So, my little black-magic strumpet, we meet alone at last. In what whorehouse did Elaine discover a choice morsel such as you?'

'I am a nun,' Jane replied gravely, 'a novice, from the Convent of St Julienne of the Scarlet Bliss.'

Hazel chuckled.

'As good as a whorehouse. I was once an ardent follower myself, you know, I am familiar with all their practices. Some would say I was even a wanton follower in my youth. Are you a wanton follower?'

Jane gasped as Hazel's hand slid below her skirt and between her thighs. The rough palm pressed against Jane's mound through the silk of her petticoats. Jane desperately wanted to cross her legs, to tighten that palm further against her, but resisted the urge. Perhaps she should try and prove that she was not quite the little slut that Hazel believed her to be.

'I am a true believer, if that is what you mean,' Jane replied stiffly. She could feel her mouth growing dry and her breathing shallow at the thought of what Hazel may have in mind. She realised she had left the haven of the Morlanby estate when she had stepped through the last kissing gate on the path. Was this attack then some kind of revenge for Elaine ordering Hazel off the estate? Some secret enmity raged between Elaine and Hazel, and Jane had stepped into the crossfire.

But the view from where Jane lay was exquisite to her. The hard planes of Hazel's beautiful face, tanned nut brown, were rigid with frustrated and long repressed lust. Jane loved Hazel's high cheekbones, her wide sensual mouth, her cropped blonde hair. She wanted to stroke those temples, smooth those frown lines, run her hands through the close-cropped hair, but her arms were pinned to her sides by her bodice.

'What black magic were you up to just then?' Hazel asked in a low purr, even as her palm ground relentlessly against Jane's mound. Jane's clit was beginning to throb at the indirect pressure, eager for more.

'I was just using some twigs to dowse for sources of power. Do you know of the practice? It's well proven to track down underground sources of water, too,' Jane replied as steadily as she could.

'Yes, I know something of the skill, but evidently I'm not as adept as you. Maybe I'll hire you to find me a spring close to my cottage. Might as well use your brains as well as your body while you are playing the holy whore at Morlanby.'

Hazel smiled wolfishly and casually felt in her back pocket. She took out a small knife she used for handiwork and protection. Its blade gleamed sharply in the sunlight.

'No need to threaten me,' Jane said breathlessly, 'I'll not scream. I'll not tell anyone about this. It's because of Elaine, isn't it?' she could not resist adding.

Jane wished she had kept silent. At the mention of Elaine, Hazel's jaw clenched dangerously. Then Hazel smiled, her eyes narrowing with lust.

'I know you are not going to say anything about this. After all, didn't Elaine send you here this morning just to snare me?'

'No, of course not,' Jane objected. Hazel shrugged as though she did not believe the denial.

'Well, you are willing enough,' Hazel observed. 'I can feel the juices dripping out of you hot and slow, like a volcano about to erupt. I know you want this.' With a quick flick to the wrist, Hazel cut through the laces to Jane's stays. Jane shivered as the cold metal just whispered by her hot flesh, but did not leave a mark.

As Hazel roughly parted the stays and exposed Jane's breasts, Jane tried to cover herself in token resistance. Hazel calmly gripped Jane's wrists, holding the wrists tight together with one hand.

'No false modesty, please,' Hazel hissed. Her blue eyes followed the contours of Jane's breasts, the thickening stalks of nipples, the blushing aureole. Her free hand took pleasure from them, stroking them, kneading the soft flesh possessively. She pinched the nipples and pushed the breasts together so that the nipples stood side by side, begging to be suckled. With a groan, Hazel licked and sucked and nipped as Jane moaned at the delicious pleasure.

Jane felt as though Hazel's coarse hands branded her, yet loved the sensation of being sullied in this way. She looked up, unable to bear the sight of Hazel's flat wide tongue lapping over her teats. Hazel's rough fingers pinched Jane's nipple tips into maddening sensitivity. Hazel's white teeth grazed slowly over the milky globes and nipped with little needle bites so that Jane bucked with the shock and the pleasure.

They were surrounded by pale-green gorse and above seagulls wheeled in the blue sky. Jane's cries mingled with the gulls' cries as she lay helpless, letting the stronger woman molest her at will. Hazel enjoyed her breasts slowly and sensuously.

'I can't bear it any longer,' Jane groaned.

'But you must,' Hazel murmured. She kissed Jane with savage passion, bruising her lips, nipping and circling her tongue, ravaging her mouth completely as she pressed her body down upon Jane's. Jane could feel the coolness of the cotton shirt, and beneath it the small breasts they contained. She felt overwhelmed by this sensual onslaught, undulating against a strong thigh, still clad in corduroy, which pressed hard between her legs. Hazel's breeches, her pubis, rode Jane's hip bone.

Jane could only guess what forces had worked on Hazel to provoke this frenzied passion but she felt lucky indeed to bear the brunt of her lust. Jane longed to suckle Hazel's hard breasts, to undo her flies and seek out her cunt, but she was tethered and reliant on the other woman's will.

Suddenly Hazel swept her up in her arms and flipped her over on to all fours in the short grass. She tore at Jane's petticoats until the girl's upturned arse was fully exposed. Jane moaned, propped awkwardly on her wrists and elbows, hips swaying provocatively in spite of herself, as she felt Hazel's palms skim over her tender arse flesh.

'How lovely . . . you still bear some shallow welts from the other day at Maiden Falls. That riding crop has a bite, does it not? Never fear, I know how much you like correction. I could tell that from the look on your face as I watched you receive your punishment. I'll give you a taste of my belt, to warn you to obey me, to make you pliant and as mad with lust as I am . . .' Hazel murmured.

'Yes, yes,' Jane muttered in response. 'Punish me, please.' She jutted her arse cheeks high, inviting Hazel to chastise them.

Jane shrieked at the first blow of the thick leather belt. The force was powerful, and left her martyred flesh hot and stinging in the sea breeze. Yet the lash sent a pulse inside her, a spasm along her tight little anus, which told her Hazel was an expert at this game.

'Again, please,' Jane moaned in spite of herself, all semblance of virtuous resistance gone. She was thoroughly enjoying being Hazel's whore.

'Be quiet, or you'll get the edge of my belt next time,' Hazel ordered roughly. Jane felt Hazel's fingers rake like talons across the tortured arse cheeks. Jane let out a long, slow sigh as Hazel licked the hot flesh. Then hard, relentless fingers sought out Jane's swollen, pulsating quim.

'Enough foreplay,' Hazel growled, even as she plunged three fingers into Jane's dripping crack, sliding in as though Jane's sex was made of butter, 'you're hot enough right now, you little hussy.' Jane bucked and writhed against Hazel's rapacious digits as they dabbled against the cushion of her sex until she felt herself quivering and her cunt walls pulsed to embrace the fingers. She welcomed Hazel's fist more deeply into her than she had ever thought possible before.

Just as she felt orgasm approach she heard Hazel spit and felt the plunge of an anointed index finger into her tight little arsehole. Yelping like a she-cat, Jane impaled herself further on Hazel's expert fingers, feeling the come explode like a star inside her head. Hazel did not relax her pressure, and Jane soon felt the rise of a second orgasm. The sensual release after Elaine's teasing and the tension of the seance was delicious and absolute.

'Please, let me suck you, sit on my face, please, I'll do anything,' Jane begged dreamily as she eased down. She was still light-headed when Hazel spun her on to her back.

She noticed that Hazel's hands, still covered with her quim juice, had now slipped through the undone flies of the corduroy trousers. Jane looked up at the handsome face, at the subtle changes of expression, and knew that Hazel was gently pleasuring herself. Those juicy fingers were now anointing her own cunt and clit with expert thrusts. Hazel came with her eyes closed, a soft feral grimace which seemed at once fierce and vulnerable.

Then Hazel's eyes opened. Their piercing blue assessed Jane's naked, pouting disarray.

'You're the second girl to offer me anything like a shameless hussy today. But I have a certain reluctance. I am slow to trust women with my cunt.' She smiled bitterly. 'Maybe at heart I am something of a prude.'

'Or maybe just unlucky in love,' Jane offered.

The change in Hazel shocked Jane. She noticed the tension in the lean face, the muscled arms, immediately.

'Maybe,' Hazel agreed, a wolfish smile on her lips, 'but since you've been so . . . accommodating, my little black-magic strumpet, I will give you a parting gift. On your knees.'

Jane obeyed, tension and excitement and a flutter of renewed lust creeping across her belly and up her spine like pins and needles.

Hazel let her trousers and long-johns drop. Beneath she was naked. Jane gazed admiringly at the rough fair curls, the pink flesh that peeped out.

'Look, but do not touch,' Hazel threatened, as she stood above Jane, her long lean legs astride her shoulders. Jane nodded obediently, even though she longed to lap at the hidden prize.

'Continue to look,' Hazel said, as she flexed her knees and parted her sex lips. Jane admired the swollen glistening cunt swaying above her.

The sudden burst of warm golden liquid made Jane gasp with shock. She was surrounded by the tang and musk of Hazel as the golden cascade continued, filling her nostrils, coursing down her cheeks, down her chin, dripping over her naked breasts on to the grass below. Jane opened her mouth and let her tongue dabble in the stream of sweet piss. It reminded her of country cider fresh oozed from the still, and just as heady.

All too soon the sparkling jet had ceased.

'Can I lick you clean now?' Jane begged, as she admired the pink slash, still laced with golden beads sparkling at the brim of those delicious sex lips.

'Next time, perhaps. If there is a next time. This will have to do for now,' Hazel replied harshly.

Jane could not hide her disappointment at not being allowed to touch the other woman's cunt.

As some kind of consolation Hazel's own lean hand wiped away the pee, mingled with quim juice. Then Hazel pressed that hand against Jane's lips. Eagerly, obediently, Jane lapped the rough skin clean, tracing the calluses of hard work left on Hazel's palm with tender thoroughness. The taste of the juices, mingled with the salt taste of skin, seemed like ambrosia to Jane.

'Thank you,' Jane said humbly.

Hazel pulled up her long-johns and trousers and fastened her thick belt. Jane watched her with respect and increased attraction. Such a quiver of repressed fury and desire was still contained within the other woman's powerful, well-honed frame. Her self-control, her passion, must be awesome to stop at this point, even more awesome when fully unleashed. She must be saving herself for some other woman, Jane thought wistfully, someone she has wanted for a long time. Then Jane felt some of the truth about Hazel and Elaine's enmity dawn upon her almost against her will.

'How long have you wanted Elaine?' she murmured sadly, half to herself. Hazel bent her face close to Jane's.

'Listen, black-magic strumpet,' Hazel growled. 'Don't speak to me about that ever again, or things will be worse for you next time we meet, do you understand?'

'I understand,' Jane whispered. 'I did not wish to anger you.'

Hazel nodded, relenting a little.

'Go home, pretty little nun. While you still can. Take care of yourself. It's the best advice I can offer you.'

'I have no home,' Jane protested weakly. 'Even the convent is lost to me.'

'Then plot and plan and get yourself one. You're not stupid. You have talent. Think for yourself a little. Don't trust everything to Lady Melmouth. If she has made any promises, make sure that she keeps them –' Hazel seemed to spit out the reference to Elaine with an effort, '– or things may go badly for you.'

Jane looked into Hazel's blue eyes and nodded gravely, registering the warning even if she considered it unnecessary.

Hazel smiled mockingly.

'For now, you best hurry back to Morlanby and dress in a fresh set of clothes. I seem to have rather ruined these.' Hazel threw the shredded stays, the torn petticoats, towards Jane. Jane caught them, huddled them across her naked form, suddenly absurdly chaste.

Hazel grinned as she noticed the modesty, but did not look unkind. Then Hazel swung on her heels, and began walking along the path, back towards her own cottage.

'Don't worry, little nun. I'm sure Lady Melmouth has plenty of pretty silk underskirts to replace those,' Hazel called without turning back.

Jane watched as Hazel's proud erect figure strode away, a lone shadow against the sun-dazzled sea.

ELEVEN

Jane stumbled back to Morlanby in a daze, splashing herself clean in a stream, huddling into her untidy clothes.

Jane had hoped to reach the privacy of her own rooms without being noticed, but when she reached her door, she found Sebastian waiting outside. He was sitting in the window seat on the landing, legs crossed, carelessly reclining as though he were in an opium den.

He raised his eyebrows.

'You are in a state of dishabille, Miss Claremont. I'll hazard a guess and say you have had an encounter with a local bit of rough behind my sister's back. I promise to be the soul of discretion – unless you want to tell me all about it, that is.'

'I would rather not recount my . . . adventure, Lord Melmouth,' Jane stammered.

Sebastian smiled. 'Of course. We really must remain on first-name terms from now on, Jane, particularly as we each know a secret about one another.'

'What secret of yours do I know?'

'Oh, several, I should think, after last night. Or none at all and I am about to trade you one.' He arched an eyebrow and grinned. 'Now, I shall give you five minutes to change. Then I shall take you on a lightning tour of this wing plus the chapel, which comprises the original Morlanby home. Are you up to it?' This last question was posed seriously by his intelligent eyes, the colour of golden tobacco, even though Sebastian wore his habitual expression of light-hearted mockery.

Jane nodded.

'Good. Don't keep me waiting longer than this cheroot, though, or the others will find me, which would be tiresome.'

Jane hastily splashed herself clean in a basin of water, changed into fresh underclothes and a dark-brown dress before she rejoined him on the landing.

'You've slipped the attention of Ashby and Barnes and Shetland, then?' Jane asked, as they climbed up to the turret together. Sebastian nodded.

'They think I am taking a nap. I suppose I should be, the amount of laudanum they gave me, but I felt this was rather more important.'

He staggered slightly, pausing to hold on to the banister.

'We could do this another time,' Jane suggested, watching him doubtfully.

'My dear Jane, if they have their way we'll never get the chance to do this ever. Now come.' He continued up the flight of stairs.

'You share your sister's determination,' Jane observed admiringly.

'But not her pride. Or I would never bring you here.'

Jane was surprised when they reached the top storey. It was not what she expected.

Here were low-beamed rooms. Plain boarded floors. The paraphernalia of childhood. Dolls and shuttlecocks, lead soldiers and their fort, wooden animals and their dusty ark. Adjoining the nursery was a schoolroom. A blackboard and a large table was still set at the front for the teacher. Three smaller desks and chairs were still laid out before them. Shelves of encyclopaedias and picture books, a map of the British Empire, a globe of the world lining the schoolroom walls.

Sebastian spun the large dusty globe. It creaked as it turned and stopped at the pink Asian subcontinent. Sebastian's lean fingers spanned the length of India, examining its contours thoughtfully.

Jane went to the window. She admired the wonderful view of mountains to the left, sea to the right, and a swathe of parkland

and woods in between. She wondered how many tutors and governesses had grown angry when their pupils gazed out at the ever-changing landscape, or sunlight on the sea, rather than paying attention to their sums.

'You want me to read the aura in this room?' Jane asked, a little bewildered. 'I would have thought this would be one of the most innocent rooms in the whole of Morlanby.'

Sebastian laughed briefly, distracted, still gazing at the globe.

'Indulge me,' he murmured, before guiding Jane to the teacher's chair and setting her down in it. Then he went over to the window and looked out at the view. He seemed calm, despite the laudanum, despite the sleepless night Jane knew he had passed since the seance. She watched his tall and lonely form, so like Elaine's.

'Please begin,' he said quietly, breaking into her thoughts.

Jane took a breath and gently laid herself open to the impressions stored in the room.

'It is winter,' she began haltingly. 'There are two young girls and a little boy sitting at the wooden desks. The boy is about seven years old, skinny, with gold hair and eyes the colour of old tobacco. This is you, Sebastian. The girls are blonde. One is dressed in a blue velvet dress, her hair is in long ringlets – Elaine. The other is more sombre, in a plain black dress – Hazel.' Jane blinked, brought herself out of the trance.

'Very impressive, Miss Claremont. Please continue,' Sebastian said with quiet authority.

Jane summoned the children's images once more. 'They all look – you all look – pinched and pale. Has there been an illness in the house which has caused you all to keep quiet? For you do not make a sound as you listen to the boring drone of your tutor describing the life of Henry VIII.' Sebastian shrugged, then gestured for Jane to carry on.

'A man walks into the room. He is burly, red-faced from the climb to the turret room. He seems angry.'

'My father,' Sebastian whispers. 'You don't have to describe everything else blow by blow. I was there already, remember? Just read it and be done.'

Jane nodded. She returned to the vision of Sebastian's father towering over the young Sebastian . . .

'Sir, you have broken into my study again, haven't you? You've rifled though my papers again, haven't you?' The red-faced man shouted into the young boy's ear.

A thin, well-dressed woman stood at the doorway wringing her hands. She had just made it up to the turret room. She was mouthing something silently to young Sebastian over his father's head. Pleading with him. Sebastian's mother, Jane gathered.

'Tried out my opium pipe, have you? Looked at my love letters? And my collection of nudes I'll wager. You always go too far, don't you?'

Sebastian's father shook his little son by the shoulders. Young Sebastian said nothing.

'You little wretch, answer me. What kind of man will you grow into? We'll have to send you to school to toughen you up. Then you won't be babied by your mother and idolised by these foolish girls. You'll learn to be a real man. Will you answer me, sir? The truth now. Have you been in my study?'

The mother nodded violently to Sebastian behind his father's back. Of course, she was asking Sebastian to cover for her. She had been trying to uncover some secret of her husband's and the evidence of her search had been discovered.

'Yes, sir,' little Sebastian said quietly.

With a roar, his father dragged him from the room almost knocking his mother off balance in the process. She followed them, distressed but silent. The girls remained quiet and unmoving.

'I should have said it was me,' Hazel said to Elaine.

'It would not have saved Sebastian,' Elaine sighed, 'when my father is in such a mood.'

The image faded. Jane returned to the present to find herself gripping the table with tension. She wondered if the tutor at that time had done the same, forced to witness such behaviour and too afraid to object or intervene.

'Oh, Sebastian,' Jane said.

'I am surprised, pleased and, I must admit, embarrassed that you managed to pick up on some of what happened in this room, Jane. It saves me the irksome task of trying to explain why the seance, why my father's voice from your lips, had such an impact on me. Perhaps now you won't think me quite as mad as my so-called friends portray me.'

'I've never thought you mad,' Jane said.

Sebastian smiled. 'Throughout my miserable childhood I had the consolation that I protected Mother and the rest of the family from the worst of his rages,' he observed with a hollow laugh. He slowly stubbed his barely smoked cheroot out on the windowsill. 'But you can understand why I am not entirely surprised to know the shade of my bastard father still haunts these walls, wanting to destroy me.'

'The only power he can have over you is what you give him. He is dead and you are living. You must drive him out of your heart by finding true love and happiness.'

'Listen to yourself! Did you learn such sentimental clichés at the convent?' Sebastian sneered. Jane did not reply, just watched Sebastian's profile as he stared out of the window. Then he relented and smiled at her. 'Perhaps you are right,' he said. 'I finally begin to think it remotely possible I may fight free of my father's shadow. Now let me show you the chapel, while we still have time. While I still have the nerve.'

Jane struggled to keep up as Sebastian thundered down the winding staircase, his shoulder occasionally glancing off the rough stone wall. At the bottom of the turret were two recessed doors. Sebastian produced a large brass key, and opened one of the doors with creaking effort.

'A secret way into the chapel,' Sebastian explained, 'one of many. My colourful ancestors recognised the value of sanctuary for forty days and forty nights once they reached the refuge of the chapel. It helped many of them fight their way back from impossible odds and retain power.'

He creaked the door shut behind them as Jane walked into the chapel nave. Rays of sunlight warmed the beeswax and polished oak, shone jewel-like colours through the stained-glass window.

She blessed herself with the holy water in the fount at the entrance.

'Come over here, Jane,' Sebastian called from behind the wooden grille which screened off the Lady Chapel.

When Jane joined him he was sitting in the ornate front pew, staring fixedly at a point above the statue of the Madonna.

'What do you make of that?' he asked simply. Jane sat beside him and followed the direction of his gaze.

It was a stone carving set high up into the wall, just below the eaves.

'I had not noticed it before,' she said in wonder.

'Some say it is even older than the chapel itself,' Sebastian whispered, 'carried here from the Irish castle which was my forefathers' original home.'

The carving was crude and graphic. A large-eyed smiling face, almost a grotesque gargoyle. Small breasts, stunted legs spread wide. Impossibly long arms which reached below the legs, so that each hand could part the lips of a huge gaping cunt that filled the gap between the thighs.

Jane stared up at it in fascination and awe. Here was the centre of the power she had sensed at the seance, this was the source of the visions of the dark woman. She could feel its power, like a faint humming inside her brain, even now.

'It's called a Sheela-na-gig,' Sebastian explained. 'It's a goddess of creation and destruction. They have a similar deity in the Hindu pantheon.'

'It's strange to see such an image here,' Jane said, glancing from the serene marble image of the Madonna to the shameless stone goddess.

'I used to stare at it for hours, when I prayed here as a child and when I sat here during each family mass,' Sebastian confided. 'Eventually I began to believe in her just as much as the Madonna. I pictured her as the guardian of Morlanby, the fertility of every harvest, overseeing the birth of every lamb or foal, and watching over me.' Sebastian glanced at Jane. 'I have to admit that half the candles I lit, the flowers and tokens and fasts I offered, were for her and not Our Lady. Are you very shocked?'

'Not very,' Jane said simply. 'That . . . stone goddess does have much power. I can feel it.'

Sebastian shivered, felt for his cigarettes, then changed his mind. All the while he continued to gaze at the Sheela-na-gig.

'Her opening is such an abyss. I used to be frightened of being swallowed by her entirely if I ever did anything wrong.'

'She has the capacity to be angry and vengeful,' Jane observed, also gazing at the upturned face, the gaping stone cunt. 'But why should she be angry at the head of the family she is meant to cherish?' Jane herself could only feel warmth emanate from the Sheela-na-gig at this moment. A sensual energy which began to flood her sinews, as she admired the wanton stone goddess. She realised she could not sense what Sebastian sensed from it right now, try as she might.

'There is a standing stone at the top of the mountain behind the Maiden Falls,' Sebastian volunteered abruptly. 'Locals say it is the answering phallus for her hole. The carved stone at the Maiden Falls is their halfway mark.' Sebastian ran a nervous finger around his collar, as though he suddenly needed air. His eyes glittered, his cheeks flushed, and his long legs jigged nervously. 'Maybe that's why the chapel was built on this exact spot, so the Sheela-na-gig could line up with the other two stones of power. It's strange for it to be outside the fortifications of Morlanby itself.'

Jane nodded. 'I traced ley lines, lines of power, between here and Maiden Falls. Perhaps I ought to go and see the standing stone you speak of also,' Jane said.

'Yes, but not today, it will be dark soon.' Sebastian turned to Jane. 'She is angry with me, the Sheela-na-gig, but you she likes. Why is that? As you say, she is meant to be my family's guardian. What will Morlanby do without her good favour? I'll be honest, Jane, she frightens me more than my father ever did.' Sebastian gripped Jane's elbow. 'Promise me you'll help me to placate her, please.'

'Of course,' Jane said. 'Of course I'll help. We'll find out what is wrong and make amends.'

'I have to leave,' Sebastian said. 'I can't bear being so close to it.' He rubbed his temples in nervous frustration.

'Sebastian?'

Father Dominic appeared. The young priest sat on the bench beside Sebastian, his dark eyes grave with concern. He spoke to the youth very gently. 'Sebastian, what is wrong?' Then he glared at Jane. 'What have you done to him?'

'Nothing,' Sebastian interjected, 'she has done nothing to me. She is helping me, Dominic. She'll find the answer, I know it.'

'Nevertheless you must rest now, Sebastian,' Father Dominic soothed. 'I'll take you to your rooms.'

'I'll stay here, and see what else I can sense,' Jane said hastily. 'You go and rest and we will talk about it later.'

Sebastian looked at her distractedly, then smiled with a ghost of his habitual charm. 'I'll give in gracefully. See you later, little nun. You have a certain stubborn will yourself, do you not?'

Sebastian chuckled as he allowed Father Dominic to help him upright. Jane watched as Sebastian leaned heavily against the tall, dark-clad figure of the priest, walking slowly out of the Lady Chapel and into the main chapel. She peered through the wooden grille anxiously as they shuffled forward at an uncertain pace. Sebastian suddenly looked very tired, his shoulders sagging. He let his golden head fall against the other man's shoulder, and Father Dominic sighed tenderly in response.

'Why do you take such risks with your health, Sebastian?' the priest whispered.

'I have to, if I am to keep my home, Dominic,' Sebastian replied dreamily. 'It's the only way to find out what is really going on. They never let me alone, that league of three gentlemen up there.'

'Then send them away. You are still lord here.'

'I have to know that I have the right.'

'You torture yourself, you who have a barely blemished conscience, while they roll in the mire. Of course you have the right to order them from your home.'

'Ah, Dominic, how little you know of me. I am very tired, my friend.'

'Let me carry you upstairs.'

'No, who knows what they would make of that.'

Father Dominic leaned his forehead against Sebastian's. They

111

stood together for a while, swaying slightly. It seemed to Jane that both struggled with strong emotions.

'Would you like to rest here a little then, in this pew, before we face them?' Father Dominic asked finally in a wavering voice.

'No. Let me sit outside a little while. I just need air. Only for a short while, then we must return to my rooms. Otherwise they will guess what I've been up to and the little nun will be in danger.'

Jane held her breath as they left the chapel. She remembered the warning that Hazel had given her and shivered. Then she sat back down on a pew in the Lady Chapel, to gaze at the Sheela-na-gig. She stared at it for some time, opening herself to its power, asking what had angered it, why Sebastian had displeased it, and how he could make atonement for any injury.

There was no reply. She did not expect such a powerful deity to respond immediately to her summons. She contented herself with feeling its energy course through her, through the chapel. It was a strong dynamo of vitality which made her ears sing even as she channelled some of its resonance.

After a while, the power she imagined flowing through her which emanated from the carving made her feel incredibly aroused. Although the chapel had been chill when she and Sebastian first entered, she found herself feeling hot and sticky. She loosened her collar, her cuffs, her waistband. She could feel the warmth like a sensual caress, surrounding her. Her limbs loosened, her neck and shoulders relaxed.

It was as though she were in a steamy jungle about to embark on some voodoo rites. She wondered dimly whether she should stop now, and leave the chapel for another day. Then she realised that she could not pull away. She must continue to gaze at the Sheela-na-gig.

She felt the warmth from the carving reach her blood, and it made her light-headed. Even as she continued to look up at the goddess she felt her nipples throb into life and longing. As for between her legs, it seemed as though her cunt wanted to swell and grow and gape as large as the stone carving above her.

Jane hardly realised where she was or what she did any longer. She felt her hands glide over her body in long sensuous strokes.

She felt the curves of her breasts, of her hips, the quivering of her belly. She grew drunk on the ripeness of her own body. She felt the afterglow of Hazel's hands upon her, the bruises she had left, the trace of Hazel's musk still on her skin, and the memory of the frantic sex that had exploded between them made her voluptuous. Her body was a finely tuned instrument which quivered constantly on the edge of orgasm.

She looked up at the Sheela-na-gig and longed to lap the circumference of that huge cunt. She longed to search the gaping pussy with both fists, to make the licentious expression on the carving yet more pronounced. She wanted to spread her legs and offer her own cunt to the goddess.

Jane looked around, squirming against the hard wooden pew. Furtively she let her fingers seek out her nether lips and stroke the fevered flesh. Then she stopped. With great effort she forced herself to sit still, and place her hands piously in her lap. After all, this was a place of God. Hardly the place to wank herself senseless. What if Father Dominic returned?

Jane looked at the ornate carvings on either end of the pew she sat upon.

A carving of a gigantic oak leaf formed the armrest, and from the end of it sprouted a huge acorn which formed the baluster that helped the old and infirm pull themselves upright after a long mass.

A smooth, glossy acorn carved from old oak, polished with beeswax and pious hands for generations.

A large phallus of an acorn. Jane ran a feverish tongue across her dry lips as she admired the smooth proportions of the carved acorn, then glanced up at the wanton Sheela-na-gig.

Dare she?

She stroked the smooth wood and it felt like solid silk beneath her fingers. She wondered if she could balance herself on the narrow bench, using the bench in front as a prop, and sit upon the delectable acorn. It seemed to be designed for exactly that purpose, she concluded, as her cunt lips ached and throbbed and hungered to slide themselves across the wide acorn dildo.

'What are you doing?'

She spun round guiltily.

It was Megan, standing at the other end of the pew, craning to watch her curiously. Jane was aware how she must appear to the maid. She was dishevelled, her cleavage showing, and panting like a strumpet, stroking the bulbous carved acorn as though it were the most arousing phallic instrument she had ever seen. Which it was, at that moment. She sat back, buttoning her blouse up quickly.

'Praying,' she answered lamely.

Megan did not disguise her contempt or disbelief of that statement. She continued to watch Jane coolly.

'What happened to your morning clothes? I found them torn at the foot of your bed,' she said.

'I . . .' Jane frowned. 'I was climbing the coastal path and fell down into a ravine filled with gorse.'

'Did you really? Was that after I saw you on the path earlier?' Megan asked, an insolence in her voice, as she sat at the other end of the pew. Jane bridled at the maid's disrespect.

'And what was wrong with you, Megan, when I saw you on the path to the beach? You seemed in a state of undress and rather distracted,' she retorted. She shifted uneasily on the hard wooden bench. She hardly noticed that her hand had stolen back to the acorn carving and was stroking it like a cat.

'Perhaps I fell into some gorse patch too,' Megan replied sarcastically, jutting out her breasts and raising her chin in defiance.

'Really? Well, I doubt you earned such bruises as these.'

Jane recklessly unbuttoned her blouse once more, and revealed a livid lovebite Hazel had branded low on her neck.

Megan slid across the length of the bench to sit closer to Jane and examined the lovebite more closely. There was a jealous glint to her eyes and an angry flush to her cheeks.

'She gave that to you? After she refused to touch me? Is that the nature of her love, that she refused to give any of those bruises to me but bestowed them on you instead? You must have tempted her in ways I know nothing of, just like the common street harlot that you are,' Megan flared. 'I'll give you more bruises if you like them, you little hussy. How about this? Does it turn you on?'

Megan gripped a slice of flesh on Jane's upper arm and twisted viciously.

'Ow, that hurt!' Jane lashed out with a stinging slap across Megan's cheek to make her stop. 'I'll have you dismissed if you lay another hand on me, you stupid peasant.'

'Aw, but I've come to fetch you for your bath, miss. I must lay my hands on you for that, mustn't I? Looks like you need a bath badly to me, you soiled slut. How you can even pretend to pray so piously in that condition is beyond me.'

Jane flushed, outraged. She grabbed a handful of Megan's hair from under her maid's cap, yanked it out and held on. Megan promptly yelled in sharp protest then took hold of a hank of Jane's short hair to drag her closer.

They twisted and pulled, staring at each other as tears started in their eyes. Jane dimly recognised that she was acting out of character, and guessed that Megan was too. Was it prompted by jealousy over Hazel? How come Hazel triggered such violent emotions in them so quickly?

Or was it the Sheela-na-gig?

Then Jane was aware of how Megan's body was pressed against hers. She surrendered to the feel of the maid's full breasts crushing her own, and felt the hardening bud of each nipple. She felt the girl's breath, hot and laboured against her neck, and she grew excited when Megan flicked a long leg across her lap to sit up and straddle her, still viciously pulling her hair. Jane was now pinned beneath Megan and losing the fight.

'Stop, this is ridiculous!' Jane protested weakly.

'I'll let go of your hair if you let go of mine. On the count of three,' Megan said huskily.

Jane nodded in agreement. She felt her body melt against Megan in spite of herself. She wanted to kiss those insolent lips even as she wanted to rake the flesh of that lovely body with nails like talons.

They released each other's hank of hair but Jane still hungered for closer contact with Megan's panting breasts, her supple body. Megan made no move to climb from Jane's lap. She was looking at Jane's cleavage, admiring the pale skin marked with that livid lovebite.

Suddenly they were kissing, long and hard. Megan's lips tasted like blueberries, sharp and sweet. Jane was taken aback by how turned on she felt. Perhaps Megan was right after all. She was nothing but a slut. But she did not care as Megan's lips and tongue traced her mouth, then her cheek, then her earlobe. The slow licks and nibbles followed the contours of Jane's ear. Then Megan traced the curve of Jane's neck with more bruising kisses which made Jane throw her head back in surrender.

Jane took Megan's wrist and licked and kissed its delicate inside skin. She traced figures of eight with the tip of her tongue and blew upon the dampened flesh so Megan would feel the gentle thrill of it. Megan sighed with pleasure.

Megan's skin tasted salty with a metallic hint to it. Jane wanted to lick every inch of its surface. Even as she realised the insanity of it somewhere at the back of her mind, she reached for Megan's other wrist to give it the same treatment.

'What did Hazel do to you?' Megan asked breathlessly as she reached into Jane's blouse to stroke her collar bone, the soft flesh above her breasts. 'Tell me, you slut, what did Hazel do?'

'She fucked me with her fist. She pinned me down and nipped and molested my breasts until I was drunk with longing, then she fist-fucked me nice and slow.'

'What else?' Megan asked huskily, one hand seeking her own breasts while she continued to fondle Jane. She dipped her hand into Jane's cleavage and massaged the firm breasts. Jane groaned, bucking against the pressure of Megan's pubis as Megan pinned her down. 'Tell me, harlot, what else happened? I'll pinch you and worse if you do not tell me.'

'She . . . she . . .' Jane was gasping, aroused by Megan's attentions and the memory of what happened.

'What did she do?' Megan pinched Jane's nipple cruelly and Jane gasped more loudly. Megan massaged her own nipple, and continued to pull on Jane's swelling teat. Jane could tell from Megan's too bright eyes and parted lips that the maid was eager to hear the rest despite her jealous rage. Jane was pleased that Hazel had, for some reason, chosen to slake some of her passion when they had met on the coastal path, moments after she had refused Megan that same privilege.

'She peed on me,' Jane whispered at last, even as she sucked on one of Megan's teats, lost to the strange sensual spell. 'Hazel peed all over my face. Don't you wish she had done that to you?'

'How dare you! Filthy little whore, letting her piss on you,' Megan said, raking nails across Jane's breasts in spite. She sniffed Jane's cleavage with perverse envy. 'I believe I can still smell it on you. You've been marked like the bitch on heat that you are.'

'Yes,' Jane admitted, even as she took Megan's palm and licked a fat tongue across it. 'And afterwards she wiped herself off with her hand, and I cleaned up her hand just like this.'

Megan groaned. Jane's blood thundered in her ears, and she quivered from the memory of Hazel's hands upon her as well as the crush of Megan's body. She wanted to drive Megan wild with envy. There was lust and defiance mingled in Jane as she gazed up at Megan.

'But she did not let you touch her, right?' Megan hissed. 'She used you but didn't let you close, I'll bet. Because she's saving herself for me.'

'You're a fool if you believe that,' Jane retorted, laughing. 'I'm not telling you any more about it. You are now going to have to bathe me and tend to my bruises and know that it could have been you but it wasn't. Let's face it, you weren't woman enough for her.'

'Liar! I'm much better than you.'

'Then prove it.'

There was a dangerous gleam to Jane's eye when she realised that Megan was incensed beyond all caution. She reached out a slim hand to stroke the wooden acorn carving.

'There's one of these on each side of the pew. We can each take one to ride. Check each other's skill at a distance.'

Megan laughed.

'You're insane, little nun. What would that prove?'

'Well, I could examine your face, your expression when you bring yourself off. I could watch your technique and you could watch mine. Then we can compare notes and maybe even plan to seduce Hazel between us.'

'What are you saying?'

'I'm saying that Hazel has used us both, and it's about time we took advantage of her if we can. Besides,' Jane said, smirking, 'I'd like to see you sitting on one of these acorn phalluses, trying to keep your balance, trying to keep your composure in front of me. I'll wager you won't be athletic enough or aroused enough to do it and brave the risks.'

All the while Jane ground her pubis up against Megan's, and stroked the maid's exposed breast. She felt insane with lust, it was true. She could not resist laying down the challenge. To lose it completely, right here in the Lady Chapel where they could be discovered so easily. She badly wanted to fuck in front of the Sheela-na-gig. She badly wanted to make Megan reveal her true sexuality, discover that she was just as sluttish as she accused Jane of being. For all the maid's insults and superior moral tones, Jane could tell that Megan was as hot as Hades and she wanted to take that to the limit.

Megan leaned close to her, then kissed her in a slow teasing manner.

'Very well,' she whispered, 'but we must be quick and quiet about it.'

'Good.' Jane smiled. 'Then let me up. Watch and learn.'

Megan stood up, retreated to the other bench armrest and stroked her own carved acorn phallus. Jane felt the maid's eyes, hot and hungry, upon her as she stood on the bench seat. Then she rested one foot on the back of the pew in front and hitched her skirts to show Megan her splayed, glistening sex lips. Jane slid an index finger inside herself, let it circle there with a stifled groan. The muscles of her legs, clad in silk stockings, tensed as she began to straddle the carved acorn. She slid a second, then a third finger into her sex, widening the swollen gap between her labia, which unfolded like lotus petals beneath her practised caress. Jane kept on glancing up at the Sheela-na-gig, and the lewd carving continued to inflame her. Meanwhile she was treated to the sight of Megan bunching up her own skirts around her waist and taking up a similar position. Jane watched as the maid played with herself, her almond eyes softening at the familiar self-caresses, her rosebud lips slightly parted. Part of Jane wanted to go forward and make love to the beautiful girl instead of continuing the masturbatory duel. Jane admired the statuesque quality of Megan's shape.

She loved her grey eyes with their long dark lashes, that glossy chestnut hair. But pride restrained her from acting upon any affectionate impulse.

Instead she eased herself gently on to the smooth wood. She felt her cunt slick over the carving, helped by the libation of juices flowing from her sex. She was so turned on, the wide girth of the carving was hardly noticeable to her. Her cunt felt almost as wide as the Sheela-na-gig's and avid for satisfaction.

She let the acorn's tip butt up against the tender cushion of heightened feeling inside her, and circled slowly. All the while she watched Megan. Megan began to pinch and pummel and roll her full breasts with one hand while her other delved into the beautiful rose-pink cunt, the same colour as her cupid's bow lips. She too was dripping with juices, ripe as a fresh peach, and Jane's eyes followed her movements eagerly.

Then Megan straddled her wooden acorn carving, and eased herself down on to it.

They were each impaled by the bench now, sharing the same unlikely dildo. They were dishevelled and hot and panting in the chapel's unnatural hot-house atmosphere. Jane stared into Megan's grey eyes, which were bright and distracted with desire. Jane slowly rocked against the wide, unyielding dildo, enjoying its curves, the carved nub at its tip, the ridges that formed the acorn's cup. It seemed perfectly sized and shaped to met her cunt's every need for sensation. She pressed against her abdomen and rubbed her clitoris as she rode slowly up and down, welcoming the leap of arousal every time she filled herself up. She watched hungrily as Megan too circled her dildo, and pressed her pubis to increase the sensation.

'Let's fuck,' Jane said. 'Quickly.'

The two girls rocked and frigged and felt an amazing volcanic spurt of come juices as they quivered and came opposite one another. They were driven to a feral peak of sensation before sliding into orgasm. The bench was solid and did not even rock slightly as their obscene acrobatics brought them off simultaneously. Even as Jane felt the burst of bliss on each upstroke subside, she could not help but think that they had been possessed by an alien lust, that they had been manipulated into acting out a tableau for someone else's benefit.

Perhaps the Sheela-na-gig was having lewd fun at their expense.

Both girls slid off their carved acorn dildos slowly, reluctantly, feeling their fever pound away to be replaced by guilt. Jane slicked her creamy come-juices across the old dark wood, dreamily thinking it would nourish the grain, before she realised she must clean up evidence of her outrageous masturbation. She noticed that Megan was polishing her acorn with a corner of her apron to remove the glossy juices she had left behind. Jane pulled out a handkerchief and spat, to wipe away the most obvious traces.

'A pretty picture, I must say.'

Both girls started like criminals.

It was Elaine, standing by the screen to the Lady Chapel, looking at them both.

'How long have you been watching?' Jane asked nervously.

'Long enough,' Elaine sneered, staring at Jane and then Megan. 'Long enough to know you need a special punishment for this outrageous and dangerous behaviour. This place stinks of sex.' She went up to the statue and lit a cone of incense, followed by a candle as some kind of atonement. 'Have you both no strand of shame or discretion?' she asked angrily.

'I'm sorry, it was as though . . .' Jane trailed off.

'As though we were enchanted,' Megan finished for her, and Jane darted a look of thanks.

'That's right,' Jane shivered, suddenly very cold. 'My apologies.'

'Megan, I order you to shave Jane's nether-hairs after you have bathed her,' Elaine said haughtily, 'and then shave your own. It may take a while to devise a suitable punishment for you both but I am sure I'll think of something.'

'Please don't be too angry,' Megan begged.

Elaine cocked her head to one side and looked at her.

'Why shouldn't I be? You were foisted upon me by Hazel Branagan, who assured me you were both modest and innocent. A few days later you're indulging in sleazy sex with my young protégée here.' Elaine raked a disdainful glance over Jane, 'Who should know better, I admit.'

'It was I who started it,' Jane interrupted, anxious to shift Elaine's attention from Megan.

'Was it indeed?'

'No, it was me,' Megan interrupted. 'I . . . I was jealous.'

'Jealous of what? Over what?'

There was a silence. Megan looked down, and Jane glanced at the marble image of the Madonna, determined to avoid even a glance at the Sheela-na-gig. If only she could shake the last of the sensual fug from her mind and concentrate.

'I'm waiting,' Elaine warned ominously, 'for an answer.'

Jane cast a warning glance at Megan. If Elaine discovered Hazel had anything to do with this, she would be furious. The real cause, Jane felt sure, was the Sheela-na-gig, leering above them in the stone wall of the chapel.

Megan shrugged, registered defeat as she failed to think of a convincing lie.

'It was over Hazel,' she blurted out. 'We both saw her on the beach today.'

Elaine's look was inscrutable. But from the way her knuckles clenched white as she folded her arms once more, it was obvious she was overwhelmed by an annoyance she fought hard to repress.

Before Elaine could respond, her expression changed, and she looked beyond them both as footsteps rang out on the stone flags behind them. Jane turned to discover Lord Ashby, dressed in Harris tweeds, looking grim with disapproval as he thundered up to them.

'Why, Lord Ashby, what a pleasant surprise. Back from your shoot so soon, I see. You have decided to pray in our ancient chapel after all?'

'I would never have stepped foot in here for the purpose of prayer, madam, for I hate the stench of Rome about the place.' He scowled at the altar, the statue, the flowers, candles and incense. As usual he did not deign to glance at Jane or Megan, as they were mere servants.

'Then to what do I owe this honour, Lord Ashby? Have you been called away on urgent business and wish to thank me for our hospitality before you leave?' Elaine continued sweetly. Lord Ashby laughed hollowly at the jibe.

121

'I am here to tell you that your brother has taken a turn for the worse. Father Dominic –' Ashby could not refrain from a sneer when referring to the priest '– is tending to Sebastian now, but Sebastian is very agitated and calling for you. From what I gather he has been indulging in more parlour tricks with your little nun, and the result has upset him terribly.'

Elaine raised an eyebrow at Jane, who nodded to confirm it.

'Lord Melmouth asked me to read a certain room and then the chapel,' Jane told her in a low voice.

'We'll speak of this later,' Elaine said. Jane admired the way Elaine's body language altered as she turned to face Lord Ashby. She looked imperious and stern, matching Ashby's overbearing manner.

'Jane has merely helped my brother when he asked her to. However, thank you for telling me. I shall go to him directly.' She put out her arm, making it clear that Lord Ashby should accompany her, even though he wanted to linger in the chapel. Jane was certain he wanted to question her more closely about what had happened, upbraid her and bully her away from Morlanby. Once more Jane was grateful for Elaine's protection. Elaine remained loyal despite Jane's latest indiscretions.

Lord Ashby's scowl deepened, but he complied with an impatient bow and escorted Elaine from the Lady Chapel.

Jane was startled when Lord Ashby suddenly paused to look back at her. She felt the weight of his contempt and hatred shine out of his bloodshot blue eyes.

'I promise you, nun, that you'll pay for the witchery that you have worked on Lord Melmouth today.'

Jane did not reply.

'My brother is waiting for us,' Elaine said coldly, and Lord Ashby nodded before they continued on their way. Jane watched the man's stiff back and shoulders and knew that Lord Ashby was afraid. Not so much of Jane, but of the subtle presence of the Sheela-na-gig.

The Sheela-na-gig was intensely angry with Lord Ashby, and on some level even he could sense it.

★

It transpired that Jane had to hastily bathe herself and prepare for evening dinner alone, as Megan was called away to help care for Sebastian. Jane dressed carefully in a pale-grey dress it was easy to button herself into. She felt tense and worried about Sebastian. But she was glad at the respite from delving into the mysteries of the Sheela-na-gig, which only exposed her to her own randy urges. She sat and meditated on her rosary, feeling cool sanity fully return to her, before she went down to dinner.

Even though she was composed, Jane was susceptible to the rich sensations of the formal meal. She watched the pool of candlelight cast a soft glow over the dark oak table and reflect dully in the silverware. Crimson curtains billowed so sensuously Jane wanted to reach out and touch them. The tapestries which hung in the dining hall beckoned her with flashes of turquoise and old gold and burnt sienna, depicting tales of knights and dragons. It was as though, after a foray into the world of spirit, the material world reclaimed her with a vengeance.

She longed to ask Elaine if everything was truly fine with Sebastian but Elaine was in resplendent social armour, beautiful but distant and polite to everyone except Sebastian. Sebastian himself certainly seemed as though he had fully recovered. His fair hair gleamed in the candlelight and if his skin was pale, his eyes were bright and animated. His hands gestured to emphasise his conversation and his cultured voice acquired a Celtic burr as he drank more vintage claret and became expansive. He was civil and pleasant and lucid, keeping pace with the small-talk around the table. It was a pleasure to hear him laugh when Elaine shared a childhood anecdote with Dr Shetland.

It was also a pleasure for Jane to feel Elaine glance towards her from time to time. She felt it like the touch of her fingertips.

'Tomorrow, if the weather holds, I vote we visit the standing stone. We could all walk there, take a picnic,' Sebastian suggested. 'Jane will be interested in seeing it, and you've never been there before, Dr Shetland.'

'I am not certain that would be a good idea,' Dr Shetland said politely. 'You are too fatigued from your recent exertions. In a day or two, perhaps.'

'But don't you think the fresh air would do us all good after the over-indulgence of the last few days?' Sebastian persisted.

'A shorter walk with the dogs down to the beach may be the best plan for tomorrow,' Elaine said calmly. 'Then we'll see.'

Jane listened to the careful words regulating Sebastian's day as though he were a child. Sebastian caught her eye and smiled, as though he guessed her thoughts. For the moment he seemed happy to humour their way of humouring him.

Jane felt tired and plucked up courage to ask for permission to retire early. Elaine raised her glass to her, in a kind of reconciliation, and bade her goodnight as Jane beat a hasty retreat.

As Jane sat in her cosy bedchamber and listened to the wind rustling the trees and rattling the casements, she began to feel relaxed and at peace. The enigma of the Sheela-na-gig faded from her mind. She almost wondered how anyone could fancy there were unquiet spirits haunting the venerable walls of Morlanby.

TWELVE

Jane was woken by someone rapping on her door. It was broad daylight. She stumbled to the door and opened it to find Elaine, still fully dressed, standing hands on hips.

'Sebastian seems fully recovered from his nervous collapse and his watchers are placated,' Elaine said. 'I managed to doze for an hour or two, but now I need some different form of relaxation. Come to my room.' Elaine leaned closer to whisper in Jane's ear, 'Did you think I would forget our unfinished business? Come. Don't bother to get dressed.'

Jane obeyed, still feeling sleepy. It was as though reality was a dream to her.

She had presumed Elaine wanted to speak of what had happened in the schoolroom and the Sheela-na-gig, but Elaine had something else on her mind. Perhaps Sebastian had already told her of what had happened the previous day.

Elaine's apartment possessed a bathroom, full of the latest plumbing triumphs – water closet and large enamel bath. A wraith of steam crept out of the bathroom enticingly.

Jane looked at Elaine, wondering if she was intending to bathe while they talked. But Elaine's clear blue eyes held a wicked glint.

'Go into the bathroom,' she ordered.

Jane obeyed.

Megan was waiting for her, naked in the large bath-tub. Jane's heart flipped as she gazed into Megan's almond-grey eyes. Megan's neck flushed prettily above the level of the milky water, and she smiled shyly.

'Good morning, miss.'

'Morning, Megan.'

'Tell her what you are to do,' Elaine said, watching from the bathroom doorway after she had closed the door firmly behind her.

'We are to bathe together and then shave each other down there.'

Jane slowly divested herself of her dressing-gown and then her nightgown. She looked doubtfully at the tub of shaving soap, white towels and cut-throat razor lying on the ceramic shelf next to the bath.

'I'm not sure I can use a razor,' she admitted with a shiver. She felt bashful, her honey skin prickling as she felt Megan's grey eyes assess her. Which was ridiculous, after all that had already passed between them. But that had been in the middle of a strange and overheated passion. Here they were meeting afresh, like old lovers, to bathe together. Jane stepped into the bath, and Megan hooked up her legs to let Jane sit down.

They began to wash each other, and to get to know the contours of each other's bodies as they soaped and rinsed in the milky, perfumed waters. Jane was soon soothed by the steamy confines of the bath. She lingered over the soaping of her breasts. Her love bruises from Hazel had faded, and only retained a faint sensitivity.

'Soap each other's breasts,' Elaine ordered as she watched. 'Slowly and gently.'

Jane's heart thudded at the command. It was exactly what she wanted to do with Megan's heavy breasts. She slowly glided her hands over the other girl's wet skin. She let her cupped palms test the weight of each breast and soap their sensitive undersides. Then she circled gently, tracing the large rose aureole and the hardening nipples.

Meanwhile she felt Megan fondle her own pert breasts, softly kneading them into glistening sensitivity.

Elaine sighed.

'I'm so glad I decided to play cupid to you both. I know what a canker Hazel Branagan can be. I am sure you would find each other much more rewarding than that bit of rough.' Her voice was silky, but there was irritation beneath its tones. 'Now, Jane, perch on the side of the bath and spread your legs so that Megan can shave your snatch.'

Jane obeyed. She always felt a frisson when Elaine's cultured voice used filthy terms. She gripped the side of the bath-tub and spread her thighs wide so that Megan could kneel in the bath water between her legs. Megan took the shaving brush and applied the lather generously between Jane's legs. The sable brush grazed against Jane's sex in a tantalising caress through the creamy foam. Then Megan took the cut-throat razor and carefully began to shave from top to bottom, scraping the discarded hair on large sheets of newspaper laid beside the bath, then tossing the paper into the waste bin. Jane watched with fascination as Megan's neat hands wielded the silver razor. She felt only the faintest rasp against her skin as the razor made contact and scooped away her lathered pubic hairs. Jane admired the bare skin thus exposed as it passed. She spread her legs still wider to let Megan have easier access lower down. Her sex lips seemed to jut out wantonly without their nest of hair to hide in, and she felt Megan's breath, cool against their wetness. Megan gently held the outer folds to one side with her fingers, then the other, to ensure she had shaved around Jane's sex completely. Then she rinsed, and patted the area with a smooth lotion which soothed the skin.

'Now, Jane, you must shave Megan,' Elaine said tersely as she watched the performance. Her arms were folded, her face impassive, but it was clear she enjoyed the show.

Jane lathered Megan as Megan sat and splayed her legs. It felt scary to handle the razor and carefully scrape the dark, curled hairs away from Megan's sex. Jane began at the outer edges and gradually worked towards the luscious pink slash. She tried not to be side-tracked by how beautiful it looked between the lather. But she noticed with fascination that the lips swelled almost imperceptibly as Jane proceeded with her task. The thought unnerved her, and she slipped ever so slightly in the final pass over Megan's skin, leaving a little bead of blood.

'I'm sorry,' she gasped, and lapped at the red pearl without thinking. It tasted metallic sweet.

'It's only a little graze, no harm done. You did very well for your first time,' Megan said in a low voice.

'I did not want to hurt you,' Jane said, even as she rinsed water over Megan's sex and smoothed her with a little of the lotion.

'You'll have plenty of practice from now on, as you must both remain clean-shaven while you are at Morlanby,' Elaine said. 'Sorry to interrupt your intimate moment, my dears, but I want you out and dried in front of my parlour fire.'

Megan and Jane smiled guiltily at each other as they towelled each other down.

It was strange to stand in front of the fire, naked and with a shaven pussy. It was strange to stand beside another naked and shaven girl while Elaine watched them. As Jane and Megan stood on the Persian carpet Elaine circled them, scrutinising them. She touched a breast, a bare bottom, and stroked a finger along the shaven pubis of each girl. Then she went to her bureau and took out the long lengths of ribbon which had been used in the seance.

'I knew that these would be useful,' she said. 'Now turn to face one another.'

Jane obeyed. She felt her clean skin glow at the sight of Megan nude. Megan's nipples protruded like cherry buds and Jane longed to nibble them. Jane began to feel the familiar wetness between her legs. Ever since she had arrived at Morlanby she had been at the mercy of her sensual appetites. She hardly knew how to resist them any more. Furtively she slid her inner thighs against one another, tested the new sensation of naked skin at the top of them.

'Stand closer together. Much closer. That's right. Jane, rest your chin on Megan's shoulder. Megan, do likewise. Ah, that's it. Keep that pose.'

Jane began to breathe shallowly. She was pressed against Megan's flanks, could feel the other girl's soft downy skin, her breasts, her shaven pubis. She wanted to kiss Megan's neck and put her arms around the girl's waist, but she knew this was not permitted.

Elaine took a length of ribbon and tied Megan's left wrist to

Jane's left wrist. She did the same to each of their right wrists, binding them tightly together. Then she looped ribbon around Jane's left thigh, wrapping it in figures of eight to Megan's left thigh. She bound their right thighs thus also.

'There,' she said at last with satisfaction. 'Now you two young lovers can be each other's whipping posts.'

Jane could not see Elaine take up her cane from her bureau drawer, but she could hear it swish through the air as Elaine tested it.

'You will both have to stand firm and comfort each other,' Elaine said, 'while I administer your punishment for yesterday's shocking display in the chapel. I hope the experience means you will later turn to each other for consolation, rather than fighting like hell cats for the questionable favours of Hazel Branagan.'

Jane could not help but tense as she heard Elaine approach her from behind. She heard the cane whip through the air twice before it sliced down to make contact with her buttocks. She yelped. She was bound so closely to Megan that she could not arch away from the bamboo's full onslaught. Her arse cheeks remained tensed and stinging for the next blow, and the next. Elaine did not spare her, and soon she felt the burning flesh of her arse spread a fierce hot pleasure over her body, through her loins. At every blow her pubis jolted against Megan's, and Jane's breasts were thrust against Megan's breasts. It was as though Elaine was controlling how she caressed Megan's naked body with her own.

Her naked clit hood swelled and she grew even more juicy under the delicious chastisement. She pressed closer to Megan so that every quiver of pain and pleasure could be recorded on Megan's skin. Jane sank her mouth against the soft triangle of flesh where Megan's neck joined her shoulders, and she sucked hard to stop herself from crying out. Megan's body swayed with hers, supporting her. Megan moaned at the feel of Jane, of the tender bruising and sucking of Jane's vampire kiss.

'That should be enough for now,' Elaine said at length, as Jane felt Elaine's cool palm stroke her stinging flesh. 'After all, we do want you to be able to sit down in polite company. Now you must support Megan while she tastes her punishment. Well, are you going to thank me, Jane? I have, after all, been quite lenient considering the circumstances.'

'Thank you, madam,' Jane whispered.

'Louder.'

'Thank you, madam,' Jane gasped, and meant it.

Jane watched as Elaine walked behind Megan's naked form. Jane could see from Elaine's flushed cheeks, her parted lips, and the glitter in her eye, that the aristocrat was fully enjoying herself. Elaine let the cane slice through the air a few times, feinting blows, and Megan tensed at every possible strike. Then she laid about Megan's arse, and Jane could feel each blow course through Megan's body as a quiver of pain and sensuous pleasure. She could see livid pink stripes appear on Megan's bottom while Megan chewed into her shoulder for comfort. Elaine was an expert, skimming the milky flesh to make it ripple and sting from each blow, but leaving no dark bruises that would last in its wake.

At length she concluded her chastisement of Megan's naked arse, and Megan was also ordered to thank her for her leniency.

Jane felt liquid fire between her legs, in the pit of her belly. She adored being bound so close to Megan, yet ached to be able to stroke and caress the girl's body. All they could do was stand stiffly, licking at each other's necks and ear lobes, pressing together and swaying slightly against one another in their bondage. Jane's arse stung mightily so that waves of heat tremored down her legs, up her spine, and juices ran unfettered down the inside of her legs. She had to admire Elaine for the deliciously randy torture she had put them through.

'Such a pretty picture,' Elaine said, circling them slowly. She savoured the ecstatic looks on her preys' faces. 'Shall I leave you two love birds alone with your predicament?' She took out her pendant watch, checked the time. 'Alas, *tempus fugit*. Never mind, you can remain tethered for a few minutes longer while I pleasure myself at your expense. I do so enjoy playing the voyeur. This is a tableau I must exploit to the full.'

Jane heard Elaine move to the chaise-longue behind her and soon heard little moans and gasps from the aristocrat. Jane's abdomen quivered in sympathy and her loins ached, honey wet with longing. She tried to rub her sex against Megan's but that only served to tantalise her more. The fact that Elaine would be the only one to orgasm after this morning's session was obviously another of her punishments.

When Elaine had satisfied herself, she cut their tight bonds of satin. Jane rubbed her chafed wrists and gingerly stroked her burning arse flesh.

'You may apply salve to each other – but make it quick,' Elaine said, handing Jane a tub of ointment. Jane nodded and tenderly smoothed a generous amount of the salve across the livid welds on Megan's beautiful bottom. Then she bent over. Jane swayed and swooned and flinched as Megan also treated her arse with the ointment.

'It's almost time for tea in the drawing room – which you must serve, Megan,' Elaine said when they had finished. 'Before you dress and leave, however, you must insert these.' Elaine looked in her dresser and took out a small wooden box, sliding open its lid. Inside the velvet lined box were two small ivory balls. Some of their surface was smooth, some of it slightly raised in little bumps. The ivory had strange foreign characters carved into it.

Megan looked at them suspiciously. 'Insert them where, madam?' she asked.

'Why, put them into your cunt, Megan. They will move in you while you walk about and serve. Between these love orbs and your stinging buttocks you will experience the most delicious frisson. But of course you must not reveal your arousal in polite company, or I will dismiss you. You may remove them after serving tea, rinse them of your juices and return them to me this evening. Is this clear?'

'Yes, madam.'

Jane watched in fascination as Megan slipped the little orbs inside her swollen sex, her hips undulating to receive them comfortably. Then the maid hurriedly dressed.

'Now, Jane, you shall wear my pearls to tea.' Elaine dangled the choker length string of wild pearls on her wrist then handed them to Jane.

'Thank you,' Jane replied, bewildered.

'But not around your neck. Inside you. They shall offer similar sensations to the love orbs. Again, this will teach you to hide your libido while in polite company. Am I clear?'

'Yes,' Jane said meekly as she pushed the bundle of pearls up into her moist crack. Their coolness against her warm insides made her tremble in excitement even as she hurried to dress.

'I hope this will teach you both to have more discretion in future,' Elaine said sternly, 'and I hope that it has also kindled a certain arousal between you both. Young pure love is to be encouraged, after all,' she continued with wicked primness.' Now let us go down.'

The high tea was exquisite torture to Jane. The company was seated around a roaring log fire in the drawing room. It was an effort to sit on an upright chair. To keep her back straight and eyes downcast, acting demure and prim while feeling randy as any streetwalker. She drank tea, ate cucumber sandwiches and petits fours from bone china, while her sex lips pouted over pure wild pearls.

Thankfully, Sebastian had gone for a short walk with the dogs, and the other three gentlemen present did not deign to talk with her. But still it was an ordeal to sit in restrained silence while those pearls slipped about delicately inside her every time she shifted in her seat, trying to ease the pressure on her stinging buttocks. She struggled to remain impassive in front of her betters.

Megan poured tea, and offered sugar with the ornate sugar tongs that brought back memories for them both, and handed round plates of food. The maid's dark lashes were lowered and there was a faint flush to her cheeks. Megan was wearing a fresh white apron, and a white lace cap on her smooth chestnut hair. She looked like the quintessential parlourmaid. And yet Jane knew that as she moved about, bent to pour and serve, those little love orbs revolved silkily up and down her cunt, and her buttocks ached against her starched cotton petticoats. Jane felt a visceral longing for Megan's body. She remembered the press of that naked body against hers whenever Megan hazarded a glance at her. It was as though they were still bound together by invisible cords. Jane was painfully aware of every move that Megan made, every laboured breath or suppressed sigh, every slight tremor in her body, even when she did not even glance in her direction.

Jane's breasts ached for the feel of her, the touch of her hands, and her lips, and her cunt.

Elaine had certainly succeeded in her plan to play cupid. Jane could almost curse her for it.

Elaine chatted amicably with Dr Shetland, while Ashby and Barnes conversed with each other. Occasionally she glanced at Jane and Megan, watching their discomfort with secret satisfaction. She would wickedly offer Jane some more sugar, or draw her into the conversation, when Jane could hardly pay attention to anything through her haze of desire.

'I am glad that Sebastian was persuaded not to visit the standing stone today,' said Dr Shetland as he was helped to another pile of delicate triangular sandwiches. 'He seems hell-bent on some convoluted theory about the reason for his distress and who knows where it will end, what conclusions he will reach? Perhaps it is time to halt the experiment, Lady Melmouth.'

'On the contrary,' Elaine said pleasantly, 'there is much improvement in my brother. He seems truly animated and involved in a purposeful course of action for the first time in a long while, and I welcome it. It is merely residual exhaustion which has affected his nerves recently. He is on the mend.' She smiled. 'The fresh air of his walk will certainly do him good too.'

'There is evidence that fascination with spiritualism can produce a morbid fascination with the dead at the expense of the living. This can in turn lead to full-scale insanity,' Dr Shetland said doubtfully, bracing his chest to emphasise his authority.

'Please just permit a few days longer. I am sure Jane will help Sebastian reach a safe and satisfactory conclusion, won't you, Jane?' Elaine patted Jane's hand in supplication. Jane's pearls jiggled as she nodded vehemently in agreement. She took a breath and ventured to speak.

'I believe I can help, sir,' she said quietly. 'Alas, the world of the spirit is not for the weak-minded, but Lord Melmouth is far from weak.'

Lord Ashby turned to them, as he overheard the subject of their conversation. 'I doubt we should let this farce continue another day, even,' he said irritably. 'The estate suffers while we fritter time away humouring a madman.'

'My brother has every right to investigate his theories in his own home,' Elaine replied icily, 'for as long as he wishes.'

'No. Only for as long as the land remains his, madam. And that may soon change.'

There was a silence as the adversaries faced each other. Then Elaine smiled mirthlessly. 'More tea, Lord Ashby?' she asked. 'I am keen to offer you our best hospitality during your stay. It will prove to you the estate is being well run despite your fears.'

'It looks like the weather will take a turn for the worse,' Dr Shetland said quickly before Ashby had a chance to respond with bald insults. The doctor stood up to glance through the leaded window, 'Those clouds gathering could bring snow by nightfall.'

Ashby stood up to join him. 'Sleet at the very least,' he said, simmering down at last. He obviously felt, with his battle almost won, he need not lower himself to an acrimonious argument just yet.

'Have another cup of tea, Jane,' Elaine said sweetly. 'You look rather pale.'

Jane could feel her bladder filling up and the pressure added to her horny discomfort.

'Thank you,' she said meekly, and took another sip. She was beginning to feel as absurd as Alice at the mad hatter's tea-party.

Finally the long formalities drew to a close. Jane was eager to retreat upstairs but instead Elaine took her firmly by the hand.

'Come for a short walk with me, Jane,' Elaine said. 'Perhaps we'll meet Sebastian on the way.'

Elaine guided her out through the main courtyard of the castle, out the back to the stables. Then she pulled Jane into an empty stable block, peering round to check no one had seen them.

'Do you want to pass water, Jane? Are you fit to burst?' Elaine crooned, pressing the palm of her hand against Jane's lower abdomen to add to the fullness of bladder.

'Yes,' Jane gasped, even as she squirmed at the sweet torture.

'To have a cunt full of pearls and a bladder full of piss is almost unbearable, is it not? Poor Jane,' Elaine said softly. 'Very well, you may squat here and relieve yourself.'

Jane backed against the whitewashed wall, gathered up her skirts, squatted and tried to obey. She had waited so long that it was an exquisite effort, especially with Elaine watching avidly, enjoying her predicament. Finally the pee descended like a golden waterfall, gushing down on to the hay-strewn floor. The perfume of it mingled with the smell of horse and sweat. The force of the fat jet of pee shooting out increased the fullness of her pussy. It stung a little against her freshly shaven lips but she let out a sheer sigh of bliss as she finally emptied herself completely.

Elaine, meanwhile, was fingering herself while she watched Jane. She looked at the stream of piss and then watched the release on Jane's face. Elaine's patrician features grew soft, and her frown lines smoothed, her lips pouting in lascivious abandon.

'I'm almost there,' she muttered at last, presenting her pussy to Jane, who still squatted against the wall in a relieved daze. 'Finish me.'

Jane eagerly probed Elaine's sex with her fingers. Her springy gold curls felt like soft sprigs of heather. She pressed hard against Elaine's clit and pubis, while letting her fingers stroke her inside. She braced her back so that Elaine could rock wildly against the pressure and bring herself to a peak. Jane was happy to be allowed to kiss and caress Elaine like this once more, and moaned in answer to Elaine's cries of bliss when she came.

'Ah, that was so good,' Elaine said as she finally calmed down and rearranged her dress. 'There's nothing like coming to clear the mind. Those stiff-necked vultures posing as our guests, who profess to scientifically investigate scientific phenomena . . .' Elaine shook her head in irritation. 'I swear they will drive me insane before long, never mind poor old Sebastian.'

Elaine helped Jane up and pecked her on the cheek. 'I'm going to go riding now, Jane, another good way to clear my head. But first, let me take back my pearls. Spread your legs wide.'

Jane obeyed. She gasped as Elaine's nimble fingers delved into her and tugged out the string of pearls one pearl at a time. Jane moaned at the sweet arousal of it. She felt strangely empty without them.

Elaine sniffed the pearls then pocketed them. 'I'll rinse them in a stream,' she said, 'so they don't lose their bloom. Maybe I'll let you wear them again some day. They are an heirloom from an ancestress, who received them while whoring for Charles II.' Elaine giggled. 'I like to keep them in practice so to speak. Now you go and rest, Jane. We'll meet up later.'

Jane hurried to her apartments, still hungry for orgasm. She wildly considered seeking out Megan for a fuck but that would, of course, be indiscreet and land them in more trouble. She flung herself on to her bed, wrapped her gown between her legs, and rode her shaven pussy against the thick swathe of material. Soon she was enveloped in the rapture of final, allover release that felt like bliss. Then she dozed in her clothes, exhausted by teetering so long on the edge of pleasure.

A couple of hours later, Jane was roused from a shallow sleep by loud knocks on her door.

It was Elaine once more. But this time she looked distraught.

'What's wrong?' Jane asked.

'It's Sebastian. He's gone missing. The dogs came back this afternoon without him.' She twisted her hands together nervously. 'I've searched the grounds around the house and there's no sign of him. No horse is missing from the stables so he must be on foot. Will you help me to look for him?'

'Of course,' Jane said, hurrying to collect her cloak. 'Do you think he may have walked to the standing stone after all?'

Elaine looked grim. 'I hope not,' she said. 'It's on high ground and it's already close to freezing out there.' She hesitated. 'It's on Hazel Branagan's property, too.'

Jane fastened her cloak about her. 'Tell me how to get there,' she said.

'No, I absolutely forbid it,' Elaine said vehemently. 'Try the Maiden Falls first. I am certain he would not have embarked on such an expedition without you. After all, the whole point of his recent obsession with the standing stone was that he wanted to show you the site.'

'As you wish,' Jane said, unwilling to upset Elaine any further.

'Thank you. I'll go down to check the beach. Let's hope to God we find him before his so-called friends do. I'll tell Father Dominic and Megan to organise the servants into a search party.' Elaine took Jane's hand, squeezed it in thanks, and hurried away.

THIRTEEN

Jane fetched a lantern from the stables and stumbled along the path into the woods, towards Maiden Falls. The waterfall thundered after the recent rain and white noise thundered in her ears. She could see the white churning waters by the silver light of a full moon. The night was now clear and cold. Stars shimmered and the Milky Way spanned the sky. Jane shivered, half wishing that she was still in her bed. Then she called out Sebastian's name. An owl shrieked in the distance, but there was no sign of Sebastian.

Jane closed her eyes and concentrated her thoughts on him, willing herself to sense where he had gone. Then she moved down to the wide pool at the foot of the waterfall, careful not to slip on mossy boulders. Where the pool narrowed before the stream continued down to the sea, there were a series of widely placed stepping stones. She balanced herself and carefully began to cross. Somehow she managed to reach the other side without falling into the fast-flowing dark waters. Then she followed a sheep track up the opposite bank, clinging to clumps of hardy heather. Soon the path grew less steep and she could walk up the mountain more easily. She knew that if she kept going she would, sooner or later, reach the standing stone.

The cold wind sliced through her clothes and whistled past her body as she struggled on. The lantern soon guttered out and she negotiated the path by moonlight alone. Sheep huddled like phantoms in the moon shadows as she passed. She hoped that Sebastian had not collapsed and fallen prey to the freezing cold. She had to force herself to climb as quickly as her heart would stand just to keep the circulation going in her hands and feet, even wrapped in her warm clothes.

Jane lost track of time with the effort of putting one foot in front of the other, blindly trusting to the angels – or the Sheela-na-gig, she thought with bitter irony – to guide her. She listened to her own breath muffled in the folds of her hood and watched it rise like incense before her. She could feel herself tiring and she grew frightened. No one would know where she was if she collapsed out here on her own. She was tempted to return to the Maiden Falls, but a stubborn intuition kept her to her path.

Eventually she saw the standing stone, a black, jagged monolith against the bleak moonlit mountainside. It cast a long shadow, and in that shadow lay the huddled form of Sebastian. Jane bent over his body, rubbed his cold hands, calling his name close to his ear to be heard above the wind. There was no response. Exhaustion and fear drove her to shake his unconscious form angrily.

'Sebastian, for God's sake, rouse yourself or you'll die!' She dragged him into a sitting position as his eyes fluttered open.

'Jane, is that you?' he slurred. 'Have you come to see the standing stone after all?'

'Yes, although I would have preferred to see it in the warm light of day.' She chafed his hands. 'Sebastian, you bloody fool, what possessed you to sneak up here on the coldest night of the year?'

He smiled sheepishly. 'My little nun, I just had to get away. They were watching my every mood, could hardly suppress their glee when I fainted from exhaustion. They listened to every mumble I made in my sleep, and when I woke they would take notes on my condition, rustling the commitment papers, itching to sign them and hurry me off to an asylum.'

'Don't you think this little stunt has only served to help their cause? Once they hear of it they'll prepare a little padded room especially for you, won't they? They'll declare you are no longer fit to look after yourself, that you are given over to whimsies which put you in peril.'

'I don't care any more. I cannot bear my visions any longer. Ashby and Barnes, they've worn me down these past days.'

'Don't be absurd. You must care. You cannot let them win. Their greed and manipulation cannot fathom your true nature, Sebastian. You must stand firm and show them what you're really made of.'

'And what am I really made of?'

'Strength, humour, compassion. Stand up, Sebastian,' Jane ordered. She felt bad about scolding him but knew that he would respond, even in his weakened state, to any bullying tactics which reminded him of his father. 'Come on, stand up, or are you going to prove me wrong and act like a spineless weakling? Now, tell me, where can we shelter before we make the return journey? You must know this land well enough to tell me if there is a sheep fold nearby we could use as a windbreak, at least. Think, Sebastian!'

She shook Sebastian until his head stopped lolling and his eyes opened once more. He frowned, trying hard to think even though the cold had made him sluggish.

'Hazel Branagan's cottage is just a little way down the mountain,' he said, as he began to shiver.

Jane took his arm over her shoulder, and with difficulty steadied him on his feet. 'Then lead the way, or are you going to prove the hopeless wretch your father expected you to be?' she yelled in desperation. 'Hurry, or we'll both freeze out here.'

Somehow they stumbled down the track which Sebastian had pointed out. Jane sent up a silent prayer of thanks as she saw the warm glow of light from Hazel Branagan's cottage.

'Almost there. Now double quick, Sebastian!' she yelled, propelling them down towards the cottage gate.

'Stop right there.' It was Hazel's voice, just audible before it was snatched away by the wind. Her tall figure stood in her front doorway, blocking out light from the room behind. She came towards them, and raised her lantern to identify them. Max growled in a menacing manner beside her. Jane noticed that Hazel was carrying a cocked shotgun.

'You two!' she exclaimed. 'I thought it was the Lewis brothers carrying out some childish prank.' She broke the breech of her shotgun and laid it against the wall just inside her doorway. 'Quiet, Max, they're friends.' She patted the dog's big head and his growl ceased. 'What's wrong with Sebastian?'

'Exposure, I think. He's been up at the standing stone since twilight.'

'Let's get him inside,' Hazel said briskly, realising there was no time for further questions. It was much easier to move Sebastian with Hazel's help, and Hazel all but carried his slim form into her cottage.

Max settled his jowls on his front paws and lay in front of the door as Hazel closed it. He seemed ready to guard them from anything. Jane began to feel a flood of relief at being safe in the warmth of the cottage.

'Now, Jane, let's get these wet clothes off Sebastian and get him into bed.'

Between them they stripped the shivering Sebastian. Hazel pulled a clean night-shirt of her own over his head, then bundled him into her narrow bed with all the extra blankets she could find. Then Hazel banked the fire high, and hung his clothes to dry before it. Finally she put a saucepan of milk on the little range to warm.

Only when this was accomplished did she glance over at Jane.

'You'd better get those damp skirts off too, you've obviously been wading across streams in them. I'll give you some clean long-johns and a jumper to change into.'

Jane nodded. She realised that she was shivering. Her limbs ached as sensation returned and she felt light-headed. She stripped off shyly in front of the fire, while Hazel calmly stirred the saucepan of milk, and then took her clothes and hung them to dry along with Sebastian's. The musty smell of heather came off them as they steamed before the fire.

Once in her dry clothes, she helped Hazel to minister the hot milk and nutmeg, with a dash of whisky, to Sebastian. Hazel propped him up and Jane put the tin cup to his lips until he had drunk it all. Jane was pleased to see a little colour creep back into his cheeks, and his hands felt warmer to the touch.

'Thank you,' Sebastian muttered as he sank back into the pillows with a sigh.

'Were you after another supply of my tisane of valerian and St John's wort, Sebastian? You know I would have delivered them to you at the estate tomorrow.'

'I'd run out,' Sebastian said simply. 'And as I explained to Jane I just needed to get away.'

Jane stared at Sebastian and then Hazel.

'I had been helping Sebastian while Elaine – Lady Melmouth – was away,' Hazel explained briefly.

'She was weaning me off the laudanum, and very successfully too, before Dr Shetland arrived and started to use it as a general cure-all once again,' Sebastian explained wearily.

'How long were you collapsed out there in the cold?' Hazel asked gravely.

'Not too long,' Sebastian said as brightly as he could. Jane shook her head at Hazel in contradiction.

'I'll make a tisane for you,' Hazel said, returning to her range to add a handful of dried herbs to the kettle of boiling water. 'You're a fool, Sebastian. Constantly risking your life for no real reason.'

Sebastian frowned. 'You don't know the crimes that torture my soul,' he muttered in response. 'In any case, you risked your life, didn't you, when you ran away to America to play the pioneer?'

'I took that risk for some purpose. I have my independence now.'

'So I see.' Sebastian looked around at the simple furnishings of the warm whitewashed room. The settle, the table and high-backed chairs, the bookcase and dresser. 'But you know that you could return to Morlanby any time you wanted. I am Lord Melmouth now, and I would welcome your company. You're so soothing, and practical. Why do you stay away?'

Hazel exchanged glances with the curious Jane. She frowned as she poured out a cup of the herbal fusion and handed it to Sebastian to sip.

'Too much time has passed. Too many old wounds,' she

explained in a low voice. 'The memories run deep. And your father –'

'My father has been dead these many years,' Sebastian interrupted. 'A fact which I am only slowly beginning to believe myself. We are free of his shadow at last, Hazel, free to love as we please.'

Hazel returned his level gaze.

'Are we? I don't see you living as your heart dictates, Sebastian. I see you frightened and anxious and running away from yourself.'

Sebastian looked down and plucked at the blankets.

'True. But I hope that after this night I will start to change.'

'Rest now,' Hazel said more kindly, taking his empty cup from him. 'Get our strength back for the walk tomorrow. You must rest until it's light.'

'They'll be searching for us,' Jane observed.

'That cannot be helped. If I know Elaine they will remain within the boundaries of the Morlanby estate. She knows nothing of the friendship, the arrangement between Sebastian and me. It began while she was away.'

Sebastian let Hazel ease him on to his back and he settled down to doze.

'Think about it,' he mumbled, 'think about coming to live at Morlanby. I know Elaine would want it really. I know she still . . . loves you.'

Hazel joined Jane beside the fire. She gave Jane a cup of the same tisane she had prepared for Sebastian. It tasted sweet and spicy.

'I did not know you were versed in herbal lore,' Jane said.

'I learned from the old woman who used to live here. It came in useful and I added to her knowledge on my travels.' Hazel smiled. 'You're not the only one to have special powers, little witch.'

The two women sat in silence for a while and gazed into the crackling flames. Max twitched his paws where he lay splayed in sleep.

'Would you like to talk about it?' Jane asked at last. 'Tell me about you and Elaine? It may help.'

Hazel glanced sideways at her and pokered the fire.

'Help who exactly?' Hazel challenged. 'Help you satisfy your curiosity?' Then she sighed. 'I suppose Sebastian has a point. It has festered unspoken for so long.'

'Then tell me. The bare details at least,' Jane urged. 'Who knows, it may help me to cure Sebastian of his malady. Even witches need to know the facts of their subject's domestic circumstances before they can provide a cure. And Elaine wants me to find a cure.'

'Persuasive, aren't you?' Hazel smiled. 'Why don't you ask Elaine herself?'

'Because she would not tell me,' Jane said simply. 'She's too proud.'

Hazel traced Jane's cheek with her rough fingers and smiled.

'That's true enough. You are astute, little nun. Very well, the history will keep us awake while we watch over Sebastian.' She settled back in her chair, propped her long legs on the fender, and let her arm trail down to stroke Max's smooth ears as she talked.

'There isn't much to reveal, in truth. It's a pretty common tale of thwarted puppy love.'

When Jane did not comment she shrugged and continued.

'I was fostered by Sebastian's father when my parents died. I was ten years old. Sebastian was six then, and Elaine was nine. Elaine and I got along together very well, and we both loved Sebastian.' Hazel grinned. 'It's difficult to refrain from being fond of Sebastian.'

'I've noticed,' Jane replied.

'Yes. But soon he was sent off to boarding school. That's where he got closer to his cousins, the ones staying at Morlanby, and met that new priest.' Hazel shook her head. 'A different world, a man's world. Meanwhile Elaine and I remained at home. As mere women, we were not worth an education. But we had the run of Morlanby.' Hazel smiled softly at the memory, 'There wasn't an inch of mountain or forest or beach that we did not explore. And we read books from the library and visited the wise old woman who lived here. Between sewing and serving tea and other such ladylike duties, we haphazardly educated ourselves.'

Jane gazed into the amber underglow of the burning logs and imagined such a carefree existence, lived through the gaps of adult control.

'And then?' she asked as Hazel grew silent.

Hazel frowned.

'And then we grew up and things became complicated. Sebastian returned from boarding school. He hosted shooting parties and lavish house parties at Morlanby before he went up to Oxford. Around that time Elaine's father insisted she become engaged to Lord Ashby. He was older than us, but he still cut a dashing figure then, and even possessed a modicum of charm.'

'Which he has since lost.' Jane shuddered. 'But he also had land, and money, didn't he?'

'Yes. Elaine's father did not mind marrying her off in exchange for a stake in such property.'

Jane nodded. She thought how the situation was now reversed, with Ashby poised to take Morlanby away from Elaine and Sebastian.

'It seemed as though Elaine was actually smitten with the man, or rather enamoured with the pretty baubles that he could shower upon her,' Hazel recounted. 'They were inseparable. He bought her furs and diamonds, introduced her to London society. She went to the opera, the ballet, was presented at Court. She sent me long letters describing every glamorous occasion. I was, of course, quite miserable. I missed her desperately.' Hazel's eyes wavered from Jane's, and she gazed into the embers of the fire to hide her emotion.

'When they returned to Morlanby for the Christmas festivities I hatched a stupid, reckless plan.' Hazel grimaced at the memory. 'You have to realise I was almost beside myself with feelings and longings I could barely name. Morlanby is like that, I am sure you have noticed. It's hard to keep a level head there.'

'Yes,' Jane admitted, as she huddled further into her woollens. Hazel threw another log on the fire and its warmth flared up once more. Sebastian mumbled, then turned over in bed.

'Go on,' Jane urged. 'What was your plan?'

'Quite simply to seduce Lord Ashby.'

'No! But why?'

'It was strange. I almost found him attractive when reflected in Elaine's eyes, when I read the way she described him in her letters. I loved the object of my love's desire. And I formulated

144

the theory that it was the only way to solve my problems. I was heartsick, desperate. If I could prove that Ashby could not remain faithful on the very eve of his wedding, proud Elaine would have to break off the engagement, wouldn't she? And then she and I would be together again at Morlanby. Spinsters but happy with it.'

Jane nodded. 'A bizarre but believable theory. But certainly a risk with a man like Ashby. I can understand now why Elaine did not want you near Morlanby with Ashby there, even if you did not carry it through. And I understand why relations may be strained between the two of them, for that matter. I did not realise there was such a history between them.' Jane sipped at her herbal tea. 'So, were you successful in your seduction?' she asked. 'How far did you get?'

'Practically all the way, I am ashamed to say. On Twelfth Night I wore a revealing dress of scarlet silk – can you imagine me dressed in such finery?' Hazel snorted in derision at the memory. Jane felt herself grow warm and sticky just imagining the Amazon beside her dressed that way, and tried hard to pretend it was just the warmth of the fire.

'And did he notice you?'

'Oh yes, for practically the first time. I laughed at all his jokes and drank all the glasses of punch he plied me with, while Elaine glowered at me from behind her ostrich fan. I must have appeared attractive to him because he so easily fell for my clumsy flirting. But that's the nature of men, isn't it?' Hazel grinned derisively. 'He carried me off to a quiet room and began to kiss me. I thought about his lips kissing Elaine, and wondered whether his hands had touched her body in the same way they now touched mine. It helped me to yield to his caresses more easily.' Hazel rubbed her hand across the back of her neck to ease its stiffness. 'It seems so strange to recall it now, as though it were a bad dream. When Elaine discovered us she found us in a state of undress. She had come to fetch us for some party game, and found us indulging in one of our own.'

'What did she do?' Jane asked eagerly.

'She told Ashby to leave the room immediately. This he did

with as much grace as he could muster. I think he was glad to get off so lightly.'

'And what did she do to you?'

'She went absolutely wild. She pounded me with her fists and called me a whore, a golddigger. She asked me how I could betray her like that.' Hazel closed her eyes, back in the moment. 'I felt her hands rail against my breasts, and even in anger their touch was so much more arousing than Lord Ashby's had been. I lost my composure, grabbed her and kissed her. Told her that I loved her. That I could not bear to lose her, that I would do anything to keep her. Even share her with a husband if needs be. Imagine my delight when she kissed me back! She admitted that while she had been in London she had missed me more desperately than I had ever realised. That she had tried hard to hide it, thinking I did not return her love in that way.' Hazel gave a small shrug at the happy memory.

'From that moment on we were inseparable once more, and this time shared our passion with our bodies. We used to sneak into each other's beds, ride up here on summer afternoons to lie in the shadow of the standing stone.' Hazel stopped short, emotion making her voice unsteady. She threw another log on to the fire before she continued. 'Elaine delayed her wedding again and again. Lord Ashby was puzzled and frustrated when I refused his further advances, suddenly virtuous once more. Then one day old Melmouth found us together, kissing and caressing in Elaine's apartments, when he returned unexpectedly from London. As you can imagine, he was not as forgiving as Elaine had been with Ashby on Twelfth Night. Melmouth senior was not by nature forgiving to anyone but himself. That old reprobate was incensed that such perversion could be carried out by his own daughter and fosterling under his own roof.

'He promptly threw me out of the house without a penny,' Hazel said simply. 'He kept Elaine locked up so she could not follow. I sheltered here at this cottage, with old Deidre. I tried to get access to Elaine but failed. I waited and waited.

'Finally I managed to see her at the Maiden Falls when she was allowed out on walks by herself again, and the routine at Morlanby had more or less returned to normal. I begged her to come

146

away with me. I told her the usual clichés about how love would find a way, and I would work hard to build a home for us. I urged her to run away with me right then, with only the clothes on her back.

'She refused.' Hazel laughed bitterly. 'And that is all there is of our little love story.' Hazel looked tired at recounting a story only too familiar to herself. 'I went away on my own, earned my fortune, returned older and wiser. Old Deidre had died without an heir, and this place was standing empty, so I bought it. Meanwhile Elaine chose to remain within the luxurious boundaries of Morlanby. Well, one could hardly expect her to do otherwise. Her blue blood is tied to Morlanby more strongly than her heart could ever be bound to mine.' Hazel lapsed into bitter silence. Her bright blue eyes stared broodingly into the fire as she replayed unpleasant memories.

'You do my sister a great disservice,' Sebastian said in a low voice from beneath her pile of bedclothes. Hazel and Jane looked at him, startled that he had been listening.

'What do you mean? I thought my version of events was very fair.'

'But you don't know what happened after you were thrown out. It was a hard struggle for Elaine to be rid of Ashby, to persuade Father to pay him off and avoid a scandal rather than just meekly go through with the marriage. It was a bitter affair, and still rankles with Ashby, I know. But she stood her ground, because she loved you.'

'Then why did she not come away with me?' Hazel rasped harshly. 'Why did she hesitate?'

'Because of me,' Sebastian replied simply. 'She wanted to protect me from my father until he died and I could inherit Morlanby. She knew that he was more temperate when she was around, even if he was angry with her. She had a way with him that I did not. She wanted to ensure that my father did not manage to destroy me. Then when he died finally, she had to try and stop me from destroying myself.'

'And this is how you repay her?' Hazel asked bitterly. 'By attempting to die of cold alone on the mountainside?'

There was a pause.

'You are right. I should prove myself more worthy of her love and loyalty,' Sebastian said bravely.

'I'm sorry, Sebastian, I spoke in haste.' Hazel ran her fingers through her short blonde hair, her face pensive. 'I had thought she stayed out of selfish complacency. I had not even considered that she may have stayed out of loyalty to you.'

'Then consider it now, and act on it. My father is so much to blame for all of this. He twisted everyone and everything around him. If I must change to find happiness, you must change too, Hazel. Give my sister a second chance.'

'And would she give me a second chance?' Hazel asked sarcastically. 'I think not.' But there was the light of hope in her eyes. 'Go back to sleep Sebastian.'

'Will you promise to think on it?'

'Yes. I'll think on it.'

As Sebastian drifted into sleep, Hazel turned to Jane.

'Now you've had your bedtime story, would you like to lie down here in front of the fire and rest? The carpet will protect you from the cold floor, and I'll bring you a blanket.'

'Only if you lie down with me,' Jane challenged. 'You'll need some rest too if you're going to help Sebastian down the mountain in the morning.'

Jane could feel sleep creeping over her, making it hard to focus. She put down the tin cup, now empty, before it fell from her hands.

'Very well,' Hazel replied, 'if it's the only way to get you to rest.'

They lay side by side, spoon-like, beneath the eiderdown which Hazel fetched from her linen chest, along with two spare cushions to act as pillows. Jane took hold of one of Hazel's hands and snuggled close. She could feel Hazel's small, hard breasts against her back, could feel Hazel's lean body and legs pressed against her for warmth.

'Don't writhe about so,' Hazel whispered, 'We'll wake Sebastian.'

Jane mumbled in reply. She longed to test the limits of Hazel's chastity even with Sebastian sleeping so close to them. But she was too tired to take advantage of Hazel's intimacy. Besides, she thought guiltily, Hazel still belonged to Elaine. That much was obvious.

Even so, Jane felt warm and comforted as she fell into sleep and dreamed of the filthy things she wanted to do with Hazel.

FOURTEEN

Early next morning, Elaine was standing in the drawing room and staring anxiously out of the window. She had not slept all night, nor had anyone else at Morlanby. There was still no sign of Sebastian. Elaine felt fear clutch at her heart. She found it impossible to eat anything. She even found it hard to breathe when she wondered about what could have happened to Sebastian. She tried not to think the worst.

She could hear activity in the next room and knew the male guests were having their breakfasts. They ate heartily while they discussed dredging the river, or checking the beach at low tide, for Sebastian's body. Elaine quivered with outrage. She imagined Ashby and Barnes appraising the crockery, dining table and chairs. Calculating how much they would fetch at auction after they had buried 'poor Sebastian' and evicted her from her home.

Was it really over? Had her brother finally given in?

She watched the hoarfrost glisten in the morning sun, spiking the lawn and shrubbery like a frigid bridal veil. She focused on the middle distance, watching the moisture rise like incense where the sun's rays warmed the crystals into vapour. She offered a prayer for Sebastian's safe-keeping.

Gradually she registered that three figures were limping down the avenue towards the castle. They moved slowly but inexorably between the shadows of the oak and chestnut trees.

She threw on her shawl and slipped out through the hallway. She beckoned a groundsman, raking gravel on the drive, and he jogged across to follow her down the avenue towards the figures.

She felt giddy with relief when she recognised Jane and Hazel linking arms with Sebastian, helping him on the final stretch home. Sebastian looked pale and haggard but he was most certainly alive.

'Thank God you are safe,' she exclaimed, putting her arms about him.

'Or the devil,' Sebastian said. 'Don't worry, sister, I'm fine.'

Elaine turned to the groundsman.

'Help Lord Melmouth to the house. Take him to his Tudor apartments, the bedroom is freshly prepared. I'll be there directly.'

'Yes, madam.'

Jane and Hazel were relieved of Sebastian who leaned against the burly groundsman.

Elaine looked from one to the other.

'Thank you,' she said awkwardly.

'It's nothing.' Hazel turned, about to walk home again now she had delivered Jane and Sebastian safely.

'Come up to the house,' Elaine said stiffly. 'At least have some breakfast in the kitchens before you go home.'

Hazel looked as though she was about to refuse. Then her expression relaxed. Her eyes, cornflower blue in the sunlight, smiled even if her lips did not.

'Very well,' Hazel said.

The three of them stole back into the castle, following the groundsman and Sebastian. Somehow they managed to settle Sebastian into the Tudor bedroom, situated higher in the turret than his usual rooms but still close to Elaine and Jane's bedrooms.

'Hazel, I need your herb tea again,' Sebastian mumbled with a wry smile.

'I'll leave some for you. Try to rest,' Hazel replied.

Don't mention anything about this,' Elaine told the groundsman. 'Just return to your work as though nothing has happened.'

'Yes, madam.'

When he had gone, she turned to Jane.

'Go down to the kitchen with Hazel,' she said. 'Have some

breakfast too. Tell Megan to come up here with some of Sebastian's personal effects from his rooms lower down. Ask her to do this without arousing too much attention.'

'How long do you think you will manage to keep him secretly here, safely away from Ashby and the others?' Jane asked, guessing Elaine's plan.

Elaine shrugged. 'Long enough to let him have a decent rest at least. They have hardly left him alone since they arrived here.'

Jane nodded in understanding.

Once alone with Sebastian, Elaine sat beside his bed and stroked his forehead. It felt hot and clammy with fever. She sighed. Sebastian may be alive but he was not yet out of danger. She would have to swallow her pride and deal with this.

'Ah, Sebastian. If only you did not take everything so seriously,' she murmured.

But Sebastian already slept. His breath rattled shallowly in the quiet room.

When Megan arrived with some fresh night clothes, toiletries and a pitcher of water, Elaine had reached a decision.

'Is Hazel still here?' she asked the girl.

'Yes, madam.'

'Ask her to prepare some tisanes and poultices for fever. She can use any herbs she can find in our kitchen or gardens. Tell her . . . ask her if she is willing to help nurse Sebastian through this. Tell her that I would welcome her help.' Elaine twisted her hands, trying to formulate her message.

Megan's eyes were the colour of slate as she glanced at Elaine and Sebastian.

'I'm sure she will agree, madam,' the maid replied.

'Sister,' Sebastian called, struggling to sit up. 'Fetch Dominic here too. I want to tell you about India and he would help me.'

'Sh.' Elaine held a glass of cool water to his lips as Megan propped him up and he drank thirstily. 'What about India?' Elaine asked. 'Is this bout of illness something you caught out there, is that it?'

'You could say that.' Sebastian laughed weakly, and then coughed until Megan helped him to lie down again. 'I'm walking on the edge of the crater and may fall into the volcano at any moment.'

'Not if I can help it, Sebastian,' Elaine said firmly. 'Don't be so melodramatic. Now rest. I'll fetch Dominic when I am sure you are fit enough.'

She folded her arms and sat beside him as he drifted back to sleep. Then she turned to Megan.

'Ask Jane to come up here also, after she has rested a little,' she whispered. 'She may help soothe him when he comes round.'

Megan frowned. 'Haven't you heard? The Mother Superior of her old convent arrived this morning. She has taken Jane back to the convent.'

Elaine swore softly.

'By whose order?'

'By Lord Ashby's, I think. He said Jane was upsetting Lord Melmouth too much.'

Jane was in a daze all the long carriage-ride back to the convent. She could tell from the faint smile that played about Mother Superior's lips that the older woman was glad to have her back. The sharp black eyes, the arched brows and cruel lips were as familiar to Jane as her own face. She dreaded yet welcomed the evidence that Mother Superior was pondering on how best to punish her faithlessness.

As always, Mother Superior was dressed in a wimple of pure white which contrasted with the long habit and veil which were both black as a raven's wing. Rosary beads and a bunch of keys hung loosely at her hips. She wore a simple wooden crucifix.

Jane, in contrast, felt wanton and sluttish. Her short auburn hair curled provocatively, its copper richness glowing in the winter sunlight. Her dress of dove-grey silk rustled about her and her corset pinched in her waist seductively. These were the clean clothes she had indulged in on her return to Morlanby before going down to the breakfast room. There she had been taken ambush by Lord Ashby and Mother Superior. It seemed they had been waiting for her expectantly. Together they had bundled her into the waiting carriage.

Jane looked out at the passing scenery and wondered if Elaine would realise she was gone, would send anyone to fetch her. She doubted it. Elaine had her hands full with Sebastian. Jane shivered with dread, and a certain quiet thrill, at what she may have to endure at the hands of Reverend Mother.

'It seems your betters were not well pleased with you, Jane,' Mother Superior said at length, looking at her disapprovingly. 'They are concerned that you may have stooped to witchery, or at least common parlour tricks, to remain in good favour with Lady Melmouth. They have asked me to do all that I can to save your immortal soul before it is too late.'

'I only did what I could to help Lord and Lady Melmouth, Reverend Mother. I only did what my conscience dictated.'

Mother Superior arched an eyebrow in disbelief.

'That statement may cover a multitude of sins,' Mother Superior replied. 'I must examine, judge, and punish accordingly. I suggest you spend the rest of your journey contemplating the venial and mortal sins you may have committed while out of my special care, Jane. Much may depend upon your honest repentance.'

'Yes, Reverend Mother,' Jane replied meekly.

They stopped only once on the journey, to lunch at a coaching inn while the horses were changed, and reached the Gothic steeples of the convent as twilight fell. Jane felt a frisson of fear and excitement as the heavy iron gates clanged shut behind them.

It felt strange to return to the convent. Yet Jane felt happy to breathe in the scent of beeswax, feel the smooth parquet floor beneath her boots. She loved the simplicity of the whitewashed walls, the icons of saints and portraits of former Mother Superiors that hung in the quiet corridors.

A few sisters hurried past, summoned to vespers by the sonorous toll of the chapel bell which marked the hours of their ordered life. They glanced up at Jane with frank curiosity then passed by in silence with downcast eyes.

'Go to your old cell, Jane,' Mother Superior ordered. 'Change out of your harlot's clothing into your simple habit, then come to find me in my office.'

'Yes, Reverend Mother.'

As Jane looked about her bare cell once more she felt a certain warmth of nostalgia. She almost looked forward to sleeping once more in the narrow bed, chanting prayers for hours on her knees, until nothing else mattered. Flailing herself with the cat-o'-nine-tails that hung upon the wall. If this was to be her fate, she had better get used to it.

But before she could return to her old life, she must face the ordeal of rehabilitation. What had Reverend Mother called it? The act of obeisance.

As she hurried back to Reverend Mother's office she tried to rehearse her answers to the inevitable questions. Her careful sentences evaporated on her lips, however, as she faced Reverend Mother.

'Much better. Much more spiritual,' Reverend Mother said approvingly. The rough woollen habit scratched at Jane's skin yet clung to her slender frame enticingly. She was naked underneath.

'Kneel down, Jane,' Mother Superior said, still looking over some documents at her desk. 'I am waiting for you to recount your list of sins while you have been away from our good influence.'

Jane closed her eyes, swaying slightly on her knees. The floor was reassuringly hard. Her throat felt very dry.

'I broke fast before mass and I had carnal knowledge of another woman, Reverend Mother,' she began in a low voice, looking down at the floor. She did not dare look at Mother Superior's face.

'How many other women did you know carnally?' the older woman asked. 'You forget how well I know you, Jane. Do not lie.'

Jane heard Mother Superior's skirts rustle as she moved to stand opposite her.

'Tell me, Sister Jane.'

'Three other women, Reverend Mother,' she murmured at last.

'This is most serious,' Mother Superior said. 'You have yielded completely to the appetites of your flesh.' Mother Superior leaned close to her. 'No wonder you have communicated with demons and spirits. We shall have to work hard and turn you from this path to destruction.'

'Yes, Reverend Mother.'

Mother Superior went to the tall mahogany cupboard that stood in the corner of her office. She used one of the many keys dangling at her hip to unlock it.

Jane gave a shiver of shameful joy when she saw Mother Superior pick out the instruments of humiliation. A pair of iron shackles, separated by an iron bar, with manacle chains attached. Only once before had she seen these used on a nun at the convent. She submitted with beatific calm as Mother Superior fastened these to her wrists and ankles. Now her ankles were braced apart by a bar of iron, and her wrist chains jangled as she hobbled in her restraints. She hung her head low in bashful shame.

'You must learn to deny your appetites, Jane, unless you are directed to release them by your betters. All flesh turns to dust, and your soul is in mortal danger. I am going to use the instrument to detect the witch's mark once more.' Mother Superior picked up a vial of water and flicked it over Jane's face.

'Does that burn?' she asked.

'No, Reverend Mother,' Jane replied.

'Good, then there is still time to preserve you from the devils that have tempted you. Prostrate yourself.'

Jane lay face down upon the parquet floor, her chains hampering her movements and digging into her flesh where she lay upon them.

'Lick the dust from my boots, Jane. Taste it, so you may understand where all flesh must end.'

Mother Superior thrust her dusty boot in front of Jane's face. Jane crawled forward a little to reach it. Slowly, tentatively, she licked. The dust was dry and stale. The leather of the boots gleamed in stripes where her tongue passed.

She felt the familiar surrender, slow and soft as honey, as she performed this act of obeisance.

'That will do,' Mother Superior said at length. 'Now you must submit to the test for the witch's mark. Strip.'

Jane felt once more the wicked iron pricks from the ancient instrument which Mother Superior stroked and pressed systematically over her body. She longed to arch her body and press harder against its sharp caress, but knew she must lay absolutely still and submit to the will of Mother Superior. Every time Jane moved even slightly, Mother Superior slapped her in punishment. Jane submitted lying face down, then turned over to allow Mother Superior to torture her breasts. She longed for Mother Superior to test her secret places, waited patiently to be assaulted there. But Mother Superior knew what she wanted and denied her until the very last moment.

This time she was cruel with her iron dildo, and Jane could not quite reach orgasm on its hard shaft. Jane panted, silent, her legs braced apart, and felt dismay as Mother Superior withdrew from her.

'It seems you still have no witch's mark,' Mother Superior said at length. 'But you are still very much the whore, with no control over your sinful body. Stand up, whore. Put your habit back on but pull up your skirt so I may still see your shameful nakedness. The way your sex parts are swollen is most unseemly, and needs to be punished.'

Jane obeyed, stumbling a little in her shackles. She dressed and bent to take hold of the habit's hem. She dragged it up until her breasts and body were once more exposed to the chill air and Mother Superior's avaricious eyes.

Mother Superior carefully traced a finger over the swell of Jane's swollen breasts, the 'S' of her belly, and dipped into the sweetness between Jane's legs. Jane felt wonderful to feel thus reclaimed even though she trembled with unsatisfied desire.

'I see you are shaven now,' Mother Superior said disapprovingly. 'Another reason to punish you.'

Mother Superior went over to the mahogany cupboard once more. She returned with a series of three iron clips, linked together by a fine chain.

'These shall remind you to sublime of the temptation of the flesh into higher thoughts, even as you suffer the punishment it brings.'

Jane felt a soft yet harsh sting, then a crazy spasm of desire, as Mother Superior attached one of the clamps to the folds of pink flesh around her clitoris. The searing sensation was repeated when Mother Superior attached the other two clips to her nipples. Jane's nipples swelled even more beneath their pressure, and throbbed as the blood pulsing through them was restricted by the iron clamps.

Mother Superior gave a little wrench to the chain that connected the clamps. The simultaneous tug at nipples and clit made Jane moan with pleasure.

'Now, slut, down on all fours again in the dust, where you belong. We are going to rejoin the sisters for your full ritual of humiliation and obeisance. You must renounce your sins and beg forgiveness if you wish to remain with us. I need not remind you that your only alternative is the workhouse.'

'Yes, Reverend Mother.'

Jane felt panic mingle with excitement as she crawled after Mother Superior in her bonds of humiliation. The chains that linked Jane's wrists and ankles dragged along the floor behind her, and it was difficult to keep her balance and she moved slowly after Mother Superior. With every shuffle forward her smaller chains tugged at her erotic places with a vicious heat which felt delicious.

Jane had thought all her acts of contrition would be made in private to Mother Superior alone. Now she knew the whole convent would witness her shame, and anticipation sent a wave of lust through her body.

'You must understand, Jane, that I do this for you, so you may live at one with us once more.'

'Yes, Reverend Mother,' Jane replied humbly, as she shuffled past the stone carvings of saints and angels that lined the corridors.

Soon they reached the refectory, where the sisters had gone to eat after mass. One of the sisters read a passage from the lives of the saints as the others ate their broth and bread rolls at long tables and benches either side of the bare whitewashed room. A crucifix hung above the table where Mother Superior ate, but the only other ornaments were candles in large brass candlesticks that softly illuminated the meal.

Mother Superior led Jane crawling to the head of the long benches. She raised her hand to halt the reader and soon the only sound was the jangle of chains which marked Jane's passage. Few even dared to glance up as Mother Superior and Jane passed. When Mother Superior reached the main table at the head of the room, she rang a brass bell to gain the attention of the sisters, who all obediently looked up towards them.

Jane knelt beside Mother Superior, covered in dust and chained like the true penitent.

'Sisters,' Mother Superior's voice rang out clearly, 'we have here a wretch who fled the confines of our blessed convent for the entrapments of the material world, and now petitions us to return. I ask your help in chastening her lustful body, upbraiding her arrogant mind and bringing her back to rightful humility so she may experience our particular peace once more.'

A murmur of excitement ran round the room, the faces of the sisters curious in the candlelight.

'Will you help your fallen sister?'

'Yes, Reverend Mother.' The response came back like a response at mass. Jane felt she was the centre of a strange ceremony and was uncertain what would be expected of her. She remembered some of what had happened to the last nun who had worn these chains, and the memory made her shiver. Now she was to discover the full ritual of abasement and humiliation Mother Superior had planned as her homecoming.

Mother Superior took out a pair of silver scissors. She roughly pulled off Jane's veil and wimple. She took hold of Jane's bent head and hacked at the small curls, until they fell like copper wires in a pile about Jane's kneeling form.

'Thus must all vanity pass away,' Reverend Mother said with satisfaction, rubbing her fingers along Jane's stubby scalp.

Then Reverend Mother took her scissors and hacked at Jane's habit, tore it away until Jane knelt completely naked.

There was a mutter of horror from the assembled nuns. The sisters kept themselves covered at all times. And now, before them, knelt a shorn and naked sister who had so recently shared the rituals of their daily lives. Not only that, but she was shackled in the restraints of humiliation. And as for the obscene little clamps that made her nipples stick out hard and red, and puckered the flesh that peeped out from her shaven loins . . .

Jane started to blush as she imagined the whispered comments pass between the nuns. Her skin itself felt translucent to their gaze. Some wore looks of contempt, some of disgust, and some crossed themselves for protection from the harlotry of naked flesh. Others held a glitter of curiosity in their eyes as they took in Jane's kneeling form. Some looked as though they wanted to reach out and touch her pale and martyred flesh.

Jane felt her skin tingle as she silently bore the stares and whispered insults.

'Sisters, this poor girl has fallen prey to the snares of her flesh. She has tasted the pleasures of the world and forgotten the path to heaven. We all know the stories of the blessed saints who avoided the terrible temptations offered by their own beauty and weak bodies. For example, St Brigid implored God to make her ugly, so she could better serve him. Now I must ask you to help in the subjugation and scourging of this poor lost woman so that she may return to us once more. Will you help?'

'Yes, Reverend Mother.' The response was eager. The sisters waited to hear what they must do.

'Firstly, each of you must pass by and spit upon the naked form of this poor wretch, so she may lose all pride in her young harlot's body.'

'Yes, Reverend Mother.'

The sisters formed a disciplined line. Each came forward one at a time to spit upon Jane. Each gazed upon Jane's naked body.

Jane closed her eyes as the first gob of saliva made contact with her face. The next landed upon her naked breast. Soon she was glistening with the saliva of the nuns, and she felt wet between her legs as she knelt and bore the ritual of humiliation. She lowered her head, feigning shame before her sisters, while she admired the gobbets of spit clinging to the marble skin, dripping from the clamped stalks of her nipples, that still throbbed beneath the pressure of the clamps.

'Now, Sisters. Listen to this abject wretch as she petitions your forgiveness.' Mother Superior could hardly suppress the tremor in her voice as she held up the Bible in front of Jane and made her repeat the stanzas.

'I thank my sisters for their righteous condemnation. I humbly beseech that they punish my frail flesh so I may offer up my pain for the sake of my soul, and those souls still in purgatory. I solemnly swear that I have no truck with the black arts.'

A murmur of consternation ran round the room at this sentence. Jane swallowed. She did not believe she had indulged in the black arts. She had merely followed her instincts. She felt certain that Reverend Mother had included this in case she required any future rituals to be performed upon Jane. Jane repeated the sentences in a clear voice.

'I humbly ask to be accepted among you once more, and throw myself upon your mercy,' Jane said at last.

'Stand up, Jane.'

As Jane slowly hauled herself upright she looked up at the crucifix hanging above her.

Mother Superior followed her glance.

'Pray for forgiveness, Jane, while you submit to the next ritual of obeisance. You are going to pass down the file of your sisters, and each of them must scourge you as you pass. Remember, you must offer up your pain for the sake of your immortal soul.'

'Yes, Reverend Mother.'

Jane slowly turned round. The nuns were arranged in a long double file. Each nun held a cat-o'-nine-tails.

Jane took a deep breath. Then, shoved forward by Mother Superior, she walked the gauntlet.

Each nun's face leered towards her as she passed, and she felt the sting of each flagellation with a shiver of ecstatic bliss. Some trailed the scourge kindly, seductively, across her buttocks or shoulders. Others lashed hard, with a vicious sting. Some tried to lash her twice or thrice before she managed to shuffle further down the line. The unpredictable pain-pleasure meant that she stumbled and tugged at her nipple and clit clamps provocatively. Once she fell, hampered by her shackles. Mother Superior dragged her up so that she could continue the ritual.

By the end of the cruel procession, Jane's back, buttocks and the backs of her thighs glowed with weals from the chastisement of the sisters. She could feel that the sisters were definitely enthusiastic about their task. The atmosphere was charged, as they wondered what else they would be permitted to do to Jane.

'Thank you, sisters,' Mother Superior said. She guided Jane back up to the head table.

'One final test I would ask you to perform upon this penitent,' she said, even as she bodily picked up Jane and laid her out on the table. 'I would ask you to come and run your hands all over her body, and tantalise her most intimate places. She must resist the weakness of her body and not succumb to any caress, if she hopes to avoid further punishment.'

This request was immediately and eagerly obeyed.

Jane felt drugged into a slow frenzy of lust as she felt hands stroke, pinch and knead her body with lewd intent. She felt wicked fingers tug at her nipple clamps and dabble against her clamped clit hood. She felt fingers insinuate themselves into her slippery cunt and slide between her arse cheeks to invade her tight little arsehole. She gasped and writhed, pinned down by her heavy chains and the nuns that surrounded her. She felt a few furtive tongues lick at her armpits, her belly button, her shaven pussy. Palms glided over the welts left by her scourging, cooling then inflaming her tortured skin in turn. Jane was flooded with sensation. Pain and pleasure mingled into a heady mixture, and the feelings of shame and horny abandonment were excruciating and exhilarating in alternating intensity. She dimly remembered that Mother Superior had ordered her to resist the rising orgasm which flickered within her. With a supreme act of will she lay supine and submissive, silently ordering her body to resist the onslaught of the sisters. Their dark woollen habits ground against her bare skin as they worked their will upon her, and their eyes glittered in satisfaction at their handiwork.

She wondered when Mother Superior would order them to stop.

The rapacious hands, tongues, fingers continued to possess her, tossing her to one side and then the other. One pair of hands massaged her neck and shoulders, one stroked her instep and calves. One soft mouth sucked at her toes, another at her fingers. She surrendered to the tug of lips and teeth on her ear lobes, on her clamped nipples. Then a hot, strident little tongue slid deep into her sex.

She tried with all her might to remain mute while she grew hot beneath that obscene tongue. But then she felt her juices lapped by one, then another, of the nuns who knelt in turn between her splayed legs. The iron bar rendered her helpless to resist, her sex was offered up to them like a ripe fruit to savour. She felt a tongue weave about the clamp around her clit, teasing her to swell even more against the constriction of the metal and her pelvis curled against the sharp ache and longing it caused. Then she gave a heartfelt cry of passion as she felt the smooth brass bobbles of a brass candlestick slide inside her, fucking her, suddenly fulfilling her in the way Mother Superior had refused to do earlier.

To Jane, it seemed like her orgasm was an out-of-body experience. She imagined herself high above the ground, looking down at her naked body, chained and clamped and caressed by a dozen lustful nuns while Mother Superior fucked her with the candlestick. She squirmed, reached out to the tender mouths and tongues that surrounded her, undulated to the pressure of their strokes. She felt her clit stir and flicker and send a white-hot signal though her belly and breasts to her brain until she exploded into the full hip-rocking shudder of orgasm.

It was some minutes before she felt sentient again. Even so she felt another, deeper orgasm begin to build up inside her. The nuns continued to caress her, could not leave her alone. They had to continue the ritual to see just how far a woman's body, overwhelmed and tortured with passion, would go, just how far Jane could lose herself in lust. Jane felt arms and hands picking her up, turning her over. She groaned and squirmed as she felt her nipples and clit slide against the polished wood of the table. Then she gave a little cry as she felt the thick candlestick leave her pussy. Next she felt someone part her arse cheeks, spit on her arse-hole, and slyly circle the candlestick in a little at a time. Meanwhile, fingers filled her pussy, and breasts pressed against her back, and fingers invaded her mouth, so that she could suck and whimper against them as another wave of orgasm stole across her martyred body.

Finally the fit of sex fever subsided, and the cruel caressing hands gradually left her alone. She lay exhausted and replete. Her arse still gripped the candlestick and occasionally spasmed against it until even that was gently removed. Jane was thoroughly spent, and felt cleansed by the perverse satisfaction that she had been treated as a vessel of lust by so many of her sisters.

Jane heard the sisters file out, and Mother Superior straddled her shoulders.

'Now you must partake of my goodness in atonement, Jane,' Mother Superior whispered.

Jane felt a renewed wave of bliss as Mother Superior's pussy lowered itself on to her face. She drank thirstily at the copious juices of the older woman. She lapped and wiggled and still could not keep up with the stream of juices that flowed over her lips and chin. Mother Superior tasted like a ripe pomegranate she had sampled while at the Ritz with Elaine. Soon the older woman bucked and writhed into her own orgasm, while Jane twisted against her bonds in sated bliss.

Only then did Mother Superior use the brass key hanging at her hip to undo Jane's shackles. She rearranged Jane's wimple and veil, and pulled a fresh habit over her naked form.

'Go to your cell now, Jane, and pray. You must continue to wear the clamps until I visit you at lights out, is that clear?'

'Yes, Reverend Mother.'

'For the next three days you will pray alone, until you are sufficiently prepared to take confession and return to mass. At each call to vespers, you must stand outside the chapel completely naked before your sisters. The first nun to claim you on the way out, you must accompany to their cell and perform every task of abegnation and abasement that they order you to do until Prime. Do you understand?'

'Yes, Reverend Mother.' Jane could not suppress a sigh at the shameful, wonderful possibilities this could offer.

'Now go, you little slut, and pray for your soul.'

As Jane hurried through the silent corridors, the clamps still throbbing against her nipples and clitoris, her hands folded piously in the sleeves of her habit, she could not help wondering what was to happen next, whether she would survive this sensual torture of rehabilitation, the full ritual of obeisance, and finally rejoin the convent. Or whether Elaine would remember to come and rescue her, keep her promise.

She wondered what was happening at Morlanby.

★

164

SHEELA-NA-GIG

Elaine had kept vigil with Sebastian for three nights. Hazel had prepared herbal infusions of vervain and camomile and countless others to soothe Sebastian through his fever. Elaine was thankful for the other woman's calm strength, as she guarded the sick room from the intrusions of Ashby and Barnes. Even Dr Shetland was only admitted once a day, to give Sebastian his suggested remedies. Usually this was a grain or two of opium, which Hazel would throw away as soon as the doctor departed.

'Sebastian needs that like a bullet in his foot,' Hazel would mutter, and administer a tisane or a tonic instead.

On the third evening, just before lights were lit, Elaine went to fetch some fresh herbs and paused on the landing window to look out at her favourite view across the wooded valley. She sighed at the familiar contours of the land she loved, wondering how long she would be able to enjoy it. Hazel passed by silently, unwilling to disturb her reverie.

Elaine drew on her courage.

'Hazel,' she said, 'we must talk.'

'Yes.' Hazel paused to look out of the window, watching the strips of salmon pink sunset fade from the sky. 'But not now.'

Elaine nodded awkwardly. 'Later then, when Sebastian is over the worst.'

'The fever should break tonight,' Hazel promised.

'I hope so.' Elaine felt at the end of her tether. The shapeless anxiety had given her a drawn look. She felt hounded by the circling gentlemen who waited below for news of Sebastian's progress. She had willed Sebastian to rally with all her might.

'Something rides his dreams like a night hag. I wish to God I knew what it was,' Elaine muttered half to herself.

'After tonight he will be calm enough to question about it,' Hazel replied. 'Trust me.'

Elaine looked up at Hazel. She looked into the blue-grey eyes that watched her, at the lights of dark grey and glints of fire that filled the iris.

'I do trust you, Hazel,' she said softly. She felt she could almost weep at the release of admitting it. Impetuously she pulled Hazel towards her. She draped herself about Hazel like the boughs of a

165

willow tree and nuzzled her neck. Hazel paused for a moment before she responded to the embrace.

'You're so tired. Why don't you rest? I'll watch Sebastian,' Hazel murmured against Elaine's hair.

'No, I must stay with him.'

'Then let's go back.'

Elaine realised that Hazel was gently reminding her of how vulnerable they were, embracing on the landing where they could be discovered any moment. She pulled away with a sigh and nodded.

Megan was at Sebastian's bedside. She beamed at them.

'He is sleeping peacefully at last. Feel his forehead, he is quite cool. And his pulse is normal. He has been thus for the last ten minutes.'

'Thank the Gods!' Elaine sank into the chair beside her, checking Sebastian's pulse. Then she seemed to revive, energised with new plans.

Sebastian was safe. Now to keep him that way.

'Megan, go and fetch Jane back. Bully or bribe the Mother Superior, do whatever it takes to bring Jane back with you. Sebastian will sleep round the clock. But when he wakes up I want Jane here, to help get to the bottom of what is bothering him for good.'

Megan's expression lit up.

'Yes, madam, I'll fetch her straight away.'

Hazel turned to Elaine as Megan hurried out.

'Do you think it was wise to send the girl on such an errand?'

Elaine nodded, rubbed her forehead.

'If anyone can extricate Jane from that convent, Megan can.'

FIFTEEN

It was dark and raining hard by the time Megan arrived at the convent.

She ran to the front door and rang the bell again and again, signalling the coachman to stand ready to gallop off as soon as she returned. The coachman nodded grimly, his oilskin slick and black about him as he huddled against the wind.

Megan muttered an oath in impatience and rang once more. She could see the hallway, still and candlelit, through the glass panel of the front door, but no sign of anyone.

Unable to wait any longer, Megan walked the perimeters until she found another door. When she tested it and it opened, she did not hesitate to step inside.

She was in a dark office of some kind. She bumped against the desk and felt about for a candle. She took a box of lucifers out of her pocket, tried three before she found a match dry enough to strike and light the candle.

She crept out of the office into the silent corridor. She paused, debating which way to go. Should she find the cells, talk to one of the sisters who could tell her where Jane was and simply take her away as quietly as possible? Or should she beard Mother Superior in her den, make a formal request?

Megan opted for the first plan. After brief hesitation she chose the right-hand corridor and hurried as quickly as she could without guttering her candle.

Soon she was back in the empty hallway. She pulled the bolt on the front door, opened it to signal to the coachman she would not be much longer.

She could hear the distant toll of the chapel bell and decided to follow it.

'Can I help you, young lady?'

Megan leaped in her skin at the loud question and looked about. No one was in the corridor. But one of the doors she had walked past, she now noticed, had opened and a slab of light illuminated the corridor.

She retraced her steps to find the Mother Superior sitting in her study. Megan's heart sank.

'Yes you can,' Megan replied, entering the room and shutting the door. 'I am here to fetch Jane – I mean Miss Claremont – back to Morlanby urgently. Lady Melmouth needs her.'

'I see.' Mother Superior did not seem concerned. Her dark eyes assessed Megan's dress, her anxiety, as though measuring how rude she could be to the girl. 'But I'm afraid Miss Claremont must remain with us. She has renounced the error of her ways. She regrets leaving the shelter of the sisterhood, and nothing now would induce her to leave again.'

'Perhaps I could talk with her myself, to check that this is the case.'

'You do not believe me?' Mother Superior braced her shoulders in outrage.

'With all due respect, my employer may not believe *me*, madam.' Megan replied quickly. 'She will punish me if I return empty-handed and she will most certainly dismiss me if I do not plead with Miss Claremont myself, explain why it is so imperative that she returns.' Megan drew herself up to face Mother Superior. Impatience had made her bold. 'My errand is a most urgent one, madam. Did you not hear me at the front door? Why didn't you answer?'

'The sisterhood is in a special week of retreat. We are not communicating with the outside world.' Mother Superior smiled, as though explaining matters to a simpleton. 'It is a week of quiet reflection and contemplation away from the distractions of the outside world. A way of welcoming our lost sheep back to the fold. Why, I am making an exception to our rules by even talking to you now.'

'I'm glad that you are,' Megan said gratefully. She decided to try a different tack. 'I have much respect for your customs . . . Reverend Mother, isn't it?'

'That's right, my child.'

'In fact I was considering conversion to your sect now that I am working at Morlanby.' Megan smiled and let the hood of her cloak down to allow Mother Superior see her face. She tried to feign guileless innocence, hoping the effect worked.

'That is to be commended, my child,' Mother Superior replied silkily. 'It means you will understand and respect our ways. It means you will obey me when I tell you to leave us in peace. Is that correct?'

Megan bit her lip, annoyed. 'How much did Lord Ashby donate to the cause so that you would fetch Jane back here? Or did he threaten to close down the sect, is that it? Whatever he did, you can be sure of renewed protection from Lord Melmouth now he is recovered from his recent illness once more.'

'But he is destined for the sanatorium, my dear. Lord Ashby will be the new owner of Morlanby,' Mother Superior replied matter-of-factly.

Megan felt a hot rush of anger at this new evidence of Ashby's treachery.

'No. That will not happen. Lord Ashby is in error. I left Lord Melmouth sleeping peacefully. He is on the mend and Miss Claremont's presence is important for his convalescence. That is why I must bring her back to Morlanby.'

'She is a sweet girl with a healing gift, it is true. But her place is here.'

Megan gazed down at the Mother Superior, who beamed back at her in a kind yet patronising manner. There was steel in those black eyes and something else. The hint of sexual challenge?

Megan took a breath. She guessed from her experience of Jane's preparations for the seance that Mother Superior enjoyed inflicting pain, and ensured those on the receiving end invariably enjoyed it too. Megan wondered what Jane had already been subjected to. She also wondered what Mother Superior was thinking now, head cocked to one side, examining Megan so closely.

'You are Lady Melmouth's personal maid?' she asked.

'Yes, madam, set with specific instructions to bring Miss Claremont back . . . no matter what the cost.'

As soon as Megan muttered those words she knew that she was lost. She could tell from the way Mother Superior's tongue tip darted across cruel lips there would be only one way of bargaining with Mother Superior for Jane's freedom.

Did she dare use that one advantage and suffer the consequences?

She thought of Jane and grew giddy with need. She had missed Jane so desperately these last few days, even though the busy duties of the sick room had distracted her. She would do anything to get her back. The truth was she was glad that Elaine had furnished her with an irrefutable reason to come here and extricate Jane from Mother Superior's clutches once more. And she would try anything to come away successful in her errand.

Megan wrung her hands, looking down at the floor in a submissive fashion. She let her breasts heave prettily to complete the effect.

'I would be so grateful if you could help me keep favour with my lady. I am sure that Miss Claremont would wish to remain a lay sister of your order and visit often to remain under your spiritual instruction.'

Mother Superior tapped her fountain pen against her desk blotter as though considering the proposition.

'That would be compulsory, as a minimum observance of her vows to the sisters. And what of yourself?' Mother Superior continued sweetly. 'Would you consider submitting to my personal instruction and also joining our sect as lay sister?'

'Oh yes,' Megan said eagerly, 'I would be happy to accompany Miss Claremont here on a feast day each half year for particular observances under your supervision.'

'I would have to insist that you visit every quarter year,' Mother Superior said slowly, 'for the good of both your souls.'

'As you see fit,' Megan said meekly.

Mother Superior stood up and walked over to Megan. Megan gave a little gasp of surprise as Mother Superior grabbed her wrists and pulled her close. She felt the full breasts and hips of the older woman press against her through the dark habit. Megan closed her eyes demurely as Mother Superior bent to kiss her slowly and possessively. Sampling the taste of her. Testing her mettle.

'Would you really be willing to go through such rigorous instruction for Jane's sake?' Mother Superior asked. 'What inspiring devotion.'

'Please,' Megan begged, 'I don't have much time. You have my promise. We both shall return.'

'Very well, my child,' Mother Superior said, even as her hands weighed Megan's breasts and palms grazed at her nipples. 'You are fortunate that I am quite replete after our spiritual retreat, and can defer my first lesson to a later date. Now follow me to your precious Jane.'

Megan gave a shallow sigh of relief as Mother Superior released her.

She followed the flapping skirts of the Mother Superior down many corridors that all looked the same. Megan was glad that she had struck a bargain rather than attempting to kidnap Jane as she would never have found her way. Eventually the panelled corridor gave way to a vestibule, with a high arched roof. A large wooden door opened into what looked like the convent chapel.

Beside the door stood Jane. Her hair was cropped shorter and she was naked. She stood head bowed and penitent, just as Mother Superior had ordered her to do each evensong.

Megan ran to Jane and wrapped her cloak and her arms around her. She kissed the girl tenderly. Jane's eyes held the glitter of one enthralled by the flesh, and her lips responded eagerly. Then she pulled away as if recognising Megan for the first time.

'What are you doing here, my love?' she asked dreamily.

'I am here to fetch you home to Morlanby,' Megan whispered. 'Sebastian is well again and you are sorely needed, Jane.'

Jane smiled as Megan kissed her cheeks and forehead.

'What a relief it is to see you! I have worried about you all while I have been here. I thought you may forget all about me. I am so glad that you came for me. But what about Reverend Mother? Will she let me go?'

'Yes,' Megan whispered, 'she will. Now we must be quick before she changes her mind.'

As Megan bundled Jane into the coach and they drove away, Mother Superior waved from the steps of the convent.

Megan did not tell Jane about the details of their bargain with Mother Superior. That could wait.

Back at Morlanby late the next evening, Jane was put straight to bed with orders to recuperate as she would be needed in Sebastian's room the next morning. But she found it difficult to sleep in her soft bed after the excitement of the last few days. She thought of Megan, and how calmly the maid had fetched her back. She tried to guess where Megan's room was – high in the attic, perhaps. Jane wondered if she could creep out and search for her, and sleep with her in her narrow bed. She longed to hold Megan in her arms, nuzzle against Megan's soft skin, feel those calm deft hands travel over her body. She was still on a high from the sensual depravities she had suffered at the convent. And she still felt the powerful attraction which Elaine had so cleverly planted between her and Megan before she was kidnapped by Mother Superior. Jane longed to share some soothing loving that would calm her down.

Eventually Jane rose and shouldered on her dressing-gown. She decided to sneak down to the kitchen and make herself some hot milk. She knew that she was meant to ring and order a kitchen maid to serve her, but it was two in the morning and she did not want to disturb the servants, who would have to be up early enough.

She took a lit candle and carried it carefully down the stairs, her slippers treading softly to avoid making the wooden floorboards creak. The house seemed calm and peaceful, as though it were waiting or listening for something.

In the kitchen a huge black range filled one wall and flung out heat into the square room. Jane stroked the big wooden table, the counter of pure marble, the cooking implements and huge copper pans that hung on the tiled walls.

She looked about her for the door to the larder, where churns of milk and butter, eggs and cheeses would be stored and kept cool. The first door she tried was the scullery, where the washing-up and dirty work would be done. A few pheasants, rank and high, were hung waiting to be plucked and cooked for dinner the following day. Jane shuddered and shut the door hastily.

Then she heard muted voices from behind a smaller, recessed door.

She hesitated for a moment then tried it. At first she thought the wooden door was locked, but at her next attempt the stiffness of the wood gave way and she opened it to find that she was in the chapel. Obviously another route to sanctuary designed by Sebastian's ancestors.

She was actually inside the confessional box. If she sat on the bench she could pull back the heavy velvet curtain and look through the wooden screen to the chapel itself.

It was Dominic and Sebastian, talking quietly. Jane was pleased to see Sebastian looking so well, dressed warmly in a quilted dressing-gown. Dominic was fully dressed, and had just turned from the altar.

'I am glad the fever has left you,' Dominic murmured. He looked at Sebastian fondly, and walked down to where he sat in the front pew. 'And I'm glad you wanted to come here to pray. But don't you think you should go back to bed now and get some rest?'

'I wanted to see you,' Sebastian replied, 'and I wanted to see the Sheela-na-gig. It was calling to me.'

'That thing?' Dominic looked up towards the carving and frowned. 'You feel its influence even now?'

'It goads me to live the way I must. To live in honesty with a clean conscience,' Sebastian said distractedly.

'As does your church,' Dominic observed.

Sebastian laughed.

'I suppose so. But this is something deeper.' Sebastian took hold of the other man's hand. 'Can you remember how you used to comfort me whenever I was homesick or bullied at school?' Sebastian asked. 'You used to climb into my bed after lights out, and hold me close until my tears dried.'

'Yes, Sebastian,' Dominic said fondly, with a catch in his voice, 'I remember.'

'I used to ache for you then in ways I could not understand. But now I am more used to the ways of the world, and no longer afraid. I love you, Dominic.'

'I love you also, Sebastian.' Dominic hesitated, then put out his other hand to stroke Sebastian's golden tousled hair.

'Not just that kind of love,' Sebastian whispered.

Jane blinked in surprise as she watched Sebastian's hand slowly stretch out and press against Dominic's crotch. She knew she should turn away, leave the two men in privacy before she witnessed anything else. But her limbs were heavy, and would not move. She feared they would discover her if she made the slightest noise.

She remained where she was, pulling her dressing-gown tighter around her, and continued to watch.

Dominic had taken a deep breath at the touch of Sebastian's hand upon him. He looked down, watching as Sebastian stroked the front folds of his dark trousers. He looked racked with guilt and desire. For a few moments Jane was uncertain whether he would back away and flee this temptation entirely. His right hand had pulled away from Sebastian and was clenched in a tight fist, even as his left hand continued to rest on Sebastian's head like a benediction. Then quite suddenly the fist relaxed, and Dominic thrust his pelvis against Sebastian's gentle insistent caress.

'Come closer,' Sebastian murmured. 'Let me see you.'

Jane could see Dominic struggle mightily with his conscience before he took a step closer, then another, until his crotch was level with Sebastian's face. Jane could feel a familiar warmth coursing through her. The power of the Sheela-na-gig. She knew the men would feel its power too.

Sebastian undid Dominic's trousers and let them fall in a dark pool about the priest's ankles. Jane could see that Dominic was already hard with desire. His thick prick sprung proudly away from his loins, eager for more caresses. His balls were covered with rough black hairs. Jane could tell they were tight and hard to an almost painful degree. Jane had never seen male genitals so clearly before, and was filled with voyeuristic excitement.

Slowly, Sebastian's long fingers followed the shaft of Dominic's prick and fondled his taut scrotum. The prick twitched in answer and Dominic groaned.

'Help me, man,' he mumbled.' I'm in hell!'

'I'll soon make it heaven,' Sebastian whispered swiftly.

Sebastian slowly kissed the very tip of Dominic's prick, and then licked it tenderly. 'I've longed to hold you like this, lick you like this, take you in my mouth.'

'Sebastian, don't,' Dominic groaned, in a tone of voice which begged for more tortuous caresses.

Sebastian's smiling lips encircled Dominic's cock and slowly, inch by inch, gobbled him up. Jane watched amazed as Sebastian's lips circled and sucked at the base of Dominic's prick, only to withdraw and suckle its very tip, or encase Dominic's hairy balls, and then repeat the process of swallowing his shaft.

Dominic's face was suffused with passion, and he groaned at the delicious sensations he experienced during Sebastian's lingering blowjob.

'I may come any minute, I can't hold back much longer,' Dominic whispered as Sebastian indulged in more wanton cocksucking, weighing the hairy balls in his fingers.

'Then come in my mouth and I'll drink every drop,' Sebastian murmured thickly as he took the whole length of Dominic's prick in his mouth once more.

Dominic let out a sharp cry and shot his load. His bare buttocks quivered as his face formed the tender grimace of orgasm. Jane could see a white gobbet of come dripping from Sebastian's overfull lips. Then Sebastian swallowed and blissfully licked his lips to collect the excess and savour its flavour.

Jane slipped her hand between her legs so that she could hold herself while she watched. She was strangely moved by the passion shared between the men.

'God forgive my immortal sin,' Dominic muttered, even as he bent to kiss Sebastian's moist lips and taste the issue of his own lust.

'It's no sin, Dominic,' Sebastian said. 'Love as pure as ours has to be blessed. If men such as Ashby and Barnes can primp their way through Sunday Service, then casually slake their gross appetites, why should we be ashamed? We have more genuine love and compassion than either of them.'

'I want to believe you,' Dominic growled, even as he sampled Sebastian's lips more savagely.

'Believe me,' Sebastian breathed. 'I am the Lord of Morlanby and this is my chapel. The Sheela-na-gig will consecrate our love.'

'Sebastian, stand up. I want to possess you as fully as you have possessed me.'

Jane started as a hand touched her shoulder.

'What's going on?' Megan mouthed to her. Jane realised she had left the doorway to the kitchen ajar and now Megan had crept beside her in the confession box.

Jane was shocked to suddenly see the object of her own affections beside her. It was as though the Sheela-na-gig was arranging things, playing cupid this night.

Jane inhaled the clean smell of the girl's skin, and the heavier scent of her hair. Jane swayed and felt the tremor of her body from Megan's nearness. She continued to stroke herself as she bent closer to the girl.

'Watch,' she mouthed, 'and be quiet.'

Megan nodded and peered out from the other corner of the curtain.

Dominic was now kneeling before the young lord. He parted Sebastian's night shirt and revealed Sebastian's hard cock. Sebastian's cock jutted against Dominic's admiring face. Dominic stroked the thick fair curls about the base of his lover's cock, and then his fist circled the shaft tenderly. Sebastian groaned to feel the priest's hand softly wank him. Dominic's lips bent to kiss the tip of Sebastian's prick, and he lapped at the pearl of juice which nestled there.

Sebastian uttered an oath with the ecstasy this caused him. Then Dominic let the whole shaft slide into his wide and tender mouth.

Jane and Megan could hear the hard slurps of his teasing tongue as he let Sebastian rock and fuck him in the mouth. Sebastian gripped the dark head that serviced his crotch with possessive joy. He would pull his prick away to stroke Dominic's cheek with it, teasing the mouth so eager to reclaim him. Then he would ease himself back between Dominic's willing lips and thrust into his throat.

Dominic's fierce sucking and licking soon made Sebastian rigid with pleasure. Dominic's hands reached round to grip Sebastian's bare buttocks, and gathered him closer. Then one hand crept to Sebastian's chest, to stroke and tug upon a hard nipple.

'Shoot your sperm into my mouth, please,' Dominic murmured, looking up at Sebastian with such tenderness even as he suckled the hard cock. Sebastian groaned and came immediately, bare arse quivering with the force of his ejaculation.

Jane could feel Megan's hand still gripping her shoulder with excitement as they watched, could hear her shallow breathing.

Jane watched Dominic and Sebastian embrace and kiss each other. It was as though they had just completed a marriage ceremony.

'Come upstairs, Sebastian,' Dominic murmured, clasping Sebastian's pale body to him. 'I'll put you to bed. You'll catch cold down here.'

'It's strange but it feels as warm as midsummer down here,' Sebastian observed, smiling up at his lover.' But I'll go to bed willingly if you come with me.'

When they had gone, Jane and Megan turned to one another.

'I had never realised,' Megan said in wonder.

'I should have guessed. Sebastian's full recovery has already begun,' Jane said half to herself. 'Why did you come down?'

'Lady Melmouth could not sleep and wanted some warmed milk taken to her.'

Jane smiled. 'I came down on a similar errand for myself.'

'I'll warm some milk for both of you, sweetened with honey and nutmeg.'

Jane followed Megan back to the kitchen and through to the pantry. Jane watched her deft hands skim cream from the top of a milk churn, then ladle out fresh milk into a pitcher and copper saucepan.

'I wanted to ask you,' Jane said shyly. 'What exactly did you do to claim me back from the convent? I find it hard to believe that Reverend Mother let me go so easily.'

Megan glanced at her, slate-grey eyes clouded with emotion.

177

'No, she didn't,' Megan said simply. She turned to carry the copper saucepan to the range but Jane stayed her. Jane placed a slender hand against Megan's chest. She could feel the girl's heart beating through her linen frock.

'What did you promise, Megan? What did you promise to rescue me?' Jane persisted.

Megan trembled as if suddenly chill. She put the saucepan down on the wide marble counter as her hands grew unsteady.

'Are you feeling well?' Jane asked in concern. 'Here.' She took Megan's hands between her own, relishing their coolness.

'Yes, I'm fine,' Megan snapped. 'It's just that I have thought about nothing but you while you were away. I would have done anything to fetch you back! I promised Mother Superior that we would both confess to her regularly if she let you come away with me. Are you satisfied now? I promised this out of love for you, you know.'

'You love me?' Jane repeated stupidly.

'Yes –' Megan bit her lip '– I believe I do. Maybe it was Elaine, or Hazel, or the Sheela-na-gig that hexed us. Maybe watching Dominic and Sebastian has made me foolishly romantic. What do you think?' Megan laughed, mocking her own innocence, half afraid and defiant as she gazed at Jane.

'I think that's beautiful,' Jane said, 'Because I believe that I love you too.'

Megan frowned and then gave a hesitant smile. 'Truly?'

'Truly. All the time I spent at the convent I dreamed of you. I desire you more than anything.' Jane wrapped her arms around Megan's waist and drew her close. Jane felt the magnificent swell of breasts, the rounded belly, press against her. They kissed languorously, glad to taste each other again.

'You know what I would like to do to you?' Jane asked in husky tones. 'I want to lay you on this marble slab, ladle cream over you and lap it all off again.'

Megan purred appreciatively as Jane nibbled her ear lobe. 'Think how beautiful the glossy white cream would look against the peach tones of your skin. And I can't wait to find out what it would taste like.'

'Stop it, you make me long to find out what it would feel like,' Megan replied. 'My sex is already melting at the thought of it.'

'Then sit up on the counter and I'll fetch the cream,' Jane ordered with sudden decision.

When Jane returned, Megan was sitting up on the counter. Her skirt and petticoat had been hoisted high so that her bare arse cheeks were resting against the cold smooth marble countertop. Jane admired the honey skin of Megan's thighs above her stocking tops, her perfect indentation of a navel, and the shaven pussy that lay between them. She let her hand smooth the plane of a hip appreciatively.

'Let me see your breasts,' she said tenderly, her heart thudding.

Megan undid her blouse and hoisted her bosom clear of her chemise. Jane circled the soft skin reverently, looping around Megan's brown nipples. Then she poured a little of the cream over each curve of breast and suckled gently. Megan gave a long soft purr of satisfaction as the velvet cream and Jane's velvet tongue danced whorls and circles across each growing nipple. Jane tasted the richness of the cream mingling with the faint salt of Megan's skin and hungered for more.

She spread Megan's knees so that she could feast upon the girl's shaven pussy. She let a smooth trickle of cream slide into Megan's belly button until it overflowed, trickled over her belly and down between her legs before dripping on to the marble counter. Megan murmured nothings beneath her breath as Jane lapped across the soft down of her belly. Jane had to lap assiduously, like a lascivious cat, to lick her clean. She continued to roll and massage the voluptuous breasts in the meantime.

Blindly, drugged sensuous, Jane followed the trail of thick cream down to the tip of Megan's sex. The pale cream gleamed against the rich coral of Megan's pouting sex lips, mixing with the girl's own honey juices. Jane lapped and lapped, as though she could never be sated of her lover. It was even better than she had imagined it would be. Jane let her tongue dip deep into Megan to sample her secret cornucopia. Jane fancied that she tasted elder flowers, and gooseberries, and cinnamon between Megan's sweet thighs, which now pressed and rubbed gently against her scalp as Megan trembled to her climax. Megan's buttocks clenched then

179

released against the cool marble. Jane guessed that the cold surface contrasted in sensation with Jane's hot and insistent tongue. Jane watched the petals of Megan's labia softly unfold to her strident caresses. She slowly plunged her fingers into Megan's slick canal, felt Megan fit about her like a silken glove, pulsing as Jane pressed her thumb hard against Megan's throbbing clitoris.

At this Megan became frenzied with pleasure, riding Jane's fist in abandonment. She bunched her full breasts together and grazed her fingers over stiff nipples so she could heighten the sensation of the full orgasm.

Jane remained inside Megan, tongue circling her shaven bush, until she felt the girl grow still and softly sigh. Jane withdrew and let her hand, silky with Megan's juices, glide over Megan's warm breasts. She let her palms rub over each plump nipple and Megan arched her back to savour the sensual massage.

'Now, Megan,' Jane whispered, kissing her lips, 'what would you wish to do next?'

Megan smiled. 'I may start by doing exactly the same to you.'

'That would be heavenly. But Lady Melmouth is still waiting for the hot milk,' Jane teased, even as she relaxed beneath Megan's expert kisses.

'Lady Melmouth needs a wild woman in her bed, not a cup of honeyed milk,' Megan replied breathlessly. 'Do you think the two of them will manage to get together?'

'Who?' Jane asked thickly, drugged by Megan's embrace.

'Elaine and Hazel. You can tell they are mad for each other but each is too proud to admit it.'

Jane shrugged, hungry for Megan's lips upon her. 'Who knows? If the Sheela-na-gig can work her magic on Sebastian and Dominic, and bring us together, she may even help Hazel and Elaine.'

SIXTEEN

By eleven the following morning Elaine had summoned Father Dominic, Jane and Hazel for a late breakfast, served by Megan, closeted away in the Tudor parlour. Sebastian still slept soundly in the next room. Ashby, Barnes and Shetland had gone out riding and would not return until lunchtime.

After breakfast was finished, Elaine glanced at Hazel then turned to Father Dominic.

'Thank you for helping us keep watch over Sebastian these last few days,' she said, 'and helping to keep the others at bay.'

Father Dominic set down his teacup and rubbed his eyes. Jane remembered watching him with Sebastian in the chapel, and thought that the priest looked more handsome and relaxed than ever before, even through his fatigue.

'It was nothing. The least I could do.' Dominic replied.

'When Sebastian first slipped into his fever,' Elaine said, 'he tried to tell me something about India. He told me to fetch you, that you would help him to explain, but by then he was too weak.' Elaine glanced at Jane, to check she was listening. 'I feel sure the thing that tortures his conscience happened there. Can you please tell us what you know?'

Dominic's dark eyes grew troubled and he frowned. 'I would rather wait until Sebastian is awake again. He could tell you better himself.'

'Please, Dominic. You know we have little time. Dr Shetland will make a final examination of Sebastian today before signing the commitment papers. Dr Shetland is a man of integrity, but if he suspects for one moment that Sebastian is still a danger to himself or others, he will sign those papers and Ashby will have won. Any information you can provide to help Sebastian prove he is still as sane as ever will be invaluable.'

Dominic hesitated then nodded. 'There are only a few incidents I can relate, I'm afraid. As you know, I went to India as personal confessor to Sebastian when he served for a year in your family's regiment. Ashby and Barnes were also serving a term as commanding officers.'

Elaine nodded.

'Well, they would hardly leave Sebastian alone. Training him hard, drinking him hard, declaring they would make a man of him.' Dominic grimaced. 'It was as if they were taking over where your father had left off. Even so, Sebastian did enjoy most of his time in India, I assure you. He loved the culture, fell in love with the temples, the bright colours, the people.'

'I know he brought back many lovely things from India, but he never talks of his time there.'

'Sometimes, in his spare time, he would wander off alone to the beach or the bazaars to soak in the exotic surroundings. So when he did not return to barracks one night I guessed he had probably taken shelter in a temple, or was sleeping out under the stars, like he often did.' Dominic paused and took another sip of tea. 'But later on that particular night I was roused from my slumber by an infernal racket. By the time I had reached the hallway the night porter had opened the door. It was Sebastian. He seemed in genuine distress. His shirt front was spattered with blood and he exhibited all the symptoms of shock. He asked me to fetch Lord Ashby. He was pale as death and shivering.' Dominic stared into the middle distance as he recalled that night. 'I poured us both a stiff brandy. He gulped his down gratefully, Then he slumped in his chair and little could rouse him.'

'What had happened?' Elaine asked sharply.

'I asked him, but he was so stunned. All he could say was it was too horrible to tell. I told him he was absurd. In my pastoral training I had witnessed terrible things, he could confide anything he wanted in me without risk of shocking my sensibilities. In fact he was required to confess everything as I was his spiritual pastor. But before I could question him further Ashby arrived.'

'Ashby explained they had gone out drinking and Sebastian had decided to come back to barracks alone. He had a look of distaste and annoyance on his face as he noticed the state Sebastian was in. I asked him what could possibly have happened.'

'Did he tell you?' Hazel asked.

'No. He just implied that Sebastian may have disgraced himself on a solitary drinking spree and we had better hide the evidence if we wanted to protect Sebastian from military discipline. He stressed that Sebastian may even be discharged from the regiment in disgrace if anyone else discovered him in his distraught state. Ashby took charge of the situation. He took Sebastian's shirt and burned it. Together we changed him into his night clothes. Ashby lit a candle and propped up Sebastian's little crucifix on his bedside table. Sebastian seemed agitated even so. He let out a moan of such anguish it disturbed me.

'Ashby told him to be still, that he would disturb everyone else. Then Ashby took from his pocket a syringe, and injected Sebastian with it before I had a chance to stop him.'

'Ashby got Sebastian addicted to morphine out there?' Elaine interrupted, her voice shaking with anger. Dominic frowned and nodded.

'He said it was a dose from his own supply to calm Sebastian. But I now suspect otherwise.'

Elaine looked across at Hazel and frowned.

'Go on,' she said curtly.

'Sebastian asked Ashby to swear upon his honour to make amends – for what I do not know – before he slipped into opiate unconsciousness. When I questioned him later, when he had recovered, it was as though he had forgotten the salient facts of the whole episode.'

'Or had just decided to keep it a secret. A secret that has since eaten like a canker inside him,' Elaine observed brusquely.

'I suspect Lord Ashby has not kept his word about making

amends for whatever happened,' Jane observed ironically. 'I agree that this must be the thing which preys on Sebastian's mind.'

'Lord Melmouth is awake, madam,' Megan reported. 'He's just asked me to fetch his morning coffee.'

'Good, thank you.' Elaine turned to the others. 'Time to ask Sebastian precisely what happened.'

'Good morning, my dears,' Sebastian said.

He was sitting up in bed. His eyes were bright and his cheeks a healthy colour. He was sipping a large cup of coffee. He wore a silk night-shirt. He looked like a sultan holding court, propped up on linen pillows.

'Welcome back to the real world, Sebastian,' Dominic said, sitting close to him. The priest's dark eyes danced, but there was no other trace of what the two men had shared that night.

'It's faintly shocking to hear a priest refer to this vale of sorrows as the real world, but I must admit I am glad to be back. Thank you all for nursing me back to health.'

Everyone shifted in their seats, awkward at his sincere gratitude.

'Now the very least I owe you is some sort of explanation for my unbalanced behaviour. That's why you're all here, isn't it?' He looked from Hazel to Elaine, from Megan standing discreet guard by the door, to Jane. They all nodded.

'Well, Dominic must help me confess it, because it is something I am very ashamed of. But thanks to Dominic I feel it may now be in my power to put some of it right. I thought that I was evil and now I realise I need not struggle against my own nature. I have the right and the power to do good.' Sebastian took Dominic's hand and squeezed it gratefully.

'Tell us, Sebastian,' Elaine said urgently, 'before our house-guests return and barge their way in here.'

Sebastian nodded. 'Dominic has told you of the incident while I was in India which started my laudanum addiction?'

'Yes, and that Ashby was involved,' Elaine replied bitterly.

Sebastian looked up at Dominic for moral support.

'I really don't know how to tell you all this. I am so ashamed.'

'Don't worry, Sebastian,' Dominic said, and patted the young man's hand. 'We all love you here. We shall understand, whatever it may be.'

Sebastian drank a little more of his coffee and cleared his throat.

'As you know Ashby and Barnes were always hounding me out in India, making me join them in stupid depravities to prove myself a true member of the regiment. That day we had drunk gin and tonics in the officers' mess for most of the afternoon, and then staggered out into the warm evening to watch the local Diwali festivities. I enjoyed the dancing and fireworks in the milling streets. My companions, however, had other plans.

'They took me to a simple apartment in the back streets and exchanged some words with a local man in a dialect I did not understand. Next I knew I was ushered into a bedroom where a girl sat, nervously waiting on the bed. She was very pretty, dressed in a vermilion sari with bangles and earrings and a thick, long plait snaking down her back.

'I started chatting to her drunkenly, but could not make her understand my English and pigeon Hindustani, though she smiled back shyly. Eventually Ashby, who was drinking with Barnes in the next room, called through that I was not meant to talk to the wench, but to bed her.

'I told him that I would rather not, that I was the worse for drink. But he joked with Barnes and he insisted I had to do it before they would let me out. This was the only way they could test my manhood convincingly and report back to my father, who had his suspicions after . . . well, after Elaine's little faux pas with Hazel, but they did not know the full details of that, of course.'

Elaine and Hazel glanced at each other.

'I understand,' Elaine said.

'I would think most men would have grown soft at such a proposition,' Hazel observed bluntly as she leaned against the mantel, hands in pockets, frowning.

'Yes, and especially one like me.' Sebastian sighed. 'I mean I tried but it just seemed so absurd. I cuddled and kissed the shy nervous thing but I could not raise an ounce of desire. It was like petting a new-born lamb. Besides, I did not even want to dishonour her.'

'So what happened?' Elaine asked.

185

'Well, in the end I communicated with her by sign language something of my predicament. She, too, confided that she had been forced there against her will. Eventually we made noises faking it, trying to suppress our giggles.

'After half an hour I emerged and called for a drink, which Ashby gave me gladly. He patted me on the back and congratulated me on joining the club. Then he said, since I had deflowered her, he and Barnes may as well sample the goods too for the same price.'

Elaine shuddered and glanced over at Hazel.

'I tried to dissuade them,' Sebastian continued, 'told them she was as cold as mutton and should be sent packing. But they ignored me and went into her.' Sebastian looked grim at the memory.

'Sad wretch that I am, I could do little further to prevent them from taking her between them. I sat in the next room drinking brandy, listening to her cries of protest and their casual obscenities as they pawed her. Once I rushed in there and tried to drag them off, but Ashby thumped me, Barnes kicked me away and my nose began to bleed, my head to whirl. I was frightened my interference would cause them to use her more violently, and eventually I backed off. Then they calmed down, told me a red-blooded man would understand what they were about, and if I was bored waiting I could make my own way back to barracks. All I could understand was the look of hurt in the poor girl's eyes. I ran from there, unable to bear it any longer. When I reached the barracks – well, Dominic has told you the rest.'

There was a stunned silence. Each of the women in the room looked at each other with quiet outrage while Dominic smoothed Sebastian's forehead in silent sympathy.

'Oh, Sebastian, how awful,' Elaine said at last.

'Since that night I have felt as though the Sheela-na-gig knew of my cowardice. As I staggered back to barracks through the town, and fireworks exploded overhead, I saw a figure in the shadows, stalking me, reproaching me for running away.' Sebastian's face crumpled. 'That figure has haunted my dreams ever since that night. I was a coward, was I not? A blind and stupid coward who pretended nothing had even happened until last night, when I finally faced the truth.'

'You did all you could in the circumstances, Sebastian. It was those two bastards who violated the poor girl. I wager they have never even given it a second thought,' Elaine said grimly. Hazel paced the hearthrug, nodding in agreement.

'I tried to get them to make amends. But you know that Ashby is stubborn and Barnes – well, he hardly possesses a personality, let alone a conscience. They thought I was mad to harp on it so. They plied me with laudanum to shut me up. When I returned to Morlanby I hoped I could forget the whole ugly incident for good but the nightmares grew worse. The Sheela-na-gig was angry with me for letting it happen while, on the other hand, the ghost of my macho father derided me for letting such a minor deflowering prey on my mind.' Sebastian shook his head. 'I was in a hell of my own making.'

'And how do you feel now you have told us all this?' Jane asked gently.

'Much better. Now I feel sure I can somehow act to make amends. For a start I can find the girl and give her money enough to live independently, or give a dowry if she wants to marry. Such help may not remove the dreadful memory of that night but it will remove the blight it will have placed on her life, give her a chance for future happiness. And I'll help her any other way I can.'

Dominic nodded. 'No doubt she still lives near the barracks. We can go back and track her down together.'

'Then the nightmare will finally come to an end for her also,' Sebastian murmured.

'We're not out of the woods yet, Sebastian,' Elaine observed briskly. 'First you must convince Dr Shetland of your sanity, or you'll be heading for his lunatic asylum, not a return voyage to India.'

'I know. But I feel so much stronger, I'm sure I'll manage it.'

Jane nodded, smiling in encouragement. 'Now you feel that the Sheela-na-gig is your protectress once more.'

'I believe it.' Sebastian grinned faintly and looked around. 'You can all wait downstairs. I'll dress and present myself for Dr Shetland's examination. Then we'll settle this once and for all.'

Two hours later, Dr Shetland and Sebastian emerged from the study. Dr Shetland folded away his stethoscope and placed it in his Gladstone bag along with copious notes on his patient. He then beamed round the uneasy company seated in front of the main parlour's log fire.

'Lord Melmouth, I am pleased to say, is the picture of physical health. There is no congestion in the lungs and he has suffered no long-term ill-effects from his fever.'

'What about his mental state?' Ashby barked. His hands clawed the armchair he was seated in, and he turned to stare at Sebastian as though assessing the health of a hunting hound.

'I am perfectly sane, Ashby, thank you for asking. Miss Branagan has weaned me from the noxious effects of laudanum with her herbal skill and I haven't touched a drink for days. You could say I am the soberest and sanest I have been for three years.'

'Sober doesn't mean sane if you're a madman,' Ashby replied, unimpressed. 'Are you saying you cannot take your drink like a man? What a morbid little fellow you are.'

Sebastian smiled serenely, ignoring the old familiar barbs.

'Yes,' Sebastian continued. 'This is the best I have felt since I witnessed you and Barnes rape that girl in India.'

'What on earth are you saying, man?' Barnes asked from the depths of his armchair. His phlegmatic face was flushed, 'Remember we are in mixed company, besides anything else. You are talking lewd nonsense again.'

'Nonsense? No, I don't think so. And don't worry about the mixed company, my dear fellow. You have never concerned yourself with such social niceties before,' Sebastian replied airily.

'There is no need to be rude, sir.'

'There is every need. This is my home.' Sebastian's voice did not waver, though his eyes danced with the effort of remaining calm. 'Dr Shetland has pronounced me sane and can provide written testimony confirming it. I know what time of day it is and what day of the week it is. I know that swallows fly south for winter and there are no such things as ghosts. I also know that both of you are corrupt and immoral. In fact you are carbon copies of my father and treat me with the same contempt. And do you know what, my dear cousins? I've finally realised that I don't have to tolerate it any longer. I can ask you both to leave right now.' Sebastian paused, took out a cheroot which Dominic hastened to light for him. Sebastian's fingers trembled only slightly. 'In fact I do demand that you pack your bags and leave right now.'

'Now I know you are mad,' Ashby spluttered. 'You can't just throw out your kith and kin. It's natural for Barnes and me to worry about you when you fly off the handle at the least opportunity, like a child in a pet.'

'Interpret it how you please,' Sebastian replied. 'But you must leave.' He waved dismissively. 'I am Lord of Morlanby, you know. And there is now nothing you can do to change that.'

He nodded over to Hazel, who quietly left and returned with her shotgun.

'You would threaten us with violence?' Barnes asked in amazement. 'Is that gentlemanly?'

'If you have any objections you can write to me after you've left. On second thoughts don't bother getting in touch at all. Don't wait to pack your bags. We'll send your things on. The carriage is waiting. Goodbye.'

The two men did not move. Hazel primed her shotgun when Sebastian nodded to her again.

'Sebastian, don't be ridiculous,' Barnes said. 'To let a little regimental prank carry so much weight with you – well, it's unmanly, isn't it, Doctor? Not to mention unbalanced.'

Dr Shetland frowned. 'I'm not sure I understand what is going on here, but I have found Sebastian to be sane and there's the end of it. If he wants us to leave, he has every right. It is quite an ordeal, you know, to be examined for one's sanity. We ought to leave Lord Melmouth in peace to recuperate.'

Elaine's mouth twitched as she tried to suppress her grin. Sebastian had certainly impressed Dr Shetland and won a new ally.

Lord Ashby's face was slowly turning an unhealthy puce colour. He stroked his whiskers and his small blue eyes darted from

Shetland to Sebastian to Hazel, who calmly trained her shotgun upon him.

'You are all unnatural,' he hissed venomously.

'*No*, you are unnatural,' Sebastian replied angrily, 'to harm a woman the way you did, as casually as you did, without a qualm of conscience.'

'But, Sebastian, the girl was nothing. Her own kind may have treated her much worse. Don't you realise it is our birthright? It's what we have done for generations. You deny your own heritage and play a mealy-mouthed sop while enjoying the land which men such as I conquered for you. You don't deserve Morlanby!'

'You're pathetic, Ashby,' Sebastian said firmly. He could not hide his contempt of the older men. 'Your values are meaningless. I hope you both come to realise exactly what you are, and begin to suffer as a result of your hypocritical lifestyles. But I doubt you possess that much sensitivity or intelligence. Now get out.' He turned to Dr Shetland more kindly. 'You may stay for the weekend if you wish, sir.'

Dr Shetland smiled. It was obvious he was enjoying Sebastian's put-down of the arrogant gentlemen even if he did not gather the full facts.

'Thank you, but no. I must get back to my Harley Street practice.'

'In that case, goodbye and thank you, Dr Shetland. I'll be sure to recommend your services in the highest circles following your exemplary treatment of my . . . nervous episode. Now if you will excuse me I must exercise my dogs. Come, Dominic.'

There was a stunned silence after Sebastian and Dominic had left.

'Such a charming fellow,' Dr Shetland said fondly. 'Very intelligent. If you will excuse me, I'll just go upstairs and pack.'

Elaine smiled and shook hands as he left.

Ashby shivered. Jane wondered if he was feeling the waves of disapproval from the Sheela-na-gig. She could almost taste his metallic fear as he turned to Barnes.

'Don't you find it cold in here?'

Barnes nodded, glancing nervously towards Hazel. Her shotgun was still trained upon both of them.

'Come on, let's be off,' Ashby said. 'I've business to attend to in London. I'll not waste another minute here on that insolent pup. Besides, I've not slept a wink since I arrived at Morlanby. Wouldn't surprise me if the confounded place was cursed. He's welcome to it for now. When he's run it into the ground we'll snap it up at debtor's auction.'

They walked out, ignoring Elaine's triumphal laughter, as Hazel continued to train her shotgun upon them in case they changed their minds. Elaine went to the window and watched them climb into the carriage waiting for them in the driveway. She waved at them grandly as they rode off to catch the afternoon train back to London.

When she turned to share the joke with Hazel, she discovered that Hazel had slipped away.

The next day Hazel awoke in her own bed once more. She stretched and yawned, slowly emerging from dreams. She patted Max, glad to have him at her side after his stay in Morlanby's kennels. When she returned home she had been relieved to discover that Megan's father must have visited in her absence, and fed her animals. All but one chicken had survived, probably lost to a fox or pine marten.

She went about her chores, trying not to dwell on the last few days. Elaine had got what she wanted, and Sebastian was out of danger. It was time for Hazel to return to her old life. But Hazel could not forget how good it had been to return to Morlanby and see Elaine every day. Even throughout those days spent dragging Sebastian back from the brink she had experienced the joy of being close to Elaine once more. Hazel shook her head. Reconciliation, after all that had passed between them, was too much to expect. She had to dismiss the hope that their embrace on the landing had given her.

In the afternoon grey clouds rolled away from the mountain top and a brilliant sun danced upon the russet ferns and swaying heather.

'C'mon, Max, let's go for a walk,' Hazel said, tugging on the mastiff's ear. 'Perhaps it will cure my restlessness.'

When Hazel climbed up to the standing stone, she was only a

little surprised to find Elaine sitting propped against the stone's base. They had always possessed an uncanny sense of each other's whereabouts.

Elaine was in a dress of pale wool lined with dark silk, and a scarlet cloak. Her best winter wardrobe. It suited her well. She plucked up a sprig of heather, broken off by grazing sheep, and sniffed. She smiled at Hazel.

'It smells of sea and sunshine and freedom.' She offered the sprig to Hazel, who sniffed it also and had to agree. 'Ever since we were children I've loved this place,' Elaine continued. 'The sky seems so close, and the clouds cast such quick shadows below us.'

Hazel nodded, gazing about her. 'It's always felt special here.'

'Remember how we used to climb up here and have secret picnics? And if it rained we would bully old Deidre into letting us in for a cup of tea.'

'She loved the company really.' Hazel smiled and pointed with her foot to the base of the stone. 'Do you remember our tokens, the ones we buried here?'

Elaine nodded. 'A lapwing skull and raven feathers. We promised that as long as they were buried together, we would always be bound together.'

Hazel grinned ruefully. 'Children's magic.'

'Perhaps it's worked too well. Here we are once more. It's destiny, Hazel.'

'Or the Morlanby curse.'

Elaine shook her head. 'We're free of any such curse, Hazel, or hadn't you heard?'

Hazel looked out at the horizon and smiled grimly 'Perhaps between us we drove Ashby to treat that Indian girl so badly and hound Sebastian so cruelly. Did you ever think of that?'

Elaine frowned, shaking her head. 'Ashby was a bastard before we ever met him, Hazel. It is foolish to even think that. Is that why you left so suddenly, you felt guilty now we finally have a chance at happiness?'

Hazel did not reply, continuing to stare into the distance at the dazzling sliver of sea.

'Let's clamber down the stream towards your cottage, like we used to as girls,' Elaine urged brightly. 'You're out for a long ramble, aren't you?' Elaine patted Max who wagged his tail enthusiastically. 'Max won't mind, will you?'

Hazel watched Elaine get up and start to run down towards the stream, which babbled throatily with the rainfall of the last few days. She shrugged and gave in to the impulse, following Elaine at a jog.

It was stupid and ridiculous fun to clamber down the mossy boulders, taking care not to slip into the sparkling waters. It was a challenge to place one foot and hand in front of the other, test the sturdiness of each foothold, balance and plot how next to descend. The pastime erased the anxieties of the previous few days. Their lungs filled with clean air and they giggled uncontrollably every time they almost slipped. Finally they reached a gentler incline near the cottage.

Elaine pulled Hazel down beside her in the soft springy heather. They lay side by side laughing, light-hearted after their exertion.

'What do you see in the sky, Hazel?'

Hazel looked up at the majestic clouds drifting across the high blue sky.

'I see a rabbit and a shrew.'

'And I see a toad sitting on a jam jar.'

Hazel laughed. Then she paused as Elaine impulsively pecked her on the cheek. Hazel scrambled up and continued to walk back towards her cottage. Elaine struggled after her, running to keep up.

'What's wrong, Hazel?'

'What's wrong?' Hazel turned round to face Elaine. She kept her hands in her trouser pockets to prevent herself from reaching out to hold Elaine's curves. 'It's just not that simple. You can't will us back to being girls again. Too much has passed. You don't know how I've longed for you all these years.' Hazel's eyes grew bright with suppressed emotion. Then her thoughts came out in a harsh gush of words. 'When I was cold in the snow field of Yukon, I'd imagine your body next to mine, hugging me like I was your crucifix, warming me,' Hazel recounted in a low fierce voice. 'I would imagine that my hands were wrapped in your soft hair, or better still, buried inside your cunt, your juices keeping me warm.' Hazel watched with satisfaction as a slow flush rose in Elaine's cheeks. 'And when I was hungry, I would imagine I was chewing on your gorgeous little pussy. I'd imagine how your juices tasted of a banquet – roast meats and vanilla. I would salivate and swallow and imagine having you over and over. First I sought solace with other women, but that soon passed. They could not compare. Did you know I kept myself celibate for years because of you? Until you started playing games with Megan and Jane down at Morlanby.' Hazel laughed then looked away. 'After all these years of waiting I want something special from you, Elaine. Even though I now understand why you stayed, for Sebastian. I want to know this is lasting, not another of your aristocratic affairs. I want to be more than a casual bit of rough.'

Elaine bit her lip. 'I can understand how you hurt still, Hazel. But I want to thank you so much for your help with Sebastian these last few weeks. You help saved Morlanby too, you know.'

'I'm glad I could help.' Hazel looked at Elaine once more. 'But if you want to start something with me now, don't do it out of gratitude, or just to celebrate. You better know how to finish what you start. You can't discard me like an empty bottle of champagne. I'm here for life.'

'I know you are,' Elaine said, 'and I want you.'

Hazel felt giddy at this bald statement. She propped her arm against a nearby rowan tree to steady herself.

'I love you,' Elaine said, even as she knelt in the grass at Hazel's feet and began to unbuckle Hazel's wide leather belt.' I've missed you so much. You are the only one who has ever been a true match for me, Hazel. I've never really yielded to anyone else.'

Hazel's hands began to stroke Elaine's spun gold hair, the delicate neck and chin, even as Elaine took down her trousers.

'Then take your fill of me, girl,' Hazel groaned with guttural longing, thrusting Elaine's face towards her crotch.

Elaine's patrician features were soft with desire as her tongue traced along Hazel's hard thighs. Hazel's muscles tensed and released at the tease of Elaine's mouth. Finally Elaine's tongue reached her pussy. Hazel groaned in satisfaction. Then her groan grew pained and she roughly tugged Elaine's mouth away from her.

'No,' she murmured, 'not like this. I want to make you suffer, just a little, my proud lady.'

'Whatever you want,' Elaine said eagerly, wiping Hazel's juices from her mouth. 'You can have me any way you choose. I want you too much to object.'

Hazel's eyes narrowed, assessing. Her loins were afire with Elaine's touch, but she was determined to savour this reconciliation. She clicked her tongue, considering. Then she pulled her trousers back up. 'Follow me down to the cottage,' she said casually.

When they reached the cottage garden, Hazel took off Elaine's cloak.

'Grab a spade,' Hazel ordered harshly. 'You're going to turn over part of my vegetable patch while I watch.'

Elaine's patrician eyebrows raised in surprise. 'If you need hired hands I'll send you over a stable boy from Morlanby,' she said haughtily.

Hazel smiled. 'I want *you* to do it, my lady. A little of your sweat will make my vegetables grow so much sweeter.'

Elaine coloured, opened her mouth to protest, but Hazel's expression made her think better of it. She trembled, as though remembering how sweet it was to surrender to Hazel's will.

Silently she snatched the proffered spade from Hazel and stalked across the lawn to the vegetable patch. She stabbed the spade into the hard earth. It took all her body strength to lever the sod up, turn it over, and repeat the process. Soon she began to sweat with the effort, despite the cool breeze. She gave little grunts and curses as she yanked and pulled at clumps of weed. Her face and neck grew pink and her armpits grew damp. She had a smear of dirt across her alabaster brow.

Hazel leaned against her gatepost, impassive to Elaine's struggle, watching the petite aristocrat pant with effort and the dainty hands become soily and abraded by the wooden handle of the spade. Elaine's pale skirts trailed in the soil, and her little boots were caked with mud.

Hazel took out her pipe, packed it, and smoked it serenely while Elaine toiled in the afternoon sunlight.

At the end of the row Elaine surveyed her work with a certain satisfaction. Then she glared at Hazel. 'You've just destroyed an outfit freshly arrived from Paris, which I wore especially to please you. Happy now?'

'Stop complaining. You know you love it,' Hazel said calmly. 'Clean off the spade and put it away.'

'Clean it off how exactly?'

'With your hands,' Hazel said, shrugging.

'I'll break a nail or something.'

'Try the flat rock by the shed door.'

Elaine scowled. She picked up the rock as though she considered throwing it at Hazel. Then she stooped to clear clods of soil from the spade and propped it back inside the shed.

Hazel could tell that Elaine had relished the hard work in spite of herself. Relished Hazel's lustful eyes upon her.

'Now come into the cottage,' Hazel commanded.

Elaine sat on the wooden settle by the fire. Hazel put a few more logs on the embers, moving in the sinuous precision of habit. She was conscious of Elaine's scrutiny as she took down a bottle of brandy from her one cupboard, and two glasses. She poured a generous measure in each.

'To us,' she toasted, and they drank.

Hazel felt the fire of the brandy hit the back of her throat, then her stomach. She could feel the heat of lust between them, the way that Elaine kept on looking up at her. She was longing for Hazel to make the first move.

'That's better,' Hazel said. 'Now I can smell your musk from here. Now I'll be able to taste your sweat on your skin. But first come here and worship me with your autocratic lips. Come and do homage with your patrician tongue. On your knees.'

Hazel spread out Elaine's scarlet cloak at her feet. Elaine crawled across to kneel on it in meek obedience. Hazel pulled down her trousers, kicked off her boots, and thrust her sex towards Elaine, buttocks balanced upon the edge of her wooden chair. She pointed down imperiously when Elaine looked up at her.

Elaine smiled.

'You don't know how many times I've dreamed of doing this,' Elaine whispered, as she parted Hazel's sex lips tenderly.

Hazel closed her eyes and gripped the arms of her chair as she felt Elaine blow on her clit very softly, then exhale a current of air which played up and down her sensitive twat. She felt Elaine blow harder, rippling her pubic hairs and bidding Hazel's cunt to open sesame. Hazel forced herself to stay very still, to savour it and keep it slow, even as the blood thudded through her temples.

She felt the slow upward lick of Elaine's tongue against her clit and groaned, clutching Elaine's head closer to her, pulling the blonde hair free of its chignon so it cascaded down Elaine's shoulders. It had been so long since she had felt another woman's tongue, another woman's lips, caress her in this way. Then Elaine circled Hazel's clitoris and flailed its very tip, concentrating all sensation in this one area until Hazel threw back her head and arched against the soft heat of Elaine's mouth. It was so sweet to surrender to Elaine's familiar loving. She could feel herself tremble as Elaine's fingers slid inside her and Elaine's tongue circled her sex. Then Hazel felt Elaine gently suck at her clitoris with practised delicacy. She groaned at the fire that spread over her body. She splayed her long legs wider and rode Elaine's expert fingers until she quivered headlong into orgasm. Elaine gazed up at her, face suffused with longing and smeared with Hazel's juices.

'That was only the beginning,' Elaine promised in a low purr. 'Tell me what else you want me to do.'

Hazel stroked her own wet quim, looking down at the beautiful woman who crouched before her. Even as her first orgasm subsided she felt renewed stirrings of lust.

'Elaine, I want to see you naked. Strip yourself and lie down on your scarlet cloak. My fire will keep you warm,' Hazel murmured. She felt satisfaction at finally being allowed to experience the fantasy she had dreamed of on Halloween.

Elaine performed a slow striptease while Hazel sat and played with herself and watched. Elaine discarded her pale gown, her corset and petticoats, her cami-knickers and chemise. Soon she stood naked before Hazel. Elaine's long hair flowed over her breasts and down to the small of her back. She knelt, then lay down on her side, stretched on the scarlet cloak. The contrast of Elaine's pale skin and golden hair with the vivid wool was ravishing. Hazel took off her waistcoat, her man's shirt, and stood naked above Elaine. Her long lean body glowed in the firelight.

Slowly she let her bare foot stroke Elaine's soft skin, tracing her thigh and her belly curves, rolling her arse cheeks and breasts. Standing over her like a Hellenic champion of victory as Elaine gave subdued murmurs and sighs of excitement.

Then she lay down beside Elaine. Finally naked flesh could touch naked flesh, hungry hands could explore, loving eyes could watch and weigh and note every change in their lover since they had last lain like this.

Elaine's body had hardly changed at all. Now she no longer went bare-armed in summer, and horserode more, her breasts and arms and thighs were pale and supple and firm. Hazel knew that her own body was also at the height of its powers, seasoned by privation and hard work and now blossoming in the healthy but comfortable life she had led since she had returned home.

They kissed, tongues lingered and tasted each other again. Elaine still tasted of Hazel's juices, and Hazel knew she tasted of brandy and tobacco. Then Hazel lapped at the tender hollow of Elaine's armpits. Hazel tasted the salt of Elaine's sweat, the tang of her musk, mingled with lavender and ylang-ylang from her morning bath. Elaine groaned in appreciation. Reverently Hazel bent to sample the breasts that had tortured her memories. Hazel marvelled at their translucency, their swell, the way they moulded to her avid lips. She pummelled them tenderly until a stalk-like nipple reached her mouth and she suckled it hungrily. Elaine gasped and arched towards her, plucking at the scarlet cloak helplessly as Hazel nibbled and licked and kissed each breast in turn like a panther dining on its favourite prey. Hazel's rough fingers reached Elaine's cunt and they both gasped at the electric shock sparked by the contact. Hazel felt juices drip slowly from her fingers as she worked her way into that honey pot. Then she nuzzled away at the gorgeous pink pussy, letting the tip of her tongue ride Elaine's stiff little clitoris, humming softly and mischievously so that her lips might vibrate against the tender flesh.

'Hazel, I've missed you so much,' Elaine gasped as she writhed helplessly, caressing her own breasts. Hazel continued to take her fill of Elaine's quim.

Hazel swung round so that her cunt danced over Elaine's lips. 'Will you let me do anything, my love?'

'Anything.' Elaine lapped gratefully as Hazel's cunt lowered into her reach. 'Oh please, I can't stand it any longer,' she moaned as Hazel's cruel fingers brought her to the brink then stopped frigging. Elaine raised her pussy beseechingly, begging for more pressure inside her.

'Very well,' Hazel breathed. She crawled over to her shotgun, brought the barrel to Elaine's face.

'I'm going to use this. Kiss it.'

Elaine looked up at her trustingly as she kissed the shotgun, tasting the oiled metal.

Hazel let the shotgun trail down over Elaine's breast and belly. She continued to frig Elaine until Elaine gasped, feeling hot and wet and wide. Then she slowly slid the shotgun barrel up Elaine's gaping snatch.

Elaine was driven wild by the feel of the cool metal inside her. Hazel smiled. She had used this dildo many times on herself and knew how to swivel and gently thrust and rock the gun to maximum effect. She clasped Elaine tight, holding her to her own naked flesh with one strong arm as she continued to fuck the aristocrat with the shotgun. She watched Elaine's face pucker, and grow even more beautiful in the throes of orgasm, rolling and rocking against the shotgun barrel.

Afterwards they lay together spoon-like in front of the fire. Hazel rained kisses upon Elaine's face, her neck and shoulders, and hugged her hard with puppy-like glee.

'And how do you feel now, my lady? Used and abused?'

'Absolutely,' Elaine said, smiling, drowsy after her physical exertion. 'You've made me forget the other reason I came here.'

'What reason could there be apart from getting fucked senseless?'

'To ask you to return to live with me at Morlanby. Help me to sort out the estate. Ashby was half right when he said the place needed an overhaul. I know you and I could do it. Will you help?'

'What about Sebastian?'

'He loves the idea. You should know that. You've been seeing quite a lot of him behind my back these past few weeks. He trusts you implicitly.'

Hazel kissed Elaine's shoulder once more.

'Let me sleep on it,' she replied, settling down for a nap.

Elaine took Hazel's tanned hand and slipped it between her white thighs. She wiggled her hips against Hazel's flat belly.

'Don't sleep for too long,' she warned huskily. 'I'll want you to take me again soon.'

Hazel's low laugh rumbled in her chest. She felt completely satiated. Happy at last to sleep in her lover's arms.

SEVENTEEN

Jane gave Megan's hand a reassuring squeeze.

'We're here,' she said as the carriage pulled up outside the convent.

The convent looked very different on this sunny morning in early summer from when Megan had last visited. There was a scent of roses from the formal gardens and the large wooden door was thrown wide open into the hallway.

They were not the only day visitors. Several richly dressed couples strolled on the lawns or into the hallway, escorted by solicitous nuns.

'It's an open day,' Jane explained. 'Ordinary followers of the sect, such as Lord and Lady Melmouth, or relatives of the sisters, are permitted to visit the convent. The library, the display of reliquaries, the chapel and gardens, are all open for inspection to our benefactors today.'

'I see,' Megan replied. She was a little overwhelmed. She had expected that this would be a discreet and private visit to Mother Superior so that they could fulfil their bargain, do their penance and leave for another three months. She had not imagined that Mother Superior would insist that they visited on an Open Day.

Mother Superior greeted them in the main hall. Her dark skirts and wide sleeves flapped as she hugged them both enthusiastically and then, for Megan's benefit, gave them a brief tour of the convent. Once this was accomplished, she turned to face them.

'Welcome, my children. First things first, now that you are both equally familiar with the environs. You must change into the pale habits of the lay sisters while you are here, and pray for a while in the chapel to compose yourself. Then you will make your confessions to me and I shall devise a suitable penance.'

Megan was bemused as they were escorted to a side room so they could change. It felt strange to wear a wimple and veil, and a long habit of pale rough fabric. Underneath, they were required to be entirely naked. This also felt novel. To move without the familiar constriction of a corset was liberating. But she was certain that the full contours of her heavy breasts and nipples were obvious through the clinging fabric, which was surely immodest and unseemly.

They were guided to the convent chapel to pray. The paintings and statues, flowers and incense were almost as lovely as those in the chapel at Morlanby. Megan tried to enjoy the peaceful serenity and to suppress her nerves at the prospect of confessing to Mother Superior. She felt certain it would be a unique experience. She tried to guess what formula the lascivious ritual would follow.

As they prayed day visitors passed discreetly through the chapel to admire its interior. The visitors were separated from the main body of the chapel by an ornate wooden grille. Megan felt almost like a caged animal, on display to the visitors as an example of pious beauty which benefited the convent.

Jane went to confession first, hurrying into the confessional box when Mother Superior beckoned. Megan wished she could watch the booth while she prayed, but soon tired of craning her neck to look behind her to check upon it. There was no sign of movement and she could hear nothing of Jane's confession above the background noise of the chapel. Eventually Mother Superior tapped Megan on the shoulder, motioning her towards the confessional booth.

'Where's Jane?' Megan asked in surprise. Mother Superior raised an eyebrow at her impertinence.

'Performing the first part of her penance of course. Now, child, you must confess.'

Megan reluctantly followed her to the booth, knelt on the hard floor to whisper into the grille that separated them.

Mother Superior allowed Megan to list her imagined sins during the last few months. Then she fell to questioning her closely about her relationship with Jane. Megan was not surprised. Jane had warned her this would be Mother Superior's prime concern.

Megan was shy at first, her answers halting and monosyllabic. Mother Superior rapped angrily on the grille that separated them.

'This will not do. You must provide as much detail as possible. Jane was most graphic in her confession, you know, so do not hold back on her account. For example, she described your lovemaking in the kitchens at Morlanby. Delectable, quite delectable. So please tell the truth, Megan. No false modesty.'

Megan proffered more expansive replies after this reproof. Maybe these confessions would prove to be the extent of Mother Superior's claim on both of them, randy recounts of their exploits which she could masturbate to later in the privacy of her cell. Somehow Megan doubted it.

Megan admitted to watching Sebastian and Dominic together in the chapel, and how much it had turned her on. She admitted that she still harboured lustful thoughts for Hazel Branagan and Lady Melmouth. Soon she almost forgot that Mother Superior was listening. It was a relief to admit all the little twinges of recalcitrant passion she felt but which she suppressed out of love and respect for Jane. Megan even admitted that she had fantasised about what Mother Superior would do to her following Jane's confidences regarding her stay at the convent.

Finally Mother Superior stopped her flow of filthy thoughts and words.

'You need not concern yourself about punishment at my hands on this occasion, my dear child,' Mother Superior purred. 'Your dreadful imaginings over the next few months will make that final inevitability much sweeter. I have listened most carefully, however, and have a arrived at a suitable penance for your despicable salacious thoughts, and your foul sins of the flesh.'

Megan waited, holding her breath, head bowed in expectation.

'You are to return to the chapel and recite a full rosary on your knees, in full view of the visitors. If a visitor or visitors select you to escort them on a tour of the convent and its grounds, you must oblige them in every way. We rely on the donations of our well-wishers, and you will be a most important ambassador for our cause. Do you understand?'

Megan blinked. 'I believe so, Reverend Mother. Thank you for your leniency.'

Mother Superior laughed. 'You may revise your opinion by the end of the day, Megan,' she observed ominously. 'Now go.'

Megan bowed and hurried to obey. She was a little disappointed that Mother Superior had not taken advantage of her immediately. Perhaps she wasn't Reverend Mother's type after all.

Megan knelt in the chapel and tried to attend to her rosary. Her mind kept wandering, however. What had happened to Jane? She tried not to look at the nuns that passed her kneeling form, or the day visitors who paused to look through the grille at her. Many obviously admired the pious image of a lay sister at her prayers.

Eventually she drifted off with the rhythm of her internal mantra, and it was with difficulty that she roused herself when she heard someone whisper her name.

An elderly gentleman, dressed in black, with a grey tonsure and soft dark eyes, was smiling at her apologetically. He held his top hat in his gloved hands out of respect and carried a small carpet bag.

'Sister Megan, Mother Superior said that you would be happy to escort myself and my wife on a tour of the convent. Will you?'

Megan nodded, glad of the distraction. She stood up stiffly and joined the gentleman.

His wife was waiting outside the chapel. Megan was surprised to note how young she was in comparison. Twenty-five at most. She was very pretty. She had thick coils and tendrils of glossy black hair that framed her face in the latest fashion. High cheekbones, high forehead and a wide, mobile mouth. Dark, intelligent eyes that looked shyly at Megan from beneath her broad-brimmed hat.

The old gentleman took her arm fondly and pecked her on her proffered cheek. Megan noticed how warm and rich her apricot silk dress was as it shimmered and moved with her slender form. It complimented her fresh complexion well.

'Sister Megan, I am Jonathan Wells, and this is my wife Larissa.'

'Pleased to meet you, Sister Megan,' Larissa said, offering a white-gloved hand which Megan shook awkwardly. Larissa's voice was musical, her accent as cultivated as Elaine's. Megan guessed that this couple were important patrons of the convent. Megan smiled.

'If you would follow me, I'll show you our library and collection of holy relics. Would you like me to carry your bag, sir?' she asked politely. Jonathan Wells replaced his hat on his head and looked down at his small carpet bag as though he had forgotten he carried it. He shook his head.

'No, thank you. After our tour indoors, may we walk in the gardens? It is such a lovely day. There is a particularly fine concentric maze which we enjoyed very much when we last visited here.'

This attraction was news to Megan, but she felt sure she could locate such a maze in the convent grounds easily enough. 'Of course.'

Megan spent the next hour accompanying the couple as they examined various reliquaries of the saints and rare illuminated books in the library. They seemed a devoted couple indeed, despite their age difference. Larissa was completely considerate of Jonathan's comfort. Eventually they moved outdoors and soon reached the maze, a tall winding path hedged with high walls of yew and box. Twice they paused at flat stone benches so that Jonathan could rest and catch his breath. Megan waited patiently, enjoying the warm summer's day, happy to keep to their slow pace. Larissa explained he had a slight heart problem.

By the time they reached the handsome pavilion at the centre of the maze, there was no sign of other visitors.

There were Doric columns of stone that supported the terra-cotta tiles of the summerhouse but the walls themselves were fashioned from seasoned slats of wood. Inside there were wide wooden benches, covered with tapestry cushions. There were busts of various saints and philosophers in alcoves about the walls. The air was warm from sunshine captured by the large picture

windows. A honeysuckle trailed about the door and was beginning to give up its heady evening scent. In front of the pavilion, a
fountain gurgled prettily.

Jonathan sat down on one of the benches; Larissa took another.
Megan remained standing out of respect.

'Mother Superior said that you would be only too happy to help
us in certain marital matters, Sister Megan,' Jonathan said at length.

'Is that so? Yes, I am instructed to oblige you in any way I
can,' Megan replied with sudden alarm, wondering where this
would lead.

Jonathan cleared his throat, and took hold of his wife's hand.

'Due to my illness it has been three years since I have been able
to carnally satisfy my wife. Reverend Mother has been very kind,
and permits us to visit here three times a year so that my wife
may select a sister who could . . . act my part, so to speak.'

'This year I selected you,' Larissa said simply.

Megan felt her heart thud with nervous excitement as the truth
began to dawn. This was the penance Mother Superior had devised.

'But I know nothing of such things,' she stammered awkwardly,
buying time.

'Trust me,' Larissa whispered, taking Megan's hand. 'You will
do very well.'

Megan felt the cool touch of the other woman inflame her.
She turned to Jonathan.

'What must I do?'

'You must pleasure my wife in the same way that I used to,'
Jonathan said, settling back upon the bench. 'First you must put
her across your lap, expose her bottom and spank her hard. She
enjoys this most particularly.'

Megan moved as though she were in a dream. She sat down
on the bench. Larissa draped herself across Megan's lap like a
dutiful wife. Megan parted her apricot skirts and uncovered the
lady's pale-skinned bottom. Megan was startled to find that Larissa
was naked beneath her skirts, like a common peasant. Even more
disturbing was the fact that Larissa was wearing a chastity belt.

The gold belt, with its gusset of golden chainmail, seemed
exquisitely fashioned and was locked at the waist by a silver
padlock.

Larissa smiled at Megan's fascination with the erotic restraint. 'It's beautiful, isn't it? Jonathan designed it specially for me, and our jeweller wrought it.'

'Will it hurt, the pressure of the chainmail against you, when I spank you?' Megan asked, as she observed how tightly the chainmail weaved between Larissa's thighs. Megan found it hard to catch her breath as her hands travelled across the smooth curve of Larissa's bottom.

'That's part of the point, isn't it?' Larissa purred, shifting her hips beneath Megan's caress.

'Please begin,' Jonathan prompted. His arms were folded but there was a predatory glitter in his eye as he waited for the spanking to commence.

Megan was about to refuse. But why should she refuse the whims of a beautiful woman? She would enjoy Larissa's body in exciting ways she had yet to discover. The fact that Jonathan would watch was incidental to Megan's enjoyment, but would obviously heighten Larissa's excitement.

And besides, how could she refuse the penance which Mother Superior had arranged for her? The alternative may be much less enjoyable.

Megan wondered how often the couple had performed this ritual, each time with a different nun as part of the triangle. The thought excited and incensed her enough to commence slapping Larissa's bare buttocks with gusto.

Megan soon warmed to her task. She ensured that she covered every inch of Larissa's porcelain arse with random, stinging blows. Larissa softly moaned and twisted herself in Megan's lap, as her pale buttocks became a bright pink and emanated back the heat that Megan imparted. Megan held on to Larissa's hips to keep her still and continued the chastisement for another few minutes, until she was sure that Larissa was wet against the filigree metal of the chastity belt. The effort left Megan invigorated and eager for more.

'That will suffice for now, Sister Megan,' Jonathan said at last with a catch in his baritone voice. 'Thank you. If you would now permit my wife to worship your breasts, while I admire her stinging buttocks, we would be most grateful. You would like that, Larissa my dear?'

'Very much, darling,' Larissa replied. She slowly slid from Megan's lap and sank on her knees in front of the nun. Her beautiful smile melted Megan even as Larissa loosened the nun's habit from her shoulders to reveal Megan's full breasts.

Megan could almost laugh at the absurdity of wearing a wimple and veil while her naked breasts were suckled by a beautiful woman in apricot silks. She could feel her own juices slick between her thighs as Larissa licked and nuzzled at her breasts. Larissa took each full breast tip in her mouth in turn and nipped each long, hard nipple with her front teeth until Megan groaned with satisfaction. Her dutiful attentions were unceasing.

'Now, if you could let my wife worship your, er, source, we would be most grateful also,' Jonathan said at length. Megan nodded in agreement, dimly aware that the old gentleman was tugging at his own impotent cock and balls as he watched. Megan pulled up her pale habit and parted her knees, so that Larissa could kneel and kiss and nuzzle her exposed crotch.

'How delightful, Jonathan, she is shaven,' Larissa exclaimed. 'And her musk is like the fragrance of apples.'

'Lap away, my dear, and take your fill,' he answered indulgently.

Larissa carefully directed little tongue stabs against the base of Megan's clit, making Megan writhe in appreciation. Larissa softly circled the base of Megan's clit, then pressed inside her with larger sweepings of her salacious tongue. Megan moaned as Larissa applied fingers and all manner of extra caresses in ways Megan had never experienced before.

'Faster,' Megan begged, all shyness evaporating in the imperative of rising orgasm. 'Harder.' Megan rubbed her mound against Larissa's eager mouth, vaguely aware that Jonathan had leaned forward to watch more closely. His enjoyment of her enjoyment gave her even more of a perverse thrill.

Larissa let her hand stray further inside Megan's willing sex and frigged her fast while she continued to dab her tongue at Megan's clit. Megan climaxed in a whole body shudder and a loud cry of joy. Larissa's own hips gyrated in sympathy as she almost came against the metal bonds of her chastity belt at the same time.

'Make her stop, Sister Megan,' Jonathan warned sharply, 'or

she'll reach her peak too soon.' Megan, still weak but warming to
their game, placed her hands on Larissa's hips to still their
gyrations.

'Please take off my wife's bodice,' Jonathan continued, 'and
dandle her breasts as you wish.'

Small and pert, Larissa's breasts and nipples stood rigidly to
attention while Megan smoothed and caressed them. Impulsively
Megan straddled Larissa's quivering body and kissed her slowly,
tasting her own sex on the girl's lips. Larissa whimpered and
responded eagerly.

'Very good,' Jonathan murmured. He leaned back, arms folded
once more. 'My poor wife has not had much of a release as yet.'
He ran his tongue across his lips as though considering the
problem carefully. Then he took a small silver key from his
waistcoat pocket. 'Crawl over here, wife,' he ordered.

Larissa pulled free of Megan's embrace reluctantly and obeyed.
Her pink buttocks swayed and her bare breasts jiggled as she
struggled on all fours, hobbled by her silks, to where Jonathan sat.

'Suck,' he ordered, as he held out his fingers.

Megan watched fascinated as Larissa suckled the long digits
suggestively. Jonathan swayed, his eyelids fluttered, and he grew
flushed.

'Very good, my dear wife,' he whispered. 'Now stand and I
will unlock your chastity belt.'

Larissa stood before her husband, skirts held high to give him
access to the little silver padlock. With trembling fingers he
inserted his key and the chastity belt fell away.

Jonathan's eyes were clouded with passion, as he hastily put the
key back in his pocket and reached for the carpet bag at his side.

'Sister Megan, would you be so kind as to wear this and
minister to my wife?'

Megan was handed a thick tusk of black rubber with leather
straps and silver buckles to attach it to the wearer's hips. Megan
took the thing, shrugged off her shift, and buckled it across her
groin. She could feel her abdomen flutter with lust and excitement. The base of the rubber tusk rested nicely against her pelvis
and the tip of her clitoral hood.

'It looks well on you,' Larissa said, admiring Megan while she fingered her now freed cunt.

Meanwhile Jonathan stroked his wife's long, stocking-clad legs.

'I agree,' Jonathan murmured. 'I think that my wife is now good and ready for you to service her from behind while I minister to her breasts.'

'My favourite position,' Larissa enthused.

Megan was not about to object. Larissa bent over, resting her palms either side of Jonathan, and braced against the bench. Husband and wife kissed while Megan again stroked and slapped Larissa's bare bottom. Then Megan delved into Larissa's moist waiting cunt with rough fingers. Finally Megan eased and butted the large rubber contraption into Larissa's hot and horny fanny.

Larissa moaned and rocked in response.

'That feels marvellous,' she moaned. 'Fill me up, Sister Megan. It has been long months since I was thus used. I feel I will crack open with longing. Ram me hard, I beg you.' Larissa yelped as Megan slid the full length of the rubber tusk into her and circled eagerly. Megan could not resist parting Larissa's arse cheeks and probing the tight little arse hole with her finger while she continued to thrust.

As the beautiful woman bucked and murmured oaths beneath her, Megan enjoyed the sharp lust of taking her pleasure in this way. She bent over and ground her distended nipples against Larissa's pale, bare back, pinching and slapping her arse and gripping her hips to control her gyrations as she continued to thrust faster. Megan withdrew the dildo before slamming its full length into Larissa's willing pussy once more. Larissa spread her legs wider to accommodate her nun lover's dildo and shivered with delight. Meanwhile Jonathan's fingers pinched Larissa's breasts hard, his impotence turning to joyful satisfaction as he watched his wife's expression change from lady to wanton whore.

'I'm glad I can watch you filled up by a woman, even if I can no longer fulfil that task,' Jonathan murmured, kissing his wife. 'Now, Larissa, I give you permission. Now you can come.'

Larissa had obviously been holding back on a hair trigger. While Megan held Larissa's hips and thrust into her fanny, and

Jonathan fondled her breasts, Larissa quivered and writhed into a violent orgasm.

Simultaneously Megan felt the dildo base and leather straps butt against and abrade her own pelvis and clitoris to such a degree that she felt the rush of a fierce orgasm.

Moments later Megan withdrew and unbuckled the dildo. Larissa was still in a semi-swoon, and was now cradled on her husband's lap.

'Thank you, Sister Megan,' Jonathan said unsteadily. 'You may leave us now. Tell Mother Superior we shall provide a substantial donation to the convent in gratitude for your service.'

Megan nodded. Quickly she dressed in her habit, discarded on the summerhouse floor, and ran back through the maze towards the convent.

She felt confused, yet could not deny that she had thoroughly enjoyed the encounter.

Back at the chapel Mother Superior was waiting for her, smiling.

'Sister Megan. Did it go well with Mr and Mrs Wells?'

'Mr Wells has promised another handsome donation to the convent,' Megan replied curtly.

'Very good. Thank you so much for helping our cause today.' Mother Superior stroked Megan's cheek fondly. 'Don't look so hostile, little one. Surely you now have some fresh ideas of how to love Jane when you are together again? It was educational, was it not?'

Megan bit her lip and nodded, stung by Mother Superior's knowing smile.

'Good. Go, now. I shall see you again in three months' time.'

Megan nodded, then hurried away to change. She smelled of sex and sweat and the summer day.

On the long carriage ride home, Jane and Megan held hands and watched the passing scenery. Megan sensed that Jane was as satiated and tired out by the day as she herself was.

'What was your penance, Jane?' Megan asked after she had briefly told of her own. Jane gave an inscrutable smile.

'I've yet to arrange the final part of mine,' Jane admitted. 'You are to help me.'

Megan could not help but shiver with anticipation.

EIGHTEEN

It was Midsummer's Day. Lady Melmouth and her estate manager, Hazel Branagan, were having a picnic at Maiden Falls. Their neighbours, Megan Lewis and Jane Claremont, had been cordially invited to join them at midday prompt. Lord Melmouth and Dominic O'Keefe were expected to drop by later.

On the smooth grass, in between wild flowers that nodded among long seeded grasses, the feast which Elaine called a picnic was arranged. Cold meats, slices of pie, fresh crusty bread and country cheeses, bottles of champagne and basins of fresh strawberries (the first crop of the season) were all laid out beautifully on a tartan blanket covered with the finest white linen.

Earlier Elaine and Hazel had walked to the falls at dawn, and met with a few of the women from the village for their yearly ceremony. They had each thrown garlands of wild flowers into the turquoise waters of the pool at the foot of the falls. Then a thin mist had crept along the hollows, and the sun had made dew-laden gossamer dance and sparkle.

Now the rustling leaves of the beech trees arched high above them, shading them from the heat of midday sun. The waterfall tinkled prettily, a thin white sliver after the week of dry, warm weather. Hazel had forecast a good harvest after such a warm and sunny early summer and Elaine had to agree.

Elaine had lain down on her front in the sweet-smelling grass, careless of her cream lace dress. She watched a bee lumber from one clump of foxgloves to another, its legs already fat with a coating of yellow pollen. Its drone added a baritone to the birdsong overhead. 'This is simply outrageous,' Elaine grumbled, kicking her legs backwards lazily. 'They are all late. What has happened to good manners?'

Hazel, dozing with her back against a tree trunk, opened her eyes. Their penetrating blue made Elaine's heart leap even now, after their months living together. She watched the other woman's strong fingers search for her waistcoat pocket and take out her fob watch.

'It's barely midday. Have a heart. You know that Jane and Megan have only just returned from making penance to Mother Superior. That always fatigues them somewhat.'

'Yes,' Elaine said, grinning at the thought. 'I shall make them show me all the little welts and bites left by their latest confession before they even get their first glass of champagne.' She checked the ice in the bucket. 'Which shall be warm if they're not careful.'

'Don't be such a schoolgirl,' Hazel scolded, raking her cropped blonde hair with one hand as she put away her watch. 'We must let our tenants keep their secrets. Now come over here and put your head in my lap. You can doze away your impatience,' Hazel added more indulgently.

Elaine sighed as Hazel's deft fingers combed through her hair, teasing tresses which shone smooth and glossy in the dappled sunlight. The fingers felt cool and calm against her scalp, yet she tingled at their familiar touch.

'You know they love to confide in us really,' Elaine maintained. 'Especially on Midsummer's Day when we give thanks to the Sheela-na-gig, or whatever nonsense Jane chooses to call it.'

'It's not quite nonsense,' Hazel replied, her handsome features inscrutable. 'Old Deidre believed in a similar goddess who protected this land. And on days like these, don't you feel something magical?'

Elaine laughed. 'I feel the warm scented breeze, the sun on my face, and your fingers running through my hair. That is magic enough for me.'

Elaine's blue eyes were smoky. She crinkled her golden lashes together to look up at Hazel teasingly.

'How can someone from such an ancient family be so modern and cynical in their views? Next you'll be buying a microscope and studying germs or rhizomes.'

Elaine smiled. 'If it meant I got better yield from the estate I'd do it.'

Hazel bent down to kiss her indulgently. 'Sometimes it is best to let things lie fallow, and return the stronger. Like our love. The estate will continue to improve, you have my word.'

Elaine caught Hazel's hand and kissed the rough palm.

'So let us celebrate and open a bottle of champagne between us at least, before the ice melts entirely.'

'We could always place the bottles in the stream to cool,' Hazel pointed out, her blue eyes mocking. But she could never resist Elaine's petulant hedonism: it always yielded such delightful opportunities, although she also liked to watch Elaine pout and toss her golden head until she finally got her own way.

'Very well,' Hazel conceded at last. 'Just one bottle.'

They toasted each other with champagne flutes of pure crystal and drank deeply. The cool amber bubbles of champagne effervesced and danced as though they wanted to be inhaled rather than sipped.

Elaine plucked a strawberry from a large silver basin at the centre of the picnic spread. She dunked it in her champagne and nibbled at the fruit slowly. First she licked the bright berry with her tongue, then her neat white teeth rubbed at the sweet pink flesh. Her lips took on the stain of the ripe fruit so that they looked bruised and wanton and scarlet.

Hazel watched all this as she sipped her own glass of champagne. Her blue eyes narrowed seductively.

'Are you playing the harlot with me, Lady Melmouth? Would you like a rude hand up your skirt, even though we expect guests at any moment?'

'Of course not. The very idea is outrageous.'

Elaine pretended to look shocked, even as she reached for another strawberry. She dunked the berry in the bubbles that winked at the edge of her crystal glass. Then she hitched her knees up and stared at Hazel as she rubbed the berry against her sex lips and nuzzled it into her with a sigh. After a little while, she pulled the berry out again. She placed the berry in the palm of her hand and offered it to Hazel as though it were Eve's apple.

'Eat,' Elaine purred invitingly.

Hazel smiled as she took the strawberry, dipped it into her own flute of champagne before she chewed at it greedily.

'Very well, you win,' she growled. 'Get down on all fours.'

Elaine slowly did so, letting her bottom waggle provocatively in Hazel's direction. Hazel cupped the curve of Elaine's hips, tightly clad with cream lace skirts. With skill she unbuttoned the waistband and let it fall, tugging petticoats away to reveal Elaine's silk knickers.

'You need a lesson in manners, Lady Melmouth,' she said sternly, as she pulled out her belt and slapped Elaine's buttocks with the leather strip, striping her buttocks severely. Elaine yelped then spread her knees wider and raised her arse higher for further chastisement. The pink marks on Elaine's arse cheeks, planted there by Hazel's belt, looked exquisite against the smooth paleness of the surrounding skin. Hazel felt the familiar tug at her own sex when she maltreated her lover's arse in this way.

Hazel's fingers stoked and probed between Elaine's parted thighs, teasing Elaine's hot mound. Her index finger circled Elaine's clit then plunged deep into her moist canal, withdrawing only to repeat the motion. Hazel pressed her own loins against Elaine's waggling chastised arse, as she bent above the long smooth back of her lover.

Elaine gave little groans of satisfaction, grinding her mound hard against Hazel's hand. Then Hazel picked Elaine up and swung her on to her back, laying her down on the soft grass. The vivid greenery framed Elaine's slender body, her flushed face.

'It's such a shame to waste the bubbles,' Hazel observed, as she pulled apart Elaine's thighs roughly and sloshed a little of the champagne over Elaine's naked pink crack. Then she knelt to lap noisily, drinking deep.

The bubbles of the champagne continued to dance against Hazel's tongue even as she invaded Elaine's sex with her tongue. Hazel could imagine what the sensation would feel like for Elaine, from the other woman's moans of bliss. Hazel frothed yet more champagne over Elaine's swollen pussy and drank from her once more. Elaine's knees parted wider as she offered herself eagerly, supine beneath Hazel's tender assault. As always, Elaine seemed suspended on the edge of lust when Hazel's fingers entered and finally fucked her: three fingers, then four, then Hazel's whole hand, sliding in and out, twisting and thrusting with such gentle insistence that Elaine cried out 'Harder,' until Hazel relented and pressed her body down, pubis against pubis. The pressure of her hand and pelvis finally let Elaine peak against her. Hazel watched hungrily as the flush subsided from Elaine's face.

'Poor darling,' Elaine murmured at last, 'I've taken advantage of you again.'

Hazel chuckled, and slapped her on the arse one last time.

'Don't worry. I'm sure our guests will help me unwind.'

'I'm counting on it.'

Elaine had just rearranged her dress into some semblance of order when Megan and Jane arrived. They both wore sunhats and pretty print dresses. They were flushed and panting after their walk from the cottage.

'Good afternoon, my dears. You look charming – don't they, Hazel? Here, have a glass of champagne to cool you down. We'll open another bottle.'

'You haven't begun without us, have you? Jane asked, glancing from Elaine to Hazel. 'We agreed.'

'Only a little preparation,' Elaine admitted with a smile. 'Now we are completely at your disposal.'

Jane nodded, sipping her champagne. She examined the glass in admiration as she registered the effect.

'Hazel is to be the altar for the ceremony this year,' she said with authority. 'Then we shall each take turns from now on, each Midsummer's Day.'

Elaine arched an eyebrow at Hazel, as if to say I told you so.

'I brought all the things you told me to fetch,' Elaine said as she emptied out her little carpet bag. 'An ostrich feather to represent air, a bottle of perfumed water, a candle, and a sachet of rare sweet-smelling herbs. There is also a vial of massage oil and lengths of green ribbon.'

'Excellent,' Jane beamed. 'Let's eat, and then we can begin the ceremony.' She picked up a crusty roll and began to smear it with thick yellow butter before she added a hunk of cheddar.

'You used to fast before all your ceremonies, Jane,' Elaine said, amused at the healthy plumpness of the lay sister, and her sharp appetite.

'This is different,' Jane said gravely. 'This is celebrating fullness, abundance. The zenith of the year. Here's to your health, and the health of Morlanby.'

The others answered her toast.

'How did you fare with Mother Superior on this visit, Megan?' Elaine asked sweetly, ignoring Hazel's warning look. Megan's eyelids fluttered down, as though she wanted to hide her sinful enjoyment at the memory of what had taken place in the confines of the convent.

'It was interesting and educational, madam. That is all I can say, as our confession and penance is confidential. Perhaps you should consider taking Mother Superior as your confessor, now that Dominic is often out of the country with Sebastian.'

'I don't think so. Hazel is a stern enough spiritual mistress, are you not, my love?'

Hazel's smile was wolfish but she did not reply.

After they had eaten, they looked to Jane once again for instruction.

'Hazel must strip and lay across the carved boulder,' Jane said, 'to consecrate the altar.'

'I'm not sure I like the idea. I don't know exactly what I'm letting myself in for,' Hazel said. 'Can't we start off more gradually?'

'Don't be such a coward, Hazel,' Elaine scolded. 'You said yourself you more than half believed this mumbo-jumbo. After all, the ceremony was found in old Deidre's book of herbal lore and charms, which you have often consulted yourself. You must give it a try.'

'Very well,' Hazel said. 'But you girls have a care.'

They all watched as Hazel took off her man-clothes and stood before them naked. Each of them admired the beauty of her long, lean body. It whet their appetites, to watch her tanned skin dappled in light and shade by the surrounding greenery. Megan was reminded of her first sight of Hazel nearly a year previously. Hazel's cropped head, her bare nape, her powerful shoulders and biceps. Her small breasts, her firm buttocks and long muscled legs were even more beautiful than ever before. She obviously flourished under Elaine's loving attentions.

'What now?' Hazel asked, businesslike. It seemed as though she was unaware of the enchantment she had already worked upon them.

'Now lay on the boulder, Hazel, spreadeagled on your back so you make the shape of a star.'

Hazel grimaced but followed Jane's instructions.

Jane took out the green ribbons and wrapped them around Hazel's wrists and ankles, before tying the other end of each ribbon round the boughs of the beeches above them. It reminded Jane of the bonds she had worn during the seance on Halloween. She was surprised and thrilled to notice a small tattoo of a swallow on Hazel's left biceps as she worked. A memento of Hazel's travels, she guessed. Its blue-black silhouette quivered enticingly as Hazel flexed her muscles and relaxed into her pentagram position.

'This is to signify your submission to our will, and to the will of the Goddess during the ceremony. You shall personify the Goddess, be possessed by the Goddess.'

Elaine smiled secretly at the hocus-pocus even as Hazel snorted her derision.

'Fair enough. What next, Jane?'

Jane smiled demurely, incanting a few lines of Gaelic.

'Now we must strip naked ourselves. The book calls it going sky-clad.'

'And then?' Elaine asked. Jane shrugged

'And then we do pretty much what comes naturally. The book suggest certain steps to carry out to intensify our celebration.'

'Wait a moment,' Megan said, consulting the small leather-bound volume. 'Aren't you meant to blindfold Hazel too?'

'I think so,' Jane said looking at the book, trying to remember.

'That sounds like a good idea anyway,' Elaine said eagerly. 'I'll fold up my petticoat to act as the blindfold.'

Hazel felt the cool cotton wrap around her eyes, blocking her view, before she had a chance to object.

Hazel felt fingers stroking her admiringly and knew that all three girls had begun to caress her. She groaned, already wet between the legs after her quick love-making with Elaine. Now fingers trailed across the insides of her forearms, over her hard small breasts, her high narrow hips, and along her legs. Someone stroked the instep of her foot, and then massaged each sole in turn. Hazel melted into sensuous relaxation, almost despite herself, as she felt each separate caress of her body.

Her sex twitched in pleasure as the ostrich feather was slowly stroked against her nether lips, then trailed over her breasts and back across her sex in a slow figure of eight. She tried to rise towards its ghostlike caress, to press her nipples and clit harder against the maddening sensation. But her worshippers were determined to take their time and she could only lie splayed and helpless, letting the feather glide across her skin and slick, wet slash at will. She felt a film of sweat cover her breasts, and her mouth felt dry with desire.

She let out a cry of surprise as she felt a drip of hot wax land on her belly, immediately followed by a splash of scented water and cool lapping tongues. The triple sensation was confusing, making her sway with pain then pleasure. To be martyred in this way was novel to her. She was surprised at the pleasurable sensations it raked up if she let herself relax.

Hazel smiled indulgently. Maybe Elaine had staged all this as an elaborate hoax, simply an excuse for an orgy on a beautiful summer's day. Hazel did not care. She was enjoying herself too much, surrendering to a sensual fugue like someone long denied the full pleasure of her body.

'What are you doing now, you Sybarites?' Hazel asked as the dripping alternate wax and water ceased. She could still feel some wax drying on her skin in the warm breeze.

No one replied. Instead hands anointed her with perfumed oils, heady with crushed herbs to represent the element of earth. Hazel felt a slow insistent craving flood her loins, fill her breasts and limbs while she enjoyed tender hands which firmly stroked and massaged the oils into every inch of her skin. It was heavenly to lie still and let her muscles be cosseted and smoothed into relaxation. Hands rolled her over easily while fingers began to knead and massage the back of her neck, the muscles that radiated either side of her spine. Then her bottom was smoothed with the oil, arse cheeks separated then squeezed together, kneaded until the muscles relaxed and Hazel's cunt juices began to flow copiously in response. Oiled hands circled and stroked the backs of her thighs, her calves. She felt blissful weightlessness replace any knots of tension. Hazel began to feel like she might truly be a goddess under such attentions. She felt her body glowing. Her skin felt warm and relaxed and perfumed in the sunlight.

She let herself be rolled on to her back once more, and gasped as her breast and belly were deftly stroked and massaged. She was lulled by the attentions of the loving hands, even as she reached a new level of sensitivity. She tried to guess whose hands were stroking her thighs, which mouth encased her breast. She wondered whose thumbs circled the centre of each of her palms so firmly that her wrist and fingers relaxed infinitesimally in response. But she could not keep track and soon just surrendered to each individual sensation as though Elaine had grown many pairs of hands, like a Hindu goddess, and played with her supine body at will in the delicious summer warmth.

When Hazel felt impertinent fingers slide into her wet cunt she was in no mood to resist. The fingers stroked and pressed and explored her with slow sensual tenderness. She cried out with strangled lust at this slow and teasing attention to her sex. She wanted the fingers to press further and harder against her but they evaded her pelvic thrusts, until she surrendered quietly to their caresses once more. Meanwhile she felt cool hands encase her small breasts and rasp against her stiff buds of nipples. Hazel could feel a wet sex sliding against her thigh, and then she smelled the delicate aroma of another pussy poised above her. She raised her head as much as she was able to lick at the moist vulva above her, and panted in eagerness for more as it danced just out of her full reach. Meanwhile a pair of oiled breasts replaced the hands that stroked her own hard breasts. The soft suppleness of oiled skin against skin, the pressure of hard nipples against her own, growing fat and large and aroused, drove Hazel into sensual turmoil.

'Hurry up and let me come,' she gasped, 'because I cannot stand much more of this ghostly seduction.'

Hazel was rewarded by the sensation of lips and mouths moving against her sex, dabbling fatly against her swollen clit. Each mouth in turn tasted her juices as if testing whether Hazel was indeed driven to the point of no return in her arousal. Hazel muttered oaths and writhed as though she were on a rack of desire.

Then she felt something wide, rounded and smooth butt against her clit, then gently ram against her sex lips as though begging for entry.

'Oh please,' Hazel said, spreading her legs wide.

The large silky dildo eased into her gradually, rocking and circling until her sex grew used to its size and it entered easily.

Meanwhile someone had taken her foot and sucked each toe in turn, another sucked each of her nipples in turn, and an insolent finger waggled into her arse crack, teasing her puckered arsehole. She moaned and bucked at this surfeit of pleasure and felt lips kiss her, a tongue seek hers, rasp against her teeth, taking and savouring her stifled cries of delight as the dildo began to fuck her hard, and her breasts were pinched and stroked and squeezed in time to its tempo.

Hazel, in a perverse frenzy, tried to hold out as long as possible against the expert fucking. But in the end there was no holding back. The avalanche of white-hot bliss made her yell and buck against the carved granite boulder and grab at her silken bounds. Her torso clenched, her clit and fanny jerked as she released the logjam of sexual energy she had been holding on to and surrendered entirely to pleasure.

Afterwards Hazel felt as soft and light as marshmallow, as though she had been thoroughly satiated. When she was untied eventually and the blindfold taken from her, the other three were dressed demurely once more. Elaine slipped her petticoat blindfold back beneath her skirts primly. They all gazed with delight as Hazel walked unsteadily down to the stream, splashed herself a little with the cool waters, then shook herself dry before dressing herself once more.

'Well, Hazel?' Elaine asked, half afraid and half eager. 'Did you enjoy that? Was it fun being a goddess?'

Hazel gave her a lopsided grin as she poured herself another glass of champagne. 'Let's just say it was interesting. I'll let you know for sure the next time I have to go through with the ceremony in four years' time.'

Elaine nodded, secretly pleased that her lover had reluctantly enjoyed herself.

'Just exactly what did you use as the dildo?' Hazel asked curiously.

'It's a fetish which Jane found in the chapel, hidden behind a loose stone. It's a carved prick designed exactly to fit the dimensions of the Sheela-na-gig's pussy.'

'May I see it?'

Jane handed her the object. It was carved out of seasoned oak and fashioned like a dragon. Its snout was the mock-glans and its tail wrapped in a figure of eight to form a mock pair of balls at its base. It reminded Hazel of figures she had seen in the borders of old illuminated manuscripts. She laughed at its beautiful obscenity as she passed it back to Jane, who wrapped it in a square of silk and carefully placed it in a box of polished walnut.

'Deidre's book says that this ceremony is a potent way to ensure the land is fertile,' Jane said gravely.

'Well, I hope that it works and gives us a good year,' Hazel replied.

'I know it will be a good year,' a voice rang out behind them. 'I can tell the estate is blossoming beautifully.'

They looked back into the shade of the trees to see Sebastian and Dominic walking towards them.

'Sebastian and Dominic, at last you bother to honour our invitation! You'll have to make do with our leftovers, I'm afraid, but we can open a fresh bottle of champagne. Welcome home, brother dear.' Elaine kissed Sebastian fondly.

'Thank you.' Sebastian took the proffered bottle of champagne and opened it expertly and poured into the waiting glasses.

'Good to see you all looking so well.' He beamed at each woman in turn before drinking from his own glass thirstily. He lay down beside Elaine and the silent Dominic sat cross-legged beside him as he also smiled greetings to the company.

'Sorry we were late. We were waylaid along the way.'

'By each other no doubt,' Megan whispered to Jane who grinned then waved a reproof with her fork before she tucked into another slice of pie.

'So, how did you fare in India? You telegrammed that you were successful and that you were coming home, but now I want the full details,' Elaine said.

'I'll give you the bare facts,' Sebastian replied blithely, 'as I'm too tired to tell the whole story now. Suffice to say we found Maya – the girl that those bastards Ashby and Barnes had molested – working in a whorehouse near the barracks. We explained that we wanted to make amends, and offered to help in any way we could. She was reluctant at first, thinking it was a trick to make her do unspeakable things for me, and that she would be much worse off after. But then she saw Dominic and me together and understood that my interest could only be entirely platonic.'

'She should have guessed that from the first time you met her,' Hazel observed.

'Well, I don't blame the poor girl for being suspicious and thinking I was probably unhinged or evil or both after what had happened. Eventually we took her and her special friend, Nadira, away from the whorehouse and took them to another town many miles away, high in the foothills of the Himalayas, where no one could possibly know their past. They have elected to live there and study to become holy women of some sort. They said that they would prefer such a life to marriage, and so I have arranged a small independent income for them which will keep them comfortably off for the rest of their lives. Much the same arrangement as we made for Jane and Megan.'

Megan smiled, raised her glass of champagne in gratitude and approval as she ate her strawberries.

'I think that is an ideal arrangement,' Elaine said. 'I'm sure Maya and Nadira will be happy together and you can finally consider your debt of honour settled.'

'They were very serene and lovely women,' Dominic volunteered. 'They now live in a simple house halfway up a mountain, some distance away from a large temple. Near the top of the mountain is a genteel settlement that the British have set up for their wives to spend the summer in, so they can enjoy the cool, while the menfolk toil away in the lowlands administrating the Empire. Which means they should be left quite unmolested by males.'

'Maya and Nadira even asked us if we could make a pilgrimage with them to the source of the Ganges,' Sebastian said, 'as they were certain our souls are far along the road to enlightenment and we would benefit from the journey immensely.'

Sebastian and Dominic exchanged fond looks.

'Maybe we shall one day,' Dominic said. 'Even though I have left the priesthood, I still feel a spiritual calling.'

'Are you back to stay at Morlanby for good?' Jane asked. She approved of how Sebastian's fair skin still held a faint tan, and his fair hair had grown paler from his stay in India. His face had also relaxed into a new kind of maturity, she noticed. He was far more sure of himself.

'Just for a little while,' Sebastian replied. 'We'll probably stay here with you for the summer. But now I know that the estate is in good hands, Dominic and I can travel with a clear conscience. We thought we may spend the winter in Algiers.'

'I've had my fill of travel,' Hazel said, looking across at Elaine. 'This is my spot. Right here.' She took a silver chain from round her neck. 'You can have my St Christopher now, to keep you safe.'

'That's very sweet of you,' Sebastian said, examining the little silver medallion. 'Are you sure you don't mind?'

'Of course not, take it. I'm more than half pagan these days anyway, thanks to the bad influence of your sister.'

Sebastian laughed. 'You were pagan long before Elaine influenced you.' He slipped the chain on and sighed. 'I propose a toast from all of us.' He raised his glass once more. 'To Morlanby, to the glorious summer and, most importantly of all, to the Sheela-na-gig. Long may she keep us safe and guard our loves.'

'The Sheela-na-gig,' the chorus rang out.

The crystal goblets clinked together, glinting in the syrupy sunlight that now shone full into the clearing where they sat.

In Morlanby chapel, the stone carving of the Sheela-na-gig seemed to stir in the shadows and broaden its grotesque smile in satisfaction.

SAPPHIRE NEW BOOKS

I MARRIED MADAM

☐ *Published in June 2000*   Daphne Adams

Anna has a blast making the rounds of North London dyke pubs with her best friend Joan, but it's no cure for the rut she's fallen into with her girlfriend Vicky. Still, life gets more exciting when she meets enigmatic Marlene: a tall dark German who wears silk suits, smokes long expensive cigarettes and is, in short, a Dietrich-dream come true. A funny, bittersweet and very sexy tale about what *really* happens when opposites attract.

£8.99   ISBN 0 352 33514 2

ICE QUEEN

☐ *Published in August 2000*   Suzanne Blaylock

Which of these women is really the Ice Queen: a horny out-of-work actress with her eye on the main chance? A beautiful, successful author whose appetite for female lovers is a famous open secret? An eccentric butch dyke with an uncompromising attitude and a sardonic sense of humour? Drawn together by an accident of time and circumstance, a disparate group of women all hide behind masks of cool deception – but when their paths cross the ice soon melts in a furnace of passion.

£8.99   ISBN 0 352 33517 3

SHEELA-NA-GIG

☐ *Published in October 2000*   Bridget Doyle

Jane Claremont, a not-so-innocent 19th century English novice, is just about to be ordained a nun when she begins to experience sensual visions – and ones that have the knack of becoming true. This news reaches Lady Elaine, a benefactress of the convent, and she entices Jane away with the promise of a better life. While Jane is greatly attracted by Elaine's beauty, she starts to feel there is a more sinister reason for the other woman's interest.

£8.99   ISBN 0 352 33545 9

ALSO AVAILABLE

RIKA'S JEWEL
Astrid Fox

Norway, AD 1066. A group of female Viking warriors – Ingrid's Crew – have set sail to fight the Saxons in Britain, and Ingrid's young lover Rika is determined to follow them. But, urged on by dark-haired oarswoman Pia, Rika soon penetrates Ingrid's secret erotic cult back home in Norway. Will Rika overcome Ingrid's psychic hold, or will she succumb to the intoxicating rituals of the cult? Thrilling sword-and-sorcery in the style of Xena and Red Sonja!

£6.99   ISBN 0 352 33367 7

'Splendid stuff' – *Diva Magazine*
'★★★★!' – *SFX Magazine*

MILLENNIUM FEVER
Julia Wood

The millennium is approaching and so is Nikki's fortieth birthday. Married for twenty years, she is tired of playing the trophy wife in a small town where she can't adequately pursue her lofty career ambitions. In contrast, young writer Georgie has always been out and proud. But there's one thing they have in common – in the midst of millennial fever, they both want action and satisfaction. When they meet, the combination is explosive.

£6.99   ISBN 0 352 33368 5

'It's HOT!' – *About.com*

ALL THAT GLITTERS
Franca Nera

Marta Broderick: beautiful, successful art dealer; London lesbian. Marta inherits an art empire from the man who managed to spirit her out of East Berlin in the 1960s, Manny Schweitz. She's intent on completing Manny's unfinished business: recovering pieces of art stolen by the Nazis. Meanwhile, she's met the gorgeous but mysterious Judith Compton, and Marta's dark sexual addiction to Judith – along with her quest to return the treasures to the rightful owners – is taking her to dangerous places.

£6.99   ISBN 0 352 33426 6

'Never again will I be able to look at an ice cube or a tube of
Wintergreen without breaking into a sweat! As for champagne . . . it's too
good to just drink!' – *Libertas!*

SWEET VIOLET
Ruby Vise

Violet is young, butch and new in town, looking for a way to get over her childhood sweetheart Katherine. And there are plenty of distractions in 1980s London, as the rarefied big-city dyke scene is both sexually and politically charged – full of everything from cosmic mother-earth worshippers to sexy girls in leather.

£6.99   ISBN 0 352 33458 4

'An easy, entertaining read, both funny and sad with believable
erotic bits.' – *Libertas!*

GETAWAY
Suzanne Blaylock

Brilliantly talented Polly Sayers has had her first affair with a woman, stolen the code of an important new piece of software and done a runner all the way to a peaceful English coastal community. But things aren't as tranquil as they appear in this quiet haven, as Polly realises when she becomes immersed in an insular group of mysterious but very attractive women.

£6.99   ISBN 0 352 33443 6

'An enjoyable fantasy read with a nice twist ending' – *Diva Magazine*

HIGH ART
Tanya Dolan

Tinisha – a gorgeous, non-monogamous painter – is queen when it comes to the high art of seduction. If only the beautiful women of Cornwall would stop throwing themselves at her, she might be able to get some portraits done, as well.

£8.99   ISBN 0 352 33513 0

'Just the book to relax those sun-warmed bones after a day on the beach' – *Libertas!*

---------------✂------------------------------------

Please send me the books I have ticked above.

Name ....

Address ....

....

....

.... Post Code ....

Send to: Cash Sales, Sapphire Books, Thames Wharf Studios, Rainville Road, London W6 9HA.

US customers: for prices and details of how to order books for delivery by mail, call 1-800-805-1083.

Please enclose a cheque or postal order, made payable to **Virgin Publishing Ltd**, to the value of the books you have ordered plus postage and packing costs as follows:

UK and BFPO – £1.00 for the first book, 50p for each subsequent book.

Overseas (including Republic of Ireland) – £2.00 for the first book, £1.00 for each subsequent book.

We accept all major credit cards, including VISA, ACCESS/MASTER-CARD, DINERS CLUB, AMEX and SWITCH.

Please write your card number and expiry date here:

....

Please allow up to 28 days for delivery.

Signature ....

---------------✂------------------------------------

WE NEED YOUR HELP . . .

to plan the future of Sapphire books –

Yours are the only opinions that matter. Sapphire is a new and exciting venture: the first British series of books devoted to lesbian erotic fiction written by and for women.

We're going to do our best to provide the sexiest books you can buy. And we'd like you to help in these early stages. Tell us what you want to read. Send your completed questionnaire to Sapphire Books, Virgin Publishing, Thames Wharf Studios, Rainville Road, London W6 9HA.

THE SAPPHIRE QUESTIONNAIRE

SECTION ONE: ABOUT YOU

1.1   Sex (*we presume you are female, but just in case*)
Are you?
Female   ☐
Male   ☐

1.2   Age

under 21 ☐	21–30 ☐
31–40 ☐	41–50 ☐
51–60 ☐	over 60 ☐

1.3   At what age did you leave full-time education?
still in education   ☐   16 or younger   ☐
17–19   ☐   20 or older   ☐

1.4   Occupation _____

1.5   Annual household income _____

1.6 We are perfectly happy for you to remain anonymous; but if you would like us to send you a free booklist of Sapphire books, please insert your name and address

_____

_____

_____

_____

SECTION TWO: ABOUT BUYING SAPPHIRE BOOKS

2.1 Where did you get this copy of *Sheela-Na-Gig*?
   Bought at chain book shop ☐
   Bought at independent book shop ☐
   Bought at supermarket ☐
   Bought at book exchange or used book shop ☐
   I borrowed it/found it ☐
   My partner bought it ☐

2.2 How did you find out about Sapphire books?
   I saw them in a shop ☐
   I saw them advertised in a magazine ☐
   A friend told me about them ☐
   I read about them in _____ ☐
   Other _____

2.3 Please tick the following statements you agree with:
   I would be less embarrassed about buying Sapphire books if the cover pictures were less explicit ☐
   I think that in general the pictures on Sapphire books are about right ☐
   I think Sapphire cover pictures should be as explicit as possible ☐

2.4 Would you read a Sapphire book in a public place – on a train for instance?
   Yes ☐   No ☐

SECTION THREE: ABOUT THIS SAPPHIRE BOOK

3.1 Do you think the sex content in this book is:
   Too much ☐   About right ☐
   Not enough ☐

3.2   Do you think the writing style in this book is:
         Too unreal/escapist   ☐   About right   ☐
         Too down to earth   ☐

3.3   Do you think the story in this book is:
         Too complicated   ☐   About right   ☐
         Too boring/simple   ☐

3.4   Do you think the cover of this book is:
         Too explicit   ☐   About right   ☐
         Not explicit enough   ☐
Here's a space for any other comments:

_____

SECTION FOUR: ABOUT OTHER SAPPHIRE BOOKS

4.1   How many Sapphire books have you read?

4.2   If more than one, which one did you prefer?
      _____

4.3   Why?

_____

SECTION FIVE: ABOUT YOUR IDEAL EROTIC NOVEL

We want to publish the books you want to read – so this is your chance to tell
us exactly what your ideal erotic novel would be like.

5.1   Using a scale of 1 to 5 (1 = no interest at all, 5 = your ideal), please rate
      the following possible settings for an erotic novel:
         Roman/Ancient World   ☐
         Medieval/barbarian/sword 'n' sorcery   ☐
         Renaissance/Elizabethan/Restoration   ☐
         Victorian/Edwardian   ☐
         1920s & 1930s   ☐
         Present day   ☐
         Future/Science Fiction   ☐

5.2 Using the same scale of 1 to 5, please rate the following themes you may find in an erotic novel:

Bondage/fetishism ☐
Romantic love ☐
SM/corporal punishment ☐
Bisexuality ☐
Gay male sex ☐
Group sex ☐
Watersports ☐
Rent/sex for money ☐

5.3 Using the same scale of 1 to 5, please rate the following styles in which an erotic novel could be written:

Gritty realism, down to earth ☐
Set in real life but ignoring its more unpleasant aspects ☐
Escapist fantasy, but just about believable ☐
Complete escapism, totally unrealistic ☐

5.4 In a book that features power differentials or sexual initiation, would you prefer the writing to be from the viewpoint of the dominant/experienced or submissive/inexperienced characters:

Dominant/Experienced ☐
Submissive/Inexperienced ☐
Both ☐

5.5 We'd like to include characters close to your ideal lover. What characteristics would your ideal lover have? Tick as many as you want:

Dominant	☐	Cruel	☐
Slim	☐	Young	☐
Big	☐	Naïve	☐
Voluptuous	☐	Caring	☐
Extroverted	☐	Rugged	☐
Bisexual	☐	Romantic	☐
Working Class	☐	Old	☐
Introverted	☐	Intellectual	☐
Butch	☐	Professional	☐
Femme	☐	Pervy	☐
Androgynous	☐	Ordinary	☐
Submissive	☐	Muscular	☐

Anything else? _____